I0817890

For Mother Earth,
the fae folk,
and the magic
inside us all.

Her soul's beginning, she need discover
A darkness within she'll ken e'ermore
But 'tis the horse's vision of Earth Mother
That lights her path to days of yore

—Scottish Scroll I, 1576

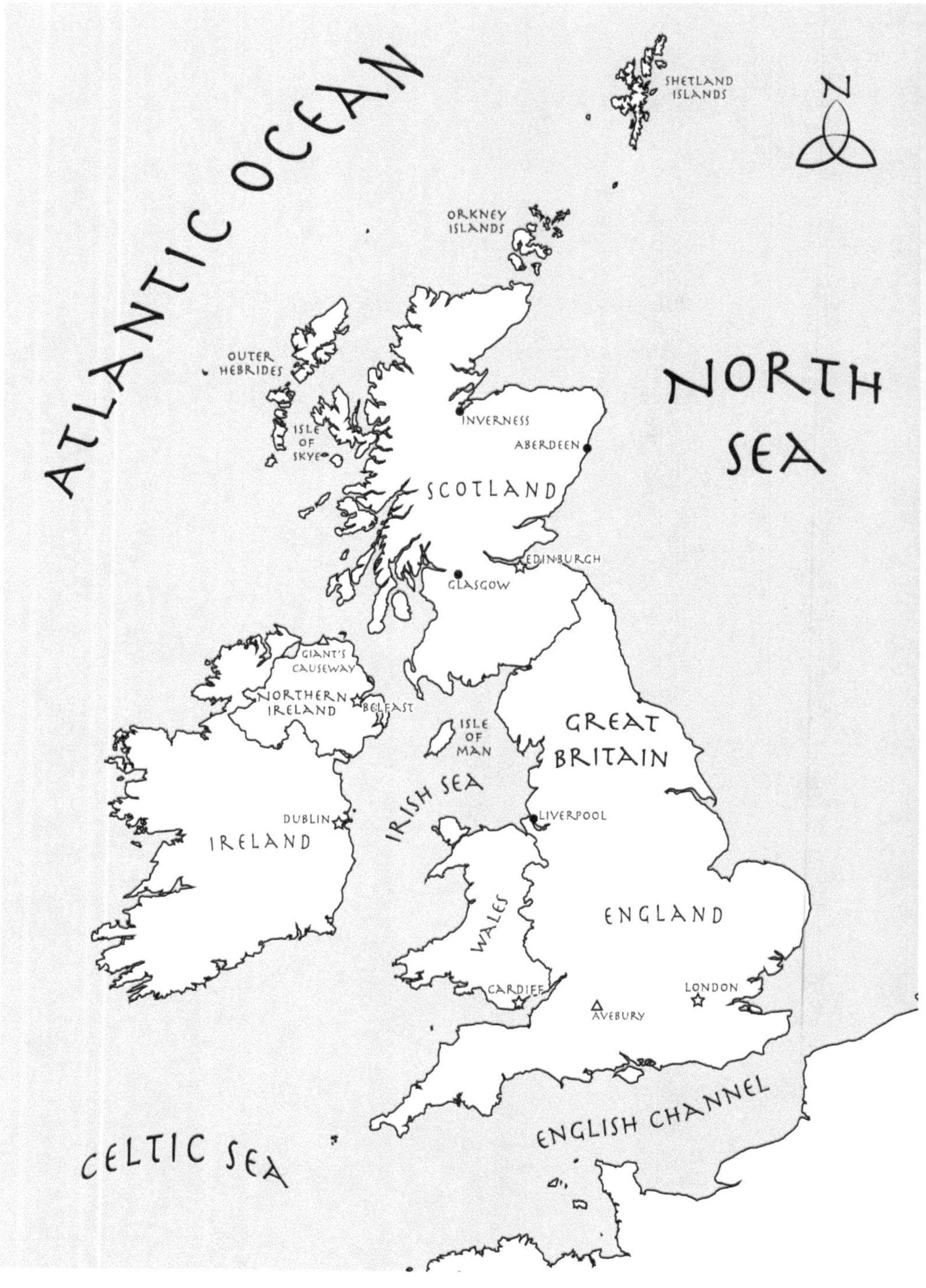

ATLANTIC OCEAN
SHETLAND ISLANDS
N
ORKNEY ISLANDS
OUTER HEBRIDES
NORTH SEA
INVERNESS
ISLE OF SKYE
ABERDEEN
SCOTLAND
EDINBURGH
GLASGOW
GIANT'S CAUSEWAY
NORTHERN IRELAND
BELFAST
ISLE OF MAN
GREAT BRITAIN
IRISH SEA
DUBLIN
IRELAND
LIVERPOOL
WALES
ENGLAND
CARDIFF
LONDON
AVEBURY
ENGLISH CHANNEL
CELTIC SEA

N

ATLANTIC OCEAN

BALLYCASTLE

GIANT'S
CAUSEWAY

NORTHERN
IRELAND

BELFAST

THE
BOYNE
VALLEY

CONNEMARA

GALWAY

DUBLIN

THE
BURREN

REPUBLIC OF
IRELAND

LIMERICK

IRISH SEA

CORK

CELTIC SEA

Praise for The Wise One

"This swift, crisply written modern-day fairytale of determination, growing up, and embracing your identity will inspire young adult readers who appreciate Irish and Scottish folklore. The environmental message resonates, and Anglehart's evocations of an Ireland where a 'lake of mystic topaz' stands 'silent and still beneath smooth mountains' are both wistful and sumptuous."

—Editor's Pick, *BookLife* by *Publishers Weekly*

"*The Wise One* is a heartwarming coming-of-age story with characters that resonate, rich European folklore, and enchanting details that tickle the senses long after the last page is read . . .as slowly as possible because you never want this hauntingly beautiful story to end. I await the sequel with bated breath."

—V. G. Anderson, author of *The Light in the Sound*

"A story of witches, magic, secrets, Ireland, a prophecy, and a yearning to know one's true identity . . . yes please!"

—Sonja F. Blanco, author of *Witch of Ware Woods*

"Much like a young adult version of *A Discovery of Witches*, this story expertly blends the folklore of the Celtic people with present-day life. This book is highly recommended to readers who enjoy young adult literature and the magical landscape of Ireland."

—Mary Lanni, *Reedsy Discovery* reviewer

"While I was reading this book, I was reminded of my first foray into Irish myths and folktales—an experience that left me in love, and a little obsessed, with this topic. *The Wise One* captures the same magic, and supported by the author's research and the heart she's poured into this story, it really sings."

—Sarah Limardo, reviewer

"*The Wise One* needs to be on all of the must-read lists for 2020. I'm so moved by the storytelling, the setting and the characters K.T. created. I consumed this in a day, I couldn't tear myself away. Not only did the author suck me into this breathtakingly visual book about magic, witches and faeries, but they stuck in so many life lessons that humans of all ages need to be reminded of."

—Sarah Bell, reviewer

K.T. ANGLEHART

THE
Magic Dwarf
PRESS

The Wise One: The Scottish Scrolls Book I

ISBN: 978-1-7773317-0-2 (Print)

Cover Design by Melissa Williams Design

Interior Formatting by Melissa Williams Design

Published by The Magic Dwarf Press

Maps designed by Riccardo Caimano | @fantacities

Note From the Author

The Wise One is an urban fantasy tale for the young and young at heart. Set against the backdrop of the Northern Ireland "Troubles", it combines environmental themes and historical events with folklore myth, earth-based magic, and new age concepts that spiritual teachers are imparting today. Some historical figures in this story include alleged witches Alice Kyteler, Petronella de Meath, and Elizabeth Dunlop (if you're compelled to research these, I recommend waiting until after you've finished this book in order to avoid spoilers).

Please keep in mind that I used creative license around some of the politics in terms of the representatives' positions and duties, and that the political views in this book do not express my own—their purpose is to portray diverse opinions during a very difficult and complex political climate.

The locations in this book are by no means accidental. During my travels in Ireland, the spots that radiated mystery and mysticism are the places readers will also be exploring within these pages.

Now, ignore everything you've just read, and sit back and enjoy the scenery!

I
The Wise One

Bruised and battered, the young woman was dragged through the screaming, unruly mob. Her wrists were bound behind her by a rope as thick as the noose she now faced.

"*Buidseach! Buidseach!*" Witch. Witch.

"*Bàsachadh!*"

Die.

She halted in front of the noose, unperturbed, for she knew her death would end swiftly. The man who held the end of her rope looked from her calm expression to the noose, and let out a shrill laugh.

"A quick snap of the neck, aye, Bessie girl? You don't think you're getting off that easy, do you? Nah, that there isn't for your kind."

The ugly man, towering and troll-like, hauled her further on like a rag doll, finally leading her to a pit loaded with broken wood fragments, branches, and logs.

She was going to be burned alive.

In that instant, her body trembled with the fear she had been trying so desperately to conceal. Of dying, no—she knew this life would not be her last, and she was ready to part ways with this physical body. But she would be lying to herself if she said she hadn't been hoping for a less painful demise.

He tightened the rope from her wrists around the wood banister that stood erect in the centre of the pit, then secured more rope round her ankles. "Spill your guts, now or never, *buid-seach*," he spat.

The woman scanned the crowd. *Foolish, blind,* she thought. They had no idea what would become of their Earth. No, she did not regret her actions. And if she had to burn for them, then so be it.

She held her chin up and addressed the spectators. Her voice was steady, knowing. "There will come a day when your fate shall depend upon a witch such as me—and you will *beg* for mercy."

The crowd cackled and spat back, simultaneously enraged and amused. But no one laughed louder than the troll-man. "Devil-worshipping hag."

He lowered his torch to the base of the pit, and the flames caught quickly. She watched them crawl towards her boots, but her eyes were forced shut by the rising smoke. In an instant, beads of sweat leaked like rain on her forehead, and her lungs swelled to twice their size.

Just when she hoped she might pass out from the heat, the flames grew larger, now licking the base of her legs. What followed was an acute, unfathomable pain. The flames travelled higher, higher, until they enveloped the lower half of her body—and she could no longer bear the sheer agony of her skin melting away.

The Wise One

ABREDONIA WOODS, MASSACHUSETTS
SEPTEMBER 13, 1991

In the dead of night, Mckenna O'Dwyer's screams forced Seán and Andre up and out of bed. They rushed over to their daughter's bedroom.

"Shhh . . . sh, it's alright, swan, you're dreaming," Seán said as he stroked her hair and cradled her against his chest.

"Another nightmare," said Andre, trying to steady his daughter's shuddering body.

Seán shook her gently. "Mckenna . . . Mckenna, do you hear me? Why isn't she waking up?"

"She seems to be in pain . . . I've never seen her like—"

She let out one long, anguished cry.

"Mckenna!" her dads called out. Her eyes shot open.

She was alive. How? Where was she now? *When* was she? Who were those nasty people?

The clock on her nightstand read 3:04 a.m. Relief swept over her, but only briefly—a lump formed in the back of her throat and rose out of her, making her sob like a colicky baby.

Andre squeezed her hand. "It's alright, Mckenna. Oh, geez, you're drenched . . ."

"I—I'm h-h-hot . . ."

"You're okay." Seán rocked her. "It's your birthday, swan, you know that? It's your birthday . . ." He said this as though it mattered, as though it would make her forget somehow. As though her skin hadn't just been crawling with flames.

"Happy birthday, Mckenna," Andre whispered.

But all she wanted to do was weep.

The High Priestess's arm was growing tired. She'd been dangling her gold chain over the globe for nearly three hours, her faithful stone secured at the end of it, sweeping steadily over every continent, country, city. Carved from an ancient Irish stone, Misgaun Medb, the pendant's magnetic power could draw in whatever the bearer pleased.

Except *her*.

The High Priestess felt Pravadi's eyes on her. "Won't you at least let me light the fire?"

"No. No fire." The Priestess wasn't fond of them. "You're certain it's today?"

"Yes," said Pravadi. "When has a vision of mine ever been false?"

The minute hand shifted. At 3:04 a.m., the log in the fireplace sparked a solo flame, making the Priestess start. A warning from the salamanders? She shuddered at the thought, and the stone grazed the globe's surface—only for a second. Then like a magnet, it shot past Canada and affixed onto an eastern region in the United States. "There you are," the High Priestess said, her mouth twisted in satisfaction.

Pravadi lowered her square spectacles on the bridge of her nose. "She's just come of age," said Pravadi, keenly. "I knew my vision wasn't mistaken."

The Priestess didn't mind her gloating. She leaned back, revelling in the stone's powers. The finest point of the stone was pinned onto a small town in Massachusetts—Abredonia Woods.

She had been waiting a long time to locate the girl, known as the Wise One. Too long.

"What about Abigail, the girl's mother?" Pravadi said. "Perhaps now the stone can track her, too, and we can be done with it."

The High Priestess rolled her eyes, wondering how a seer could be so forgetful. "The spell Abigail cast when her child was born protects her from being traced by anyone other than the

Wise One. She is our only hope."

"And if the Wise One finds her before the first Scottish Scroll is fulfilled? And once she does, if they *both* disappear . . .?"

Really, she should get a head scan. "My protégé will see to it that the Wise One fulfills the first Scroll before she locates her mother, then will keep them both close 'til I step in. *And so shall it be,*" she said with longing, imagining the hour the Scottish Scrolls would be fulfilled.

"And if there are delays? We have until—"

"I ken our deadline," the High Priestess snapped. "Have faith," she said mostly to herself as she tied the chain back around her neck.

II

THE BOOK, THE BIRD, AND THE BULLY

Mckenna awoke that morning with a splitting headache. She wasn't sure whether it was from the lack of sleep or residual pain from the vivid nightmare. Either way, all signs pointed to yet another chirpy day in this shit town.

Abredonia Woods was that "quaint" town you stopped by for an afternoon getaway. You hiked in the woods, grabbed a root beer float in the town square, then left before you realized all that was left to do was visit the library.

She threw on whatever sweater hung closest to her and dragged her body downstairs.

Seán stood behind the kitchen island sporting his favourite apron—stained with fresh pancake mix—while Andre—suited up and dashing—sat across from him, crosswording away and sipping from a mug that read *I'm the nerdy dad.*

"There she is!" Andre met her at the threshold and kissed her squarely on the forehead. "Happy birthday, my almost-adult—*who shall remain as such until the day her fathers are ready . . .*"

"Thanks, Dad."

"Come here!" Seán gave her a tight squeeze, his stubble brushing her cheek. "You alright?"

"Yeah, just tired," she said in a hoarse, pre-coffee voice. "Give it to me neat."

Already on it, Andre poured her a cup of black coffee and filled it right up to the brim. "You had us worried; it was like you were completely somewhere else . . ."

"Was just a bad dream, swan, wasn't it?" Seán interrupted.

Mckenna nodded, gulping down her coffee like juice.

Andre shifted. "Maybe we should talk about—"

"None of that, none of that," Seán interrupted with a wave of his hand. "It's Mckenna's special day today, so . . ." Seán placed a stack of boxty—Irish potato pancakes—in front of her with two candles, a one and a seven, perched in the centre, and belted out *Happy Birthday* in Irish. They chuckled at Seán's theatrics.

"And as the Irish saying goes," said Seán, raising his coffee mug, "may you live as long as you want, and never want as long as you live!"

"Here, here!" said Andre, giving in.

Mckenna raised her cup, too. Her dads were the biggest dorks.

Seán was her biological father. He arrived here in Massachusetts from Ireland in his twenties hoping to find work as an artist ("If I wanted to tend sheep all day I'd have gladly stayed."). Funnily enough, Andre was his immigration lawyer. It wasn't long after they fell for one another that they wanted a child. Dear Mckenna was the result of a surrogacy—their "absolute miracle."

Coffee and pancakes must've been the perfect nightmare hangover breakfast because her headache was finally ceasing.

"If you're ready, I can drop you off at school," said Andre, buttoning up his royal blue blazer, which Mckenna always found flattered his ebony skin the most.

"You only teach this afternoon." Andre taught at Harvard Law, about an hour and a half north from town. "I've got a pretty large foot in the door, just so you know," he'd say to her oh-so-subtly every other month or so; no, she didn't want to become a lawyer. She couldn't imagine ever being forced to prosecute an innocent person, nor defend a world-class scumbag. And every other field of law seemed boring as hell. Truthfully, she'd been considering journalism. Being out there in the thick of the action, telling it like it is. No sugar-coating, no cowardly lies.

"I don't mind," Andre said, picking at a lint ball. "I have to go in for an early meeting."

"Mhm. With who?"

"With, uh, the department head."

"About . . .?"

"The—the copy machine fiasco. Something's got to be done."

"Right, heard about that. People all over Boston are rallying."

Andre sighed, and Mckenna grinned in triumph. "A lawyer who can't lie. I think it's poetic."

"I lie *fine,* just not so well to my family. Don't I get points for that?"

"I think it's endearing, luv," Seán said, giving Andre's shoulder a squeeze, then topped off Mckenna's coffee. "You're sure you still want to turn down a lift, though?"

"Don't worry, really. Weather's nice—I'll walk."

Mckenna loved the sound of rain pounding on the pavement, the way it trickled away, satisfied, like it had done its job. She took the long route to school with the hopes that Mother Nature would wash away her sullen state of mind. She welcomed the dampness, looking forward to the clear, crisp air that would follow the rainfall.

But even the rain couldn't clear her thoughts of last night's dream. She tried listening to the droplets hitting the trees, but the image of the mocking crowd and troll-like man, the flames crawling towards her, wouldn't dissipate. Mckenna had been living with nightmares ever since she could remember. She'd been beaten, nearly drowned, but never . . .

A chill shot up her spine. How disgusting that being burned alive was once deemed proper punishment. And for what—knowing your herbs and skipping out on church?

Another thing. *Buidseach*—how had she known the meaning of the word in Gaelic? Was it even *Irish* Gaelic? Her knowledge of the language didn't extend beyond the basics, such as "Hi, how are you" and evidently "Happy birthday", plus a couple of curse words—easy to pick up around Seán.

She had sensed this morning that Seán was avoiding the topic of her nightmares—night terrors, whatever they were. He'd been doing that a lot lately, and a voice inside her head told her it was because something wasn't right. About the nightmares, but also about her. It was like he knew something she didn't. Did they run in the family? Were they a symptom of something bigger? It would explain why she'd always felt off. Wrong. Like hail in the summer.

She remembered a time, at least ten years ago, when Seán tried to hide the fact that he was seeing a therapist. He had a lot of pride, so it wasn't something he'd admit to, but she knew he was going through something dark. Mckenna never saw anything wrong with his getting help—who the hell didn't need help? But her dads were intent on keeping it from her. The truth was she had always had an underlying fear that these dreams were manifestations of some sort of mental disorder that would develop in her adult years.

She often did this—spiraled downwards, thought the worst. At least she was aware of it, but perhaps it was a sign that she should stop reading psychological thrillers.

Deep in her sinister thoughts, she stepped off the footpath and rounded the corner to her school. Her head hung forward as she walked past herds of students huddled under their umbrellas, blissful and content in their cliques, chitchatting about the next quiz or brainstorming costumes to wear at the Halloween dance.

Bullshit like that.

"How about I dress up as a wise ass with two gay dads?" said Jared, a brawny boy Mckenna despised, just as she walked past him. She ignored him, like she did all the others, and wondered if teenagers in this so-called modern era would ever outgrow their bigotry.

She swung open the heavy front doors a little too roughly, nearly knocking over something flimsy; a small girl with a pixie-like haircut had run straight into her, squeaked, "So sorry!" and scrambled past her and into the school yard. Mckenna spun round and noticed a couple of pink streaks poking out beneath the girl's dirty-blond hair. She watched the flash of pink and honey run to the massive tree over near the fence, where a book bag hung on one of its low branches. But the girl was about three inches too short—she reminded Mckenna of Tigger as she bounced up and down to reach for her bag, which was drenched from the rain. A group of students stood idly by, snickering. Mckenna was making to go help her when Ms. Zhou, the PE teacher, came to her rescue.

Mckenna could barely keep her eyes open during homeroom, which made no real difference. Ms. Silcock—whose unfortunate last name usually incited rather nasty remarks—sat behind her desk and read while students glued their desks together and copied each other's history homework. Ms. Silcock heaved a heavy sigh.

A feeling of hopelessness came over Mckenna like a rooftop on the verge of collapse. She looked back round at Ms. Silcock, who appeared as wretched as Mckenna felt. Wretched and hopeless . . . like her entire career was a joke.

Mckenna shook the feeling away. *Weird.*

By the time the bell rang, the classroom had already half-emptied. Ms. Silcock didn't care to look up.

Everyone knew Mr. Heathley hated world history. He himself felt history books were nothing more than biased accounts written by attention-seeking common people suborned by the American government. That was why he elected to ignore the school board's curriculum and teach instead about conspiracy theories—usually involving Apollo 11 and extraterrestrials.

"Great read, wasn't it?" he said, holding up a copy of *UFO Crash at Roswell,* a dramatic and extensive account of the Roswell incident, published earlier that summer. "Weather balloon, my ass . . ."

In all the years she'd had Mr. Heathley, he'd rarely referred to the actual textbook. He only forced his students to bring it to class "just in case" they needed it—but they all knew very well he meant "just in case" the principal decided to pay them a spontaneous visit. Even so, everyone knew Mr. Heathley had been there as long as the rusted tiled walls, and therefore wasn't going anywhere.

Mckenna wasn't as keen on conspiracy theories as she was on historical facts. So while Mr. Heathley denigrated the military, she flipped aimlessly through this term's textbook, until a dreadful image caught her eye: It was a black and white sketch of four frightened-looking women seemingly begging for mercy at the foot of a royal. The description read:

> *Suspected witches kneeling before King James; Daemonologie (1597)*

She began to read:

> *The North Berwick Witch Trials took place in 1590 and were the first mass witch trials to occur in Scotland. Between seventy and two hundred "witches" in North Berwick were accused of sorcery and high treason—they had been found guilty of working with the devil to bring about the death of King James VI. Two women were burned as witches at Kronborg in Denmark . . .*

A slightly hunched shadow appeared across the page. She glanced up to see Mr. Heathley hovering over her holding a stack of graded tests.

SLAM.

She jumped in her seat. Her textbook had folded shut, as though by a blast of strong wind.

What the . . .?

Mr. Heathley didn't seem to notice; he merely shook his head disapprovingly, and addressed the class. "If you get curious about what's in these things," he said, picking up Mckenna's textbook and dangling it in the air like it was infected, "though I can't understand why you would, do it on your own time."

He handed Mckenna last week's pop quiz; ninety-four percent—she had lost points for relating JFK's assassination to the hatred the president had incited due to his civil rights advocacy among a large number of Americans, like Lee Harvey Oswald. Heathley had crossed the latter name out and scribbled beside it: *No! Oswald was just a pawn. Read* Crossfire: The Plot That Killed Kennedy *(film coming out December 20).*

But Mckenna's attention was still on her textbook sitting closed on her desk. She continued to stare it down, as though it might suddenly burst into flames.

A hard knock at the classroom door made Mckenna's head shoot up—it was the pixie-haired girl from this morning, standing at the threshold and looking like she'd already recovered from being picked on.

"Are you late? You don't look familiar," Mr. Heathley said.

"No, sir. I'm new here, my name is Nissa." Her voice was a little pitchy, but not in an annoying sort of way.

A few students seated in the first row erupted in snorts. The girl's shoulders drooped a little, but she appeared determined. "I was wondering if I could have your class's attention for a minute."

Mr. Heathley shrugged. "Good luck."

She smiled gratefully and faced the bored-looking students.

Mckenna straightened up. Nissa had a zest about her that she immediately liked.

"I'm here to talk to you about recycling."

More snorts. Nissa carried on. "Last year, thirty-three *million* tons of recyclable materials like glass, metal, and plastic were recovered from landfills all over the United States."

"Your point?" said Becka, a snotty tyrant, if there ever was one.

"All garbage goes somewhere. It doesn't just disappear,"

Nissa said, looking around at their blank faces. "My point is that that's *tens of millions* of tons of materials we should never have thrown away in the first place. Our planet can't hold all of our human waste forever. Recycling is the least we can do—"

"'Scuse me, um, can you please get on with it? I have a class to teach," Mr. Heathley grumbled.

"Sorry, sir." Nissa shuffled her feet. "I'd like to urge you all to sign a petition to order recycling bins for all the classrooms."

Most people didn't hear a word she said; some merely pointed out her pink hair and asked if she was a human by day and My Little Pony by night. Nissa's cheeks turned the same colour as her streaks.

Mckenna lifted her hand. "I'll sign." Thirty-something heads turned towards her. "Shouldn't we all sign, Mr. Heathley? I mean, the, uh . . . *government* has clearly been neglecting to regulate something that is detrimental to us all. Shouldn't we, uh . . . stick it to them?"

He looked up as though there was suddenly hope for the future generation. "Absolutely, Miss O'Dwyer."

Mckenna fought hard not to roll her eyes.

"Why don't you pass that around, Miss . . ." He scrutinized Nissa's patchy jumper. " . . . strange little girl."

Satisfied, Mckenna sat back down. Nissa beamed at her.

Seconds before the lunch bell rang, Mckenna swung her legs over the side of her chair, ready to bolt, almost stomping on a gleaming object that lay sprawled beneath her feet: a gold link bracelet. She picked it up and examined the single charm that hung from it, a flat round pendant on which was engraved what looked to be a head with three legs attached to it. On the back of it, etched in small cursive, was a short phrase in a language she didn't recognize. She pocketed it, telling herself she would bring it to the lost and found after lunch.

Her usual spot outside on the bleachers was free. She took a bite of her cold mac n' cheese—last night's leftovers—replaying the incident with the book over and over again. Had she imagined it? She could've sworn she didn't, though. Even the *sound* of the book slamming had been crystal clear.

Mckenna shook her head. There she was, justifying a book acting of its own free will and dismissing all other plausible explanations. Her sanity level today has dropped to a D.

She took a deep breath, trying to quiet her muddled thoughts. It was just an off day. That was all. She'd been having a lot of those lately. Breathe in, and release. Like Andre had taught her . . .

But her focus was interrupted by a shrill *churrr;* the sound had emanated from a small bird that had landed right by her thigh. It had a distinct, tiny cocked tail and rounded body, which was a combination of brown and light grey tones; its bill was finely pointed, and a white stripe arched over its eyes like tiny eyebrows. *So peculiar,* she thought. She didn't think she'd ever seen this sort of bird around Abredonia Woods before.

"You hungry?" Feeling a little silly, she held out a piece of Seán's homemade soda bread. The little guy tugged on it gently.

Out of the corner of her eye, Mckenna spotted Nissa reading under a birch tree while Becka and Jared hovered nearby, looking about ready to be assholes.

"HEY!" Jared shouted at Nissa loud enough to reach Mckenna's ears. "We're talking to you."

Nissa paid no attention. *Good,* Mckenna thought.

"You live on the street or something? Is that why you love trees and wear those patchy rags?"

Becka doubled over. Nissa kept her eyes fixed on the page as she made to stand, but Becka kicked her heels down. Mckenna strained to hear the next words out of his mouth.

"Where're you off to, tree humper? Come on, bet I'm a treat compared to those lunatics you live with. They must have brain damage to agree to keep you around. I guess that cheque they get from the government every month is enough to buy whatever drugs they're on . . ."

It was as though a volcano erupted in Mckenna's chest, spewing an inexplicable need to retaliate. She fixed her gaze on Jared, her eyes piercing through him as if the act alone would cause him physical damage.

And then something unbelievable happened. The bird took off like a bullet and darted straight into Jared's head.

Becka screamed as Jared dropped to the ground. He began writhing in pain, blood dripping from his temple.

"What—the—HELL?" Becka shouted.

Nissa looked round, and her eyes met Mckenna's. They both watched, bemused, as the bird landed back at Mckenna's side, unharmed, and stared up at her, apparently waiting for some kind of recognition.

"I didn't ask you to do that." The bird chirped back (angrily?) in response, and flew away, leaving behind one of its feathers, light brown with tiger-like stripes. Mckenna picked it up and tucked it into her coat pocket, unsure of what had just happened, and half-convinced that she had offended the little critter.

"You're a huge freak, you know that?" Becka hissed at Nissa as she threw Jared's arms around her neck and helped him to his feet.

The bell rang, and students began shuffling towards the door. Mckenna found herself rooted to the steel bench, watching the scene before her—Becka dragging Jared's half-conscious body across the running track while Nissa stared after them, flabbergasted.

She knew it was impossible, and yet Mckenna still felt responsible for the incident. She had *intended* to hurt Jared . . . and then the bird just . . .

Now who has brain damage.

Mckenna pretended she hadn't spotted Nissa walking towards her. She wasn't mentally prepared for the conversation that would unfold, which, Mckenna imagined, would involve many awkward pauses and lots of "I don't knows."

She sprinted down the steps and leaped over the last three, nearly falling flat on the ground. She felt Nissa's eyes on her as she scrambled to her feet and took off across the field.

III

A Note Forgotten

Noon was Seán's favourite time of day. The sun was at its highest and brightest, and the house at its quietest; the good talk shows ended, meaning the TV was no longer a distraction; and next door, Mrs. Claiborne usually took Pickles, her miniature pinscher, out for a lengthy walk, granting Seán a break from his incessant barking. He had a good three hours before a hungry, irritated Mckenna would return home from school, followed by an overworked Andre.

Seán was a children's book illustrator, and the kitchen was his office of choice. He had a perfectly good desk up in Andre's study, but the vibe wasn't right—much too stuffy for his taste. There was something comforting about letting his imagination run wild in the room that inspired his most delectable meals.

Just as Seán settled into his usual chair and spread out all of his sketching materials, the phone rang. He decided it was most likely a telemarketing call, so he ignored it and got to work.

The machine beeped and the voice of Mckenna's high-school principal, who by now he recognized only too well, spoke soberly.

"Hello, Mr. O'Dwyer, this is Mr. Ramirez. I'm afraid Mckenna hasn't shown up for third period. That's already twice and school only just started a couple of weeks ago . . ." He sighed over the loudspeaker. "Now, Mckenna's grades are clearly not the issue here, but I'm afraid she can't continue this way. Her record can't afford to have as many absences as last year . . ."

Seán stopped listening after "third period" and swore under his breath. He buried his face in his hands and wondered how he was going to ever get through to his daughter—the stubborn, impulsive, reckless person that she was.

As though on cue, the front door burst open. Seán heard a backpack hitting the ground and shoes being kicked off, then tumbling against the hardwood floors—quickly followed by the unmistakable sound of Mckenna's footsteps thundering up the stairs.

"And just *where* do you think you're going?" he shouted towards the stairway.

Mckenna stopped halfway up the stairs and hung her head back in frustration.

"Not now, Dad," she called back.

She heard the kitchen chair scrape the tiles beneath it, and in seconds, Seán was on the landing. She turned around to face him; his hands were crossed over his chest, and he was staring up at her with an expression that suggested she had just flung her shoe at him.

"Can you please let this go? I just need to lie down." Her energy was spent, which came across in her feeble-sounding voice.

"Come downstairs," he insisted. "Go on, let's talk. I'll put the kettle on . . ."

"You and your goddam tea, I don't want tea—"

"*Christ,* Mckenna, get your arse downstairs."

Mckenna may not have inherited Seán's looks, but she had definitely—and unluckily—inherited his short fuse. "I said later, okay!" she roared back.

He clenched his jaw. "*Not* okay."

She muttered a curse word before taking a seat at the kitchen table, half her bottom hanging off the chair, and watched as Seán filled up the kettle with water and started pacing up and down.

"You know . . ." he began, water dripping from the kettle's spout as he jerked around. "You were an easy kid; you learned fast, you ate your vegetables—you even liked hanging around with your dad and me. But socially . . ."

Mckenna knew what he was getting at. He was always reminding her of the little to no effort she put into making friends.

"You've just never wanted to be around other people—even the ones who are decent. And I think that's why you've always avoided going to class."

"Other people aren't so great," she said dryly.

"I'm not arguing with that, but some are tolerable," he said, trying to lighten the mood. "But for you to leave mid-day, something must've happened."

"Nope," she lied. "Nothing in particular."

"Swan, I realize growing up in this . . . situation didn't exactly make it easy for you in the beginning—"

"In the beginning?" she said, raising her voice another octave. "Are you under some kind of impression that teenagers get wiser as they get older?"

"Watch your manner—"

"I honestly don't even care, Dad. If you think a few inane comments from some half-witted kids get to me, they don't. Frankly, my upbringing isn't anyone else's business."

"Alright, that's grand. Then, what's the problem?"

Mckenna could practically hear her heart hammering inside her chest.

"The problem is *there's something wrong with me!*" she shouted, surprising herself.

Andre had just appeared behind her. Bearing an expression of great concern, he tossed his briefcase aside. "I cancelled my afternoon class as soon as the principal called," he said in a low voice. "Mckenna, I didn't expect you to be home. What's going on?" He looked from Mckenna's sombre face to Seán's.

Seán spoke first. "She's bunked off school again."

"You don't understand," said Mckenna, defeated.

"Then help us to," Andre said, pulling up a chair.

Mckenna hesitated. "I just feel like . . . I'm alone. Like I can't relate to anyone, and no one can relate to me. Like I'm made up of a bunch of pieces that don't actually fit together."

"I'm not sure what you're saying, swan."

Mckenna sighed. "I just . . ." The trouble was she didn't quite know either. She thought about telling them what had happened with the book in history class and outside with the bird. Surely, they would think she was going mental. Though the way this conversation was going, they probably already did.

"Whatever it is, you can tell us." Mckenna always found Andre's soft eyes convincing.

And so she told them. She described how the book slammed shut as soon as Mr. Heathley drew nearer to her desk. She went on to explain what led up to the bird flying straight for Jared's head, as though in Nissa's defence, and how in that moment she wanted nothing more than to hurt him.

Seán pushed his chair back, nearly knocking it backwards. "Christ almighty . . ." he hissed under his breath.

Mckenna frowned, confused over his reaction, and looked to Andre, whose sympathetic gaze told her that he understood.

"Seán, I think—"

"No," he said firmly.

Mckenna looked from one anxious face to another. "This has something to do with my head, doesn't it? My head's not right." Her voice was trembling. "You saw a psychotherapist a while ago, and you were trying to hide it from me—"

"I dunno what you're saying—"

"Is it because you have some sort of episodes, too? Is that what this is? It started with nightmares, but now I think . . . I think I'm hallucinating—how else would you explain the things I saw today? Does schizophrenia run in our family? Maybe it's in your DNA. Yours or . . . my birth mother's." She was doing it again—escalating her thoughts to a dark place.

Seán's face fell. "Now, what in God's name makes you think that?"

Mckenna couldn't explain how. "All this time, maybe my mother's the one you're afraid I'm taking after," she said, seeing Seán's panicky expression. "I'm convinced I closed a book with my *mind,* Dads. And that I told a freaking bird to fly into someone's head. Just tell me if I'm on the verge of a psychotic break."

"Mckenna, of course not," said Andre quickly.

"Then what's happening to me? What are you not telling me—and why did Dad flip the second I mentioned my mother?" She gestured at Seán scratching the back of his neck and staring at the tiles on the floor.

He looked up and slammed his hands on his knees. "All this suspicion, where is it all coming from? And it's none of your beeswax that I needed help to get through something all those years ago—no one's schizo, and you *don't* have a mother! Stop finding excuses for acting up," he said irritably.

Mckenna couldn't believe how lightly he was taking this. "Right, so everything I'm feeling isn't valid? I'm just an angry teenage girl," she shot back.

Seán took a deep breath. "We've talked about this," he said, adjusting his tone. "Your dad and I sought an egg donor and a surrogate. We don't know who your mum is."

"The thing is . . . I can feel that you're lying." On some level, Mckenna had never believed their story. And today, she was sure it was just that—a story.

She turned to Andre. "Dad? You'll tell me. You want to tell me, right?"

Andre closed his eyes as if to wish away a headache, and then Mckenna felt it—guilt. Blatant, penetrable guilt seeping out of every fibre, every pore. Mckenna could practically see it closing in on him, like a net trapping its prey.

Her head felt suddenly like it had split open. It was a kind of pressure she had never experienced before, and it was followed by an urge that was not her own—an urge to confront Seán . . .

She glanced at Andre, the pleading in his eyes telling her that he needed to speak with Seán alone. She was feeling Andre's feelings.

"I'll leave you two to talk," she said, and headed upstairs to her bedroom.

Andre rounded on Seán as soon as he heard Mckenna's bedroom door close upstairs.

"You're not actually considering letting her think she's having episodes?" Andre began in a hushed tone. "This can be severely psychologically damaging . . ."

Seán wasn't listening. "This can't be happening. What brought this on? She completely snapped!"

"The signs have been there all along . . ." Andre stared at his partner with deep sorrow. He knew how difficult it was for Seán to leave this part of his life behind.

Seán was beside himself with anger. He hit the table, hard. "We're *not* telling her a fecking thing—"

"Would you keep your voice down—"

"We'll just make up whatever it is we have to make up to convince her that we don't know who her mum is, and all these odd incidents are coincidences."

"You can't be serious. Have you met our daughter? You saw how fast her thoughts jumped to her mother. That was not regular human intuition you just witnessed. It's something else entirely. She knows—"

"I am *not* letting her go down that path. I won't let her!" he hissed and lowered his voice again. "You know what—you have no right to judge this."

"Excuse me? I'm her *father* . . ."

"Oh, don't do that, you know perfectly well that's not what I mean. You weren't there," he signed exasperatedly. "You just can't understand the danger involved."

"I may not understand it the way you do, but this is her

blood, Seán. She has a right to know who she is."

"That's where you're wrong—she can't know about any of it! She'll get sucked in, just like her godforsaken mother." There was deep, undeniable hurt in his eyes. "I've worked too hard keeping her safe from it all. Her life will be ruined."

"And if you don't tell her, she'll find out some other way and we'll lose her for good. She's already halfway there, and you know it."

Mckenna's stomach was churning with anxiety, but she knew for the time being, her dads needed to be alone.

And so she lay on her bed, staring up at the ceiling for what felt like hours. Twice she almost marched downstairs to demand answers, but instead she examined her room's bad paint job, thanks to Seán. When Mckenna turned thirteen, he had insisted the room needed a good sprucing up ("You're a teen now! Your room needs a trendier look"), even though Mckenna was rather fond of her old decor. Her bedframe wall had been covered with a wallpaper of the night sky; the stars even glowed in the dark. Though Mckenna was certain that Seán just wanted her to have a typical teenage girl's room—in the hopes that she would someday become a typical teenage girl. It was now a much-too-vibrant pink.

She felt a twang of guilt; was she a disappointment? Perhaps not to Andre—he had always been on board with whatever strange phase she was in. But Seán was much more disapproving; it was important to him that Mckenna blended in. She had always suspected it was to make up for her unique upbringing. As he pointed out earlier, being the kid with two gay dads—one of whom was Black—tended to become a main feature, like some kind of extra, exposed limb. Now she suspected he had other reasons for his overprotectiveness—reasons, she believed, that had to do with who her mother really was.

Seán and Andre's surrogacy story was sweet, but it was too

neat, too perfect. Almost ordinary. And she, Mckenna, was, if anything, extraordinary.

Extraordinary. The word generally had a positive connotation, usually synonymous with remarkable and astonishing. But Mckenna had always felt extraordinary in the "outside the norm" sense of the word. Whereas most teenagers could find happiness in the simplest of things—dances, football games, house parties—she couldn't help but feel none of it mattered. She was on the outside looking in, trying dreadfully to appear fine, like a snowflake fallen flat on a windowpane, exposed and seemingly intact, but seconds from melting away.

How she knew that they were hiding the truth about her mother, she didn't know—not in any concrete way, anyway. But this miserable, lonely feeling that was amplified tenfold today was begging to be confronted.

Before she knew it, she was downstairs standing at the kitchen threshold; her dads sat at opposite ends of the table, looking like they had reached a deadlock.

"If there is any chance—any chance at all that you could help me understand whatever is happening to me, I need you to please, please take it."

She entreated with her eyes, first to a reproachful-looking Andre, and then to Seán, who she could see was fighting hard to keep his expression neutral.

"There's . . . there's nothing to tell, swan. I'm sorry."

Mckenna felt as though she had been punched in the stomach and then thrown into a bottomless chasm. It was an inscrutable emotion, somewhere in between disbelief, hurt, and betrayal.

And then all at once, anger. Anger at all the years her dads knew she'd felt like an outcast, and still treated her like she wasn't. Like she was the same as any other awkward, developing teen.

Her body froze the way it often did when she was struck with rage. And then for God knows what reason, she thought of *A Journey to the Centre of the Earth,* where she read about a volcano in Stromboli, Italy that sometimes erupted several times a day. She took comfort in the fact that she wasn't the only living organism that might have blown up more than once in the past few hours. And so there it was again—another outburst about to surface. But she didn't want to hurt Seán like she did the bully, she told herself, as if the thought would prevent another head injury. She only wanted to understand him . . . terribly.

An image of him was thrust into her mind, except it wasn't really an image. It felt more like something she already *knew* . . . similar to experiencing a déjà vu.

It was a twenty-something-year-old Seán folding a piece of paper into a tiny square, then tucking it inside his wallet.

Mckenna blinked and came back to earth. She dove for his pockets.

"What the hell . . .?"

They were empty. "Shit!"

Andre placed a hand firmly on her shoulder. Before he had a chance to open his mouth, no doubt to reprimand her on her erratic behaviour, she shrugged his hand off and sprinted for the stairs.

She was barely a foot away from Seán and Andre's bedroom door when it blasted open, as though on command. And there on the nightstand lying open was Seán's mangled wallet, which he'd had for as long as Mckenna could remember.

Just as her dads' footsteps reached the landing, she snatched the wallet, spun her body around, and slammed the door in their puzzled faces.

"Mckenna!" Andre shouted out in the hall. "What are you doing?"

"Have you completely lost your marbles?" Seán barked over his own fist banging on the door.

She took in a deep breath and dug out a tiny piece of crumpled paper. Her anxious fingers shook uncontrollably as she unfolded it.

The handwriting alone, a hurried scrawl, was enough to stop the Earth rotating. Her thoughts quieted, the room faded away, and then her mother's voice—pure and sweet in her mind—echoed:

Seán,

You know how I feel about you, so I won't spend time telling you how much I love you. You have to understand that I'm doing this for your safety and for hers.

By the time you find this note, I will have already left Ballycastle. I might even be dead. You must please promise these three things: That you will leave the country immediately and never return, nor try looking for me. That you will never tell our daughter about me or who she really is. And that you will name our precious Wise One Mckenna.

I will love you until the last full moon,

Abby

What the hell was Ballycastle? What did *who she really is* mean? About a dozen more questions rushed through Mckenna's head, and then like she'd just come out of sleep paralysis, she lost all feeling in her body, and her face was frozen in shock. She caught a glimpse of herself across the room, and the colour drained from her face. Even her auburn curls seemed to dangle lifelessly. But her eyes, normally a dull brown, were no longer void, hollow; they glinted, instead, with something utterly new. They sparked with hope.

Her mother was not an egg donor. She was very, very real.

The door behind her blasted open, and Seán and Andre ran in like there was a fire. They had managed to kick the door in.

Mckenna held up the note. At first they both squinted at it, noticeably confused. Until Mckenna uttered three words that must have been so dreadful to Seán that he literally sank to his knees: "My mother's letter."

Seán had lost his ability to speak. Andre looked sideways at him with incredulity. "What's she talking about? A letter from *her?*"

"Yes," Seán mumbled.

"But I thought . . ." Andre was at a loss for words. "When?"

Seán hoisted himself up. "I think you should sit for this. Both of you."

IV

A Pact Between Strangers

Seán suggested they make tea and move to Andre's study, where it would be more comfortable. Mckenna rarely entered the study, but when she did, she would see Andre sunk into his leather brown armchair poring over one of his encyclopedias or writing his next lecture; it was a comforting feeling—calming, like watching a stream run under a small bridge, or observing a creature frolicking in nature. But that evening, there was no such feeling. The room was just a room. Even Andre seemed a stranger to it.

Mckenna took her place on the Persian rug, facing them. She hugged her knees and waited for Seán to speak. The scene brought her back to when she was a child and Seán, the gifted storyteller that he was, would narrate tales of Irish folklore that he learned from his grandad. Though, this time around, she braced herself, for the story he was about to tell would not obtain the same reactions.

"After I graduated from Trinity College in Dublin, I took a year off to do some travelling," he began, staring at the tea leaves as they descended to the bottom of his porcelain cup. "I backpacked around Europe—Italy, France, Spain, Germany, Switzerland—all over. Looking to 'find myself' and all that idealistic stuff," he said, using air quotes. "Figure out what it was I wanted to do, you know what I mean? Was the best time of my life. Complete freedom. There's absolutely nothing like breathing in the air around the Alps . . ."

Mckenna had never seen him wear such an expression of longing.

"My last stop before heading back home was England. That's where I met your mum."

To Mckenna's surprise, Andre chimed in. "At the stone circle, right?"

At last, Seán looked up. "Yeah, Avebury—in Wiltshire. A henge from the Neolithic period. It has three stone circles . . . You'd love it, swan."

So Andre *was* familiar with Seán's past. But did he know everything, Mckenna wondered.

"An unbelievable site," Seán continued. "The largest stone circle in the world, I reckon. That's when I saw her—Abby Douglas. Abigail was her full name. Spotted her red hair from across the monument. She had curls like yourself, swan."

Mckenna's eyes welled up. She gulped, hoping to swallow the lump that had formed in her throat. She glanced round at Andre, who was staring at his partner unblinkingly.

She looked back at Seán. "I don't understand. Are you saying you also . . .?"

"What attracts me to a person is who they are in their heart, regardless of their gender. Yes, I loved her, but that was before I met Andre. And that's that."

Andre furrowed his brow and appeared momentarily stunned.

"She was Irish, too?" Mckenna wondered.

"Nah, Scottish. Tell you the truth, I was afraid she'd be English. Thank Christ she wasn't—that would've been that, right?" He laughed in spite of himself. "We hit it off right away. She was an artist too, you see. A writer. On our first date we were already talking about creating children's books together. 'I want every child to know the world is full of light before they discover there's such a thing as darkness,' she'd say. I think so, anyway—her accent was bleedin' thick sometimes." He smiled with his eyes at the memory. "That was her passion—guiding others. But it was only until after we'd gotten married that I understood the extent of it . . ."

"You were married?" said Mckenna in disbelief. From the look on Andre's face, this was no surprise to him.

"Yes. After spending some time together in England, I brought her back to the farm just outside Dublin to meet my family. We'd decided to get married shortly after. My mum went mad—hated her from the start. And Dad just thought I was being thick, that I was too young. So we eloped. We got married in a small town along the northern coast, and Abby instantly fell in love with it. Thought it was as gorgeous as her hometown in Scotland."

"Why not move to her hometown?"

Seán hesitated. "She . . . didn't want to go back."

Mckenna grew impatient. "Okay, and then what?" she demanded. "What does all of this have to do with her letter? What does she mean by having to leave for our safety? What aren't you telling—?"

"Mckenna, please," Andre said. He turned to Seán and held his gaze. "So, the real reason she left was to protect you both."

Seán looked somberly back at him. "I'm so sorry . . . I should've been honest with you."

"What was she protecting us *from?*" she said through gritted teeth. "Why did she make you promise these things—" She pulled out the letter. "' . . . *you will leave the country immediately and never return, nor try looking for me. That you will never tell our daughter about me or who she really is. And that you will name our precious Wise One Mckenna.'* Was she an international spy or something? And who am I that even *I'm* not allowed to know about it? What the hell is a Wise One?"

Seán bit his lip.

"Your mom was magical, Mckenna," Andre blurted out.

Seán rounded on him. "*Amadán!*" he cursed under his breath. Mckenna had heard the Irish word enough times to know that it meant "fool."

"What do you mean *magical?* Like, she cast spells and stuff?"

"Spot on." Seán jumped to his feet. "Lovely woman, but mad, she was. More tea, anyone?"

Andre let out a long, exasperated breath. "Not exactly, Mckenna. Well, sort of. But that's not what I meant."

"Would you just leave it, Andre—"

"Tell me!" Mckenna shouted.

Seán threw his hands in the air. "Yeah, alright. Your mum was—what she liked to call—a mystic. A very spiritual being . . . a kind of witch, you might say—call it what you like." He began pacing around the room. "She joined a coven after we were married. Not knowing a thing about magic and such, I thought it was a little weird, of course. Didn't believe in any of it. But I saw that it was good for her. She knew her herbs like I know my spices—had remedies for everything. And she had this Zen thing about her . . . can't explain it. But it was almost contagious. So, I thought, this can't be all that bad. Let her do her thing, right? Wrong.

"Your mum had gifts, you see. She could sort of heal—I won't say more than that because I don't really understand the technique. She worked with energy, that's the extent I know. She said she felt things others felt, too." That explained her newfound empathic abilities. "She also, erm, saw things. But I won't go there . . .

"Then I noticed as the months went by, she started keeping things from me. Bad things. She was in trouble. I tried to understand . . . to be there for her, but . . ."

Seán's voice began to shake, and Mckenna felt her heart (or was it his?) shatter to pieces.

"Anyway . . ." He swallowed. "By then, Abby was pregnant. And things only got worse. She was paranoid all the time, staying indoors and skipping her gatherings. She even stopped writing altogether. But when you were born, oh, you've no idea . . . She was the happiest I'd ever seen her. And then one day, without warning, I came home to find her gone and that note in your Moses basket."

"The what?" Mckenna and Andre said.

"What do you call it—the bassinette."

Mckenna tried to take it all in. Could this be true? Before she could react, Andre, whom Mckenna could tell was staying composed for her sake, leaned forward in his chair and uttered six words that destroyed any bit of rationale she had left.

"We think you have gifts, too."

Had she spoken without taking a second to consider this, the next words out of her mouth would have been, "Sure, and aliens did land in Roswell." But instead, she reflected on the inexplicable events that had occurred around her that day—how it seemed as though she and the bird communicated, how she willed the book to slam shut and the bedroom door to fly open . . .

And then she thought of how peculiar the past several months had been. At times, her vivid nightmares consumed her to the point that she would avoid human interaction for days, as though the terrible people she had dreamt about would manifest in real life. She thought of her inborn ability to read people and how strong her intuition was.

To her astonishment, she responded, "I know." But something still wasn't making any sense. "Did she ever mention other mystics or witches? People with abilities . . ."

"All the time. Her coven was full of them, supposedly. Why?"

"Okay, what else aren't you telling me?"

The wrinkles on Seán's forehead doubled. "That's all of it, swan. I dunno what you mean."

"Abby didn't want you to tell me all of this for a reason. She wanted to keep me away from magic. Why?"

"I told you, she was in danger. She thought we—you—were safer without her, without magic."

"Except you skipped the part about the 'precious Wise One.' What's so special about that? After all, there are other witches, other people with abilities . . . Are they all called Wise Ones?"

"Honestly, Mckenna, I have no idea what a Wise One is. She never mentioned it."

"And yet she wrote it. It must mean *something*. Also, why couldn't she just go into hiding, take these guys out, and come find us later?"

"I can't answer that."

"You can, though!" Her voice touched every volume shelved in Andre's collection. "Why did we have to run away forever? It was me she was protecting." Seán covered his face with his hands, and she knew. "I was the one being hunted, wasn't I?"

His fingers pressed against his eyes, Seán nodded.

"Am I still?"

"I don't know," Seán whispered.

Andre placed his hand on hers. "He's telling the truth. You're special, Mckenna. You've always been. We just don't know why."

Mckenna spent the weekend researching witches and avoiding her dads—especially Seán. Regardless of his so-called honourable intentions, she could not accept the fact he had lied to her about who her mother was—who *she* was—all these years.

She had grown up thinking she would never get to meet the woman whose genes she had inherited. Besides Seán's straight nose and hard head, she hadn't taken after much else from him; he was cautious and jovial, and she impulsive and introverted. His skin was dark in tone, while hers was milky and lightly freckled; his hair tame and fair—her curls wild and chocolaty with red pigment, passed on by her mother, it would seem; his eyes green—hers brown. Mckenna wondered if Seán saw a bit of her mother in her.

When she had asked Seán that night if her mother was still alive, he said he didn't know. While she did believe he was telling the truth, she also sensed he was holding back a lot more about his and her mom's past than he let on.

Seán still claimed he had never heard the term "Wise One."

He supposed it was just a pet name, but Mckenna didn't believe that for a second. It wasn't exactly common, and Seán had never heard Abby use it before.

"There's nothing more I can tell you, swan. But I thought . . . well, you might like these." He tossed a black velvet pouch on her bed, secured with a gold, twisted cord. "They were hers."

She waited for him to exit before emptying its contents; they were a deck of cards, each with a vibrant, intricate illustration, and a word or phrase, like *Solitude* and *Mixed Feelings,* etched in gold lettering, echoing the shimmering edges. One by one she took in their unique artwork and message. When she felt her eyes grow heavy, she closed them and began to shuffle, thinking longingly of her mother, wherever she was. A card slipped out of the deck, landing face-up on her bedspread. It read *Intuition.*

Mckenna spent most of Sunday researching the term "Wise One" in Andre's encyclopedias. Nothing. The only instance of "Wise One" was in a song by John Coltrane from his 1964 album, *Crescent*—Andre was a huge Coltrane fan.

She wasn't the only one avoiding Seán. Mckenna hadn't seen Andre speak to him since her birthday. That Friday night, she overheard some arguing in their bedroom, but she couldn't make out what they were saying.

Seán knew what was coming.

"You told me you stopped having feelings for her," Andre said.

"Yeah. No, well . . ." Seán searched for the right words. "We—we grew apart."

"And that's not even the worst of it. All this time, you *actually* made me believe that she ran out on you and Mckenna when you told her you were gay. Do you realize how screwed up that is?"

"There was no point in you thinking I had eyes for . . .well, any person, no matter their gender. I didn't want you to have any doubts about us!"

"Well, shouldn't I? You kept her letter in your wallet for seventeen years. She was clearly the love of your life."

"Oh, c'mon, you're joking, I forgot that was in there; I haven't had a new wallet since! You know I don't like to waste—I haven't changed my socks in three days."

"Really not in the mood, Seán."

"Andre, *you're* the love of my life. You are, understand? When she started slipping away, it distanced us, and nothing I did was good enough to fix it—and that's no lie! I wouldn't have gone on like that."

"I'm sorry if I'm not convinced. You wouldn't be either if you were me, sitting across from you like a fool, seeing your face . . . the way you talked about her . . ."

"Andre . . . please. It was a long time ago. The memory of it all . . . it just made me feel so many things. But mostly sad and wretched. She left me alone to raise our newborn child, for Christ's sake, and no reason is good enough to justify that! Anything I ever felt for her is gone."

At least two minutes went by before Andre spoke. "You should've told me about the letter. This involves *our daughter*."

"Of course. I'm sorry, luv, I was wrong. I was wrong."

Mckenna remembered a long silence following the muffled arguing. For a moment, she thought they had made up. But next, she heard the bedroom door open and close, then Andre's footsteps crossing the hall and disappearing downstairs.

By Sunday, Mckenna had lost all hope of discovering anything on magic and sorcery that might be of some use or meaning to her. She had gone through nearly all of Andre's encyclopedias, researching witch-related words like *Wicca, pagan, spells, supernatural, occult, coven,* even *stone circles*, which many scholars believed were prehistoric structures of ceremony and worship associated with the ancient Celts and druids, or spiritual leaders.

How curious that Seán and her mother happened to meet at one. And not just any one—the very oldest stone circle in Europe.

She found nothing concrete, only some general information on infamous witches, trials, and the history of the occult. As drawn as Mckenna felt to it all, she knew it wouldn't be enough to unearth what was really going on inside of her, who she really was.

Who her mother really was.

When dusk settled on Sunday, Mckenna's melancholy worsened. The entire weekend had gone by, and she felt as confused and miserable as ever. All she craved was some kind of sign, something that would help her find answers. Who was after her? Why? Were they *still* after her?

Mindlessly, Mckenna grabbed another encyclopedia off the shelf and cracked it open on her lap. Her eyes roamed the page and settled on the very last word: *veiled.*

Her heart gave a jolt, and a loud buzzing sound built around her ears. It lingered for a beat, urging her to acknowledge it, then faded.

Veiled . . .

"Dad!" Mckenna shouted as she bolted down the hall, skipped the last three stairs and landed on her feet with a loud thud.

Seán emerged from the kitchen, looking like he hadn't slept in ages, and Andre appeared from around the corner; both appeared surprised that Mckenna was speaking to either of them.

"I think my mother is still alive."

Seán and Andre exchanged worried looks. "I haven't heard from your mum since. I'm afraid you're going to have to accept that she won't be coming back."

"Okay, but what if the fact that my 'gifts' are surfacing is a sign? What if she's been in hiding all these years—what if she wants *me* to find *her?*" Her mind jumped to the *Intuition* card that appeared the night before.

Andre spoke for the first time in almost two days, his tone severe. "Someone who's gone through great lengths to stay hidden from her family doesn't want to be found, Mckenna. That, or—"

"No," she said firmly. "She's not dead."

Seán stared pointedly back at her. "You can't know that. She left, alright? And what does it matter?" His voice rose. "Your dad's right—if she's alive then she wants nothing to do with us, so leave it be! *We're* your family. We're all you need."

Mckenna wished that were true.

She nodded, not in agreement, but in understanding; she would not gain the insight she needed from Seán and Andre.

She walked past them and marched straight out the door.

Her feet carried her to the woods. The leaves, gradually turning as autumn loomed, sparkled in the moonlight, which flooded the narrow walkway. She walked on, past the wild shrubs, towering trees, and park benches. She would have felt like the only person in the whole town if a sudden movement hadn't caught her eye.

She turned her head slowly. Her eyes searched among the trees and fell on a particularly large hedge. She examined it and thought for a minute she spotted the shadow of a small child crouched behind it.

It was a little late to be playing hide and seek, Mckenna thought. Squinting, she took a step closer, but a rustling sound at the end of the path tore her gaze away.

There leaning against a massive tree trunk near the walkway's only lamppost was Nissa, the pixie-like girl that Mckenna—or rather the bird—had saved from the bully.

Mckenna almost hadn't spotted her; she was nestled like a small animal inside a kind of nook the trunk had formed, her face buried behind a book, straining to read under the faint glow of the lamplight.

Nissa lowered it and smiled warmly. "I guess three really is a magic number."

Mckenna's heart stopped at the word *magic*. "Sorry?"

"This is the third time we've run into each other in three days, isn't it?"

Mr. Heathley's class, the schoolyard, and now, Mckenna thought. "Yeah. Small towns, right?" Nonetheless, it was a strange coincidence. But strange seemed to be the case when Nissa was around, and that included her choice of attire: Nissa was wearing blue-jean overalls, patched-up in some areas with what looked like pieces of quilt. As if this weren't enough of a fashion statement, her socks were mismatched, one green and one bright orange—though Mckenna was also guilty of occasionally throwing on whichever ones she could dig out of her messy drawer.

Hoping Nissa didn't notice her gawking, Mckenna gestured at the book she was reading. "Must've been really good."

"Oh, yes. I started it this morning and couldn't put it down. The author's a genius!" She held it up for Mckenna, who nodded in thanks and took it in her hands. The words *The End of Nature* were printed in bold black letters across a green and yellow cover. An image of a small bird's lifeless body rested on a pile of fallen leaves.

"He talks about humanity's effect on the environment. His theory is that our planet's survival depends on the way we relate to nature."

It was easy to warm up to her enthusiasm. "Sounds provocative."

"Yes, *I* think so! McKibben will become a sensation . . . He's from right here in Massachusetts, you know. Says so on the inside cover."

"You seem to care a lot about this environment stuff. I mean, we all should. But you more than most."

"Well, yeah," she said as though Mckenna's statement was absurd. "I get that it's easy to overlook what's right under our nose, but we can't afford to do it any longer. Where would we all end up if we destroyed the only home we have?"

Mckenna hadn't thought much about it before now. She supposed she had always been drawn to nature—the sound of a breeze, a thunderstorm, and moving trees always did the trick when her mind was flooding with negative thoughts or she was low on energy. But she never stopped to think about a time when it might all go away. She had always considered the Earth limitless in what it could sustain.

"I can lend it to you if you want," she offered.

Mckenna gave a slight smile. "Yeah, sure. As soon as you're done with it." She handed it back to her. "Do you live nearby, or are you just stalking me?" she joked.

Nissa let out a deep, frog-like chortle. "You caught me! I actually live, uh . . ." She looked down at the ground. "Just a little south of here."

Mckenna sat on a flat rock opposite the tree. Construing this as an invitation, Nissa settled back into her nook.

"I just moved in with my foster family," she said suddenly.

Mckenna nodded. "Are they nice?"

"They're okay. Better than most, worse than some." She forced a laugh.

"Sorry," was all Mckenna could think to say.

"Oh, others are worse off."

Mckenna hesitated. "Do you mind if I ask . . .?"

"Go ahead," Nissa said.

She was going to ask what happened to her parents, but she didn't want to pry. "Do you find it hard living without your real parents?"

"I never knew them, really. I was about three when I was placed in Boston's foster system. I arrived by ship. That's all I know."

"But they had to have brought you here, no? Or someone would've had to. Have you tried looking up your last name? To find them, I mean."

"My record doesn't even have my last name."

Mckenna wanted to hit her forehead against the nearest tree trunk.

"Oh, don't worry," Nissa said lightly. "I've learned to live with it. I only wonder sometimes where the ship actually came from. I've never felt this was home for me. Do you ever get that feeling?"

"Sometimes," Mckenna said, thinking of wherever her mother might be.

"I don't really know how to go about researching passenger lists. I once called some government office in Boston and they asked to speak to my guardian, so I hung up."

"If you still want to look, I can help."

"Oh, that's okay. It seems like such a complicated process."

"Funny, you don't strike me as someone who gives up easily. I mean, you spent your first day at a new school telling everyone off for not having recycling bins."

Nissa grinned and shrugged her shoulders. "I don't! I'd just rather focus on stuff that's important right now. It's funny how hard it is to get people to care about the things that we need, and not the things that we want."

Nissa was now recalling the class's mocking and Becka and Jared's bullying. Mckenna would've bet her favourite purple jacket that Nissa was used to getting made fun of.

"Well,"—Mckenna slid off the rock onto the ground, stretched out her legs, and rested her head on the surface—"you got me to care." Nissa's face went from solemn to hopeful.

Mckenna came to the conclusion that Nissa was way stronger than she looked. The former could hardly live with the fact that she didn't know her mother—she couldn't imagine going about her life wondering who both her parents were and why they gave her up.

"You don't need to feel bad for me," Nissa said, reading her expression. "We all have our troubles."

A cool breeze carried away some of the leaves surfacing the path, settling them around Mckenna's boots. She scraped the ground and formed a small pile with her heels.

"I thought I didn't have a mother," Mckenna heard herself say.

"And now you do?"

"I'm not sure, to be honest. I don't even know if she's alive."

Nissa nodded empathetically. "And it's impossible to go around living as if everything is normal. As if *you're* normal."

Mckenna glanced up. "Yes. That's exactly it."

"Then you shouldn't have to," Nissa said simply.

"No . . ." she said, pondering this. "I shouldn't. Thanks."

Nissa beamed.

"And you shouldn't have to either."

Mckenna couldn't believe she had just met Nissa. They chatted for hours on end about nothing in particular, sharing fragments of their imperfect lives, each of their stories a separate piece of sharp, tinted glass that together made up one chaotic mosaic of failures, feats, and dreams.

"I try not to think about it much—the fact that I don't have anything that really belongs to me," Nissa said after Mckenna learned that this was Nissa's eighth foster family in fourteen years. "And just my luck, I lost the one thing that actually *did,*" Nissa said, closing her middle finger and thumb around her wrist.

"Oh!" Mckenna dug into her coat pocket. "Is this yours?" She dangled the gold bracelet in the air.

Nissa leaped for it. "Yes! I can't believe it. Where did you find it?"

"On the floor right beside my desk—Friday. I guess it fell off when you were handing out the petition?"

"Weird. It's never broken off." She frowned at it for a moment, and as Mckenna watched, something—a thought, feeling—entered her consciousness and lingered like an uninvited guest. It was knowing and persistent, and it didn't seem to belong to Mckenna at all; it was a sensation of utter elation that Nissa had reunited with the precious trinket that her three-year-old self was wearing when she arrived by ship all those years ago.

Was she feeling what Nissa was feeling? Was she in Nissa's consciousness?

And then she remembered homeroom on Friday, when a hopeless feeling had overcome her without warning. She must've somehow entered Ms. Silcock's head.

Nissa looked up. "You have no idea how much this means to me, really. I've had it for as long as I can remember, and I never went a day without it when I finally had enough money to get it resized."

Mckenna looked down at the ground, taking a moment to

shake off Nissa's emotions. "I'm just glad you have it back."

Under the dim light from the lamppost, she could make out Nissa's warm smile. The two lay back, gazing up at the moon.

"Wow—is it midnight?" Mckenna said at last, breaking the silence.

"Can't be." Nissa followed her gaze and hung her head back, squinting at the sky. "How can you tell?"

"When the moon's phase is in its first quarter and positioned in the east-west, it's midnight."

"How do you know *that?*"

"Can't remember where I read it . . ."

Nissa let out a "Ha!" and then held up her wrist. "Off my watch, maybe?"

Mckenna's explosive cackle echoed through the trees, followed by Nissa's, which resembled that of a five-year-old. The two were on their backs, dissolving into a fit of giggles like they had inhaled an obscene amount of glue.

After Mckenna admitted that she did indeed read the time off Nissa's watch ("I wasn't lying about the moon's phase, though!"), Mckenna spotted a faint glow the size of a mosquito beyond Nissa's head.

"Don't move," Mckenna whispered.

Nissa froze. "What . . .?"

Mckenna squinted at the spot until the light behind her gradually faded.

"I think there might be someone here. Let's go."

They jumped to their feet, dusted themselves off, and walked swiftly back up the path.

It turned out Nissa only lived two blocks south of Mckenna, who walked her to the door of a shabby-looking home with an unkempt lawn. All the lights were out.

"This is me," Nissa said, looking a little glum. "It was nice to meet you . . .?"

"Mckenna," she said, musing at the fact that they hadn't

actually introduced themselves this entire time. "You're Nissa."

"Good memory! I'm not too great with names, but I'll never forget a face," she said. "And I want to thank you."

Mckenna's mind instantly jumped to the bird flying into Jared's head. "For what?"

Nissa scrutinized her for a moment. "For finding my bracelet, for one. And for getting everyone to sign my petition."

"Oh, don't mention it." Mckenna breathed out in relief. "You know, if you want to be liked at school, you shouldn't be seen with me."

"Hmm . . . I always felt being liked was as important as Scotch Tape."

Mckenna didn't have a clue what that was supposed to mean, but she decided it was catchy. "You're a little odd, Nissa."

"Yeah. So are you."

They stood in silence for a moment. Mckenna suddenly snickered at a distant memory. "When I was a kid, my dad would always say, 'If it's drowning you're after, don't torment yourself with shallow water!'"

Nissa snorted at Mckenna's imitation of an Irish accent. "What does that mean?"

"I was never *entirely* sure, to be honest. But now, I think it means to leave your comfort zone. To dive right into what you're most afraid of—because living a shallow life is worse than drowning."

Mckenna could tell Nissa was absorbing this. "How about a pact? I won't give up my fight if you won't give up yours." Nissa was referring to finding her mother.

Someone who before that night had been an utter stranger to her had somehow understood Mckenna's yearning to know her mom more than her own fathers did.

She held out her hand. "Sounds fair to me."

Nissa gripped it and gave it an exuberant shake.

Mckenna's gut told her to wait until Nissa had gotten in safely. She watched as she entered the house, and her small silhouette appeared on the other side of the cracked upstairs window. As soon as the light turned on, Mckenna heard doors banging and voices blaring in anger—"You woke us!" The light switched off, and seconds after the voices quieted, Mckenna made out a feeble light flickering on in the darkness—no doubt a flashlight used to finish the last few pages of her book.

V

The Feather's Message

Mckenna tiptoed down the hall and was startled by a truck starting in her living room. As she suspected, the ghastly sound was coming from Seán; in a deep slumber, his legs were stretched out greedily on the three-seater sofa while Andre's tall, half-conscious body was upright on the adjacent armchair, his head slowly slipping off his palm.

She crept upstairs, careful not to step on the three creaky floorboards, and then made to go to her bedroom. In the stretch of corridor between her room and Andre's study, she stopped dead. She felt wide awake. There was no sense in going to bed now. She entered and closed the door quietly.

Her eyes swept over the bookshelf she'd always admired and settled on Andre's newest encyclopedias—a thirty-two volume set published just last year, in 1990. Mckenna scanned each gold letter embroidered on the leather binding. Though her weekend of research had proved inconclusive, she couldn't help but wonder if she had missed something . . .

The door burst open, and Seán appeared, looking dishevelled

and worried. "Thank God you're home! We were waiting up for you." He strode towards her.

Mckenna shifted behind the armchair. "I was taking a walk."

He stopped short of the chair. "For over three hours?"

Mckenna's jaw tightened.

He sighed miserably. "I'm just relieved you're safe. And I just want to say . . . I'm sorry. I'm sorry about all of this. I wish things were different."

"You wish you had been honest with me?"

"I wish you weren't involved in any of this. I wish things were back to normal. Before that letter."

Right. "Things were never normal," she muttered.

"What's that?"

She looked down at her hands. "Goodnight, Dad."

With another heavy sigh, he walked over to kiss her on her forehead and muttered a fatherly "go to bed" before giving her one last longing look and heading to his room. He wasn't at all apologetic about the fact that he had lied to her her entire life. He was only sorry she had found the letter.

The letter.

It's easy to overlook what's right under our nose. Nissa's words rang softly in her ears. She scrambled for the small piece of folded paper, digging her hands into her pants' back pockets, and then re-read her mother's parting words to Seán four or five times; of all the peculiar things it contained, it was this sentence that Mckenna found most remarkable: *By the time you find this note, I will have already left Ballycastle.*

Ballycastle was where Abby and Seán had started their married life together. It was the place Abby felt the most drawn to; where she had joined a coven, and people knew her; where she had started sensing she was in trouble; and where she had left her family behind.

If Mckenna wanted to gather clues as to who her mother was, Ballycastle was the only logical place to begin. Perhaps she'd find a part of herself there, too.

Full of adrenaline, she tugged at the encyclopedia referencing the letters *A* and *B,* and yanked it off the shelf, perhaps with a bit too much excitement because it fell to the floor with a loud thud.

Something downstairs shifted, and then she heard Andre's footsteps approaching. She tiptoed to her bedroom, the book secured between her arms, and slipped underneath her bed cover just as the door cracked open. She kept her eyes squeezed tight as Andre planted a light kiss on her forehead, and then, to Mckenna's surprise, sauntered to his room for the first time in three days.

As soon as she heard her dads' bedroom door close, she kicked the cover off, flicked on her lamp, and flipped impatiently through the pages until her eyes found *Avebury Henge.*

She was torn. This was, after all, where her parents met. Maybe this strange and magical place had answers. She hung her head back, overwhelmed by the idea of travelling so far without knowing for certain that something—someone—was waiting for her. She wished for something to happen, some sort of knowing feeling that this was where she needed to go.

Tearing off a sheet from her science notebook, she saved the page and moved on to the *Bs,* though she was quite sure Ballycastle was not a renowned place, like Dublin or Galway, or even Avebury Henge. And yet there it was, black on white: *Ballycastle, Northern Ireland.* The description was only a few lines of text, but it was all Mckenna needed to know.

> *Ballycastle (from Irish: Baile an Chaistil, meaning "town of the castle") is a small coastal town in County Antrim in Northern Ireland, located on the eastern end of the Causeway Coast. Rathlin Island and the Mull of Kintyre in Scotland can be viewed from the coastline. The family-friendly picturesque town is recognized for its beautiful beaches and bays, natural attractions, and historical sites (see Kinbane Castle: Volume 9).*

There it was. That pull—a deep-rooted longing to smell the scents of the seaside town that her parents once called home.

And here she was, in a town where she didn't belong, living a half-truth. Was she expected to go on like this every day for the rest of her life?

The walls were closing in on her. It felt as though her room was contaminated with recycled air, like being stuck on an airplane for hours on end. She took two long strides to the window and stuck her head out, inhaling and exhaling deeply. The night was still—nothing but the soothing sound of crickets.

And then—

Churrr.

The shrill chirp was instantly recognizable. Mckenna's head darted around for a sign of the plump bird, but there was nothing in sight—until a strong wind sent something soaring into her room.

A brown, tiger-striped feather. It had stuck onto a photograph of her, Seán, and Andre in front of Fenway Park.

In Boston.

Mckenna gaped in disbelief at the feather's remarkable pattern. She picked it up and stroked the delicate plumage, identical, she was sure, to the one that was tucked inside her coat pocket. Astounded, she dug it out and compared the two.

If someone had crawled inside her head that very second, they would have thought her senseless. This strange and extraordinary sign was all the reassurance she needed to do what she was about to do next. She decided this was not a mere coincidence; she knew precisely which bird this feather belonged to.

And what it was urging her to do.

Mckenna had always had excellent hand-eye coordination, so she wasn't at all surprised when the rock hit Nissa's bedroom window on the first go.

It slid open with a loud *squeak* and Nissa stuck nearly half her body out, scanning the front yard. When she spotted Mckenna sporting her deep purple jacket and lugging a large backpack, she furrowed her brow and slid the pane closed.

Mckenna stood there uncertainly for about a minute until Nissa appeared on the porch, wearing a thick, baby blue robe covered in cartoon images of bunnies. She ushered Mckenna around the side of the house.

"Is everything okay?"

"I'm going to Northern Ireland. To find my mother. Hopefully."

Nissa's face formed a brilliant smile. "I'm so glad!"

Mckenna started. "I was hoping . . ." She hesitated. Was she doing the right thing? If people were indeed still after her, she would be putting Nissa in harm's way.

Nissa scrutinized her. "Are you asking me to come with you?"

"Yes. No—I don't know. Maybe this wasn't a good idea . . ."

"No, go ahead. Whatcha thinking?"

Mckenna took a breath. "Well, I thought we could help each other. There must be immigration records somewhere. Your ship landed in Boston, right? I have a hunch we should start there." She fingered the feather in her coat pocket.

Nissa looked stunned. Mckenna had a feeling this was the first time anyone had showed any interest in Nissa's past. "I . . . but then—how will we get to Ireland?"

"I don't know yet. Grab a cheap last-minute flight from Boston maybe?"

"I don't have a passport . . ." Nissa said, her head down.

Mckenna wasn't surprised. "We'll figure it out," she said, having no inkling as to how. Nissa stood there irresolute, tinkering with her bracelet, which glinted in the moonlight.

"Do you believe in signs, Nissa?"

"I'm not sure."

"Well, I do. I don't connect much with—with anyone. And then you come along and it's like . . ."

"We've known each other forever," Nissa asserted.

Mckenna beamed. "Exactly. And then there's this bracelet." She tugged at it. "What are the chances that it broke off you for the first time the other day, right at my feet? And then I run into you again tonight? What if . . ." She paused. She was never one to be so forward, so candid with anyone but her dads. But there was something about the person standing before her. She was the Phoebe to her Holden—one of the few people Mckenna didn't consider a phony.

"What if you're meant to come with me?"

Nissa's eyes widened—at first, Mckenna thought, in alarm at what she had just said; but their sparkle indicated understanding. And then, to Mckenna's utter amazement, Nissa glanced back at the dilapidated house behind her and nodded.

"Let me just grab some things."

VI

Signs and Faith

As they walked through the quiet town and towards the freeway, Mckenna was feeling both hopeful and uncertain. She was relying a lot on her gut these days, but it would take a lot more than that to get them across a freaking ocean.

At least money wasn't an issue—for now. Mckenna had known the combination to her dads' safe since she was nine. Seán had punished her for walking to the convenience store by herself after dark one evening ("I was craving a Mr. Freeze!"), so he locked away her Walkman; knowing her father had a terrible memory, she had attempted a series of easy-to-remember combinations until she managed to crack the "uncrackable" code—4-3-2-1.

She showed Nissa the wad of cash.

"Whoa. Your dads will be pretty pissed, huh."

"It's the least they can do," Mckenna said without an ounce of remorse.

Nissa looked at the ground. "I don't have much with me."

"Don't mention it, we have more than enough to cover us for a while. There's a cheap motel close to the highway towards Boston," Mckenna said, remembering the tacky sign on their drives out to ballgames when she was little. "I'm thinking we head there now, and first thing tomorrow we take a bus." Unlike their small town of Abredonia Woods, Boston had possibilities, she thought. They could begin by finding a passport office.

She continued to strategize on the way, the two of them lugging backpacks full of clothes—tightly rolled the way Andre had taught her—Dunk-a-Roos, Nature Valley granola bars, and any other sustenance they could grab. Finally, they reached a nondescript two-storey building with a flashing neon sign that read *Motel 495*.

Mckenna approached the front desk, Nissa following closely behind her. A middle-aged balding man with rat-like eyes sat behind a glass panel (bulletproof?) fiddling with the antenna of a ten-inch television, the sporadic static noise making the dingy interior feel eerie as hell.

"Um . . . sorry . . ." Nissa began.

The man didn't flinch.

"'Scuse me . . ."

Rather than respond, he opted to thrash his TV set.

"We would like a room, sir," Mckenna said firmly.

He lifted his fat chin, his dull eyes bearing zero enthusiasm.

"We're full," he said, then continued the beating.

Nissa frowned. "But there's a *vacancy* sign right outside the door."

He looked them up and down with annoyance, like they were mere toddlers who lost their mommy at the mall food court. "There's no more rooms."

Nissa scoffed and whispered to Mckenna, "He's just saying that because we're young and thinks we don't have any money."

Mckenna's insides burned. She banged the glass hard, startling him. "I'm sorry, are we disturbing you?" she said in her most sardonic tone. "Let's start again: Hello! We would like a double room, please. And before you say you're full, there isn't a single car in your sad-looking lot, so we all know that's not true, and I'm afraid if you don't serve us, my lawyer daddy will sue you for discrimination so fast, this place will shut down before you could say 'no vacancy.'"

The man's jaw hung open slightly. Mckenna smirked and handed him a few bills. "That should cover it."

Their room was straight out of a horror film: There were cracks in the wall, like veins on an ugly, wrinkly forehead; the floors were covered wall-to-wall with a salmon rug that looked like it hadn't been vacuumed, ever; the bedspread was vomit-coloured, with the odd swirly, pea green pattern; and a single flickering lamp was all that lit the cramped space.

"This is . . . cozy," Nissa said.

Mckenna snorted, and the two were caught in a fit of giggles. Once they caught their breath, Mckenna sighed. "I'm exhausted."

"Ditto."

They lay on their backs shoulder to shoulder over the bedspread (they didn't dare touch the sheets), and within seconds, drifted off.

By 9:00 a.m., they were on an express bus on the Interstate 495 towards Boston. After nearly two hours of dozing off and on, the elderly couple across the aisle bickering incessantly, Mckenna opened her eyes to an important-looking building, where the bus came to its final stop.

They swung their backpacks over their shoulders and squeezed into the tight aisle behind the infamous pair—who, amazingly, were still at it.

"This isn't the harbour, you old crack."

"You've told me at least *six times* that you wanted to go to the McCormack Building first, John."

"Right. Yeah, that's what I said,"

" . . . Jesus, John . . ."

Mckenna had been to Boston enough times to know that its

largest ancestry group was Irish, so she wasn't at all surprised when she heard the familiar accent, which had a quicker pace and was far more nasal than Seán's.

She thought of how they must've reacted when they discovered she was gone . . .

At 8:30 that morning, Andre straightened his tie in the entrance mirror, packed his briefcase, and called Mckenna downstairs for the third time, offering to give her a lift to school.

He got no response.

"Maybe she took off early," Andre said hopefully, after he and Seán checked her room. Her backpack, purple jacket, and Converse were gone.

"Or maybe she just *took off,*" Seán reasoned.

"She couldn't have gone far without a passport and money . . ."

They exchanged worried glances and darted for the basement. Inside the safe, in place of their pile of emergency cash, there lay a note:

> *I'm sorry, but I need answers. Please don't come looking for me.*
>
> *Don't worry—I'll be okay.*
>
> *Mckenna*

Seán stared at the note in disbelief. "That's it? Two lines? DOES SHE WANT TO *KILL* ME?"

Andre pulled him against his chest. "Everything is going to be okay. She'll be okay. Let's look in her room again, see if she left any clues."

It took seconds to spot the encyclopedia on her desk, where a torn loose leaf stuck out of its pages.

Seán flung it open. "She bloody well went to Avebury Henge."

"Oh, come on. She wouldn't."

"She would. That impetuous little—"

"We don't know that for sure, maybe she was just researching it." He placed both his hands on Seán's shoulders. "I think we need to stay calm and wait for her to reach out to us."

"What are you talking about—our daughter's alone. Gone!"

"She's not gone for good. She's going through something normal people can't even imagine; we have to be patient and trust her. She'll come back home eventually . . . when she's ready."

Seán shoved Andre's hands off his shoulders.

"You're daft, you know that? If you want to wait around and hope for an angry teenage girl whose inherited abilities we can't understand to suddenly come to her senses, that's grand. But me, I'm going to find her."

And he stormed upstairs, leaving Andre standing in the dark basement listening to the old pipes making that awful racket they had never gotten around to fixing.

BOSTON, MASSACHUSETTS

Mckenna and Nissa hopped off the bus and found themselves in a wide square paved with red stone and packed with people coming and going. In front of them, dozens of enormous steps led to an odd, Lego-looking building, behind which stood a cluster of much taller buildings. Boston's business district.

"That better not be the McCormack building," the elderly man, John, said to his wife loudly. "There's no way I'm climbing all those—unless you want me to take a hopper."

"It says Boston City Hall on the front, don't you see?" His wife pointed at the front entrance, and pulled out a map large enough for both her and John to sit on. "We've got to go . . ." she began, squinting at the small street names.

Nissa mouthed "aw" to Mckenna, and stepped forward.

"Excuse me, ma'am, can we help?"

"You from here, luv?"

"Well, no, but I can help you read the map if you'd like."

"Please do!" John cut in. "Me wife is as blind as a bat."

She pinned him with a glare that suggested she would blind *him* if he didn't bite his tongue, then turned back to Nissa. "We're trying to get to the McCormack building, luv."

Mckenna glanced over Nissa's shoulder and studied the map, recognizing a few of the main streets. "Well that's Congress Street . . ." she began, following the streets with her finger, "so you just need to cross, and then take Cornhill down, and then cross Court Street to Tremont, and—"

"For feck's sake, we'll get there tomorrow," John said, throwing his arms in the air and releasing his hold on his and his wife's wheeled carryon baggage, making each fall forward on the ground with a thud.

"Oh, don't worry, mister, it's not very far," Nissa said kindly. "We can walk with you, can't we?" she added, awaiting Mckenna's nod of approval.

"Actually, we should really get goi—" she started to say, but stopped mid-word, gawking at the small, brown bird that was now perched on John's shoulder.

Impossible.

It was unmistakable: The tiger-like plumage was identical to the two tucked inside her coat pocket; its beak sharp as a needle; its chest stumpy like a fat cartoon chef; and its chirp as piercing as a baby's cry.

Nissa glanced at Mckenna and then back at the bird. Did she recognize it from the schoolyard, too?

"Shoo!" John's wife shouted, waving the bird away. It gave a last *churrr* before it flew off. "Them wrens are so noisy. Surprised to see them in America at all! Isn't it odd, John?"

So, it was a wren, Mckenna thought to herself, a bird native to, or at least common around Ireland, she gathered from the lady's reaction. That couldn't be coincidental. Were these signs—this magic—coming from her mother?

"Are you talking to me?" said John, who apparently hadn't noticed a thing. His wife rolled her eyes.

"You know what—yes. We'd love to show you the way," Mckenna said, deciding not to mess with the little wren's persistence.

Maybe the third time will be a charm, she thought, Nissa's words playing over in her head.

They learned that John's very patient wife was named Brigit—"After Saint Brigid of Kildare, of course!"—and that they had come from County Limerick, Ireland to visit their daughter and newborn grandchild; she lived about an hour outside of Boston, some thirty minutes away from Abredonia Woods.

"Mckenna's half Irish!" Nissa pointed out as they rounded the corner on Ashburton Place.

"Who isn't," John grunted.

"Are you, now?" Brigit said eagerly, as though this meant they were now related.

"Yeah, my dad's from just outside Dublin."

"Oh, that city's pure mank," John scoffed. Mckenna and Nissa exchanged confused glances. Even Mckenna hadn't heard that one, but it wasn't all that hard to decode.

They walked up for a few minutes longer and reached the top of Beacon Hill, according to the map. There stood a distinct-looking building—a black and white, glass and concrete high-rise, on its façade the words *John W. McCormack Building* in gold block letters.

"Lovely of you young ladies to accompany us old folk," said Brigit, a warm smile spread across her overly made-up cheeks.

"Aren't they coming with us, Brigit?" John said, wrinkling his brow and looking mildly confused.

"Does this look like a *Penneys* to you, John?"

Mckenna snorted, knowing Nissa wouldn't get the reference to the Irish department store.

"That bleedin' *Penneys* is everything wrong with the world . . ."

They thanked Nissa and Mckenna and gave them a final wave good-bye. Mckenna watched as John and Brigit strolled at a snail's pace up the stone steps towards the entrance, then stopped abruptly just before the revolving doors, which they were now pointing violently at.

Mckenna and Nissa exchanged curious looks and proceeded towards them to check that everything was "grand."

"Is everything alright?" Mckenna asked.

"This old man's downright loopers," Brigit said angrily, and pointed her finger in John's face. "You dragged me here for apricots, John. *Apricots.*"

In all his antics, John explained that their daughter's neighbour had grown an apricot tree over her fence, which according to John, meant those apricots were rightfully hers—and he was here to settle it once and for all.

"And I'll prove it to that caffler!" Mckenna assumed this meant "idiot", or something fouler. Livid, John stormed into the building.

"I swear to you, I'll leave him here!" Brigit said.

Mckenna glanced at Nissa, who looked as confused as she was, but nodded towards the doors anyway. Sighing, Mckenna followed John inside, Brigit babbling behind her, something about shoving an apricot up something. They approached the front desk, where a young woman greeted them in a mechanical voice.

Mckenna had to bite her lip to stop herself bursting out laughing as John explained the tree situation at length to the front desk clerk, and how if he didn't fax a copy of the bylaw to his daughter today, her nasty neighbour would never stop going after her apricots.

The clerk's blank expression told Mckenna she was possibly as unenthused as the ratty motel man.

"You're looking for the State Publications and Regulations Department. That's at the State House." She pointed to a bulletin hanging on a nearby column.

As John went off on the innocent worker and Nissa attempted to mediate the situation, Mckenna scanned the bulletin.

Secretary of the Commonwealth
State Publications and Regulations
State House, Room 117

But it was the department listed just above it that caught her eye:

Secretary of the Commonwealth
Public Records Division
McCormack Building
Room 1719

Public records. Mckenna rushed towards John and Nissa and cut in front of the former, promising him that she and Nissa would accompany them to the State House later. "I just need to check something first . . . Would you mind? We'll try not to be too long."

Brigit appeared at his side. "Not at all—I think *this one* could do with a tea to settle his nerves. Take your time, luv."

She watched them head out towards the café next door, then turned to the clerk. "'Scuse me—does your Public Records department include immigration ship records?"

"You mean, like, passenger lists?"

"Yes! Exactly."

"Sure it does."

Mckenna spun around and nearly knocked Nissa over.

"Why are John and Brigit leaving?" Nissa asked, pointing back at the entrance. "What's up?" she added, studying Mckenna's keen expression.

"Look." She nodded towards the sign.

Nissa's mouth fell open. "Talk about signs."

Mckenna was surprised by two things: firstly, how easy it was to gain access to public records—apparently, rarely anyone sought these out, so those who did were let by without much of a hassle, and secondly, the system in which the files were kept—as in there was none at all. They sifted through vaguely labelled files, hoping to obtain information on where Nissa's ship left from in 1977 and who accompanied her. So far, they had only managed to find immigration records to the port of Boston from the last five years.

"This could take a while," Nissa said, tossing aside another pile of dusty folders. "Who knows if we're even looking in the right place. Maybe the older files are in the immigration department, or the Massachusetts archives. Plus, I don't know how long John and Brigit will last alone," she added with a chuckle.

Mckenna was at a loss. She leaned back in her chair and wiped her forehead.

"Girls, I'm such a kook!" said the department clerk Lucy, popping out from behind a shelf; she had been their screening process up until now, handing them the files that contained passenger list records.

"My colleague, Jason, who has the night shift, does some kind of, uh . . . like, entering data thingy—and he's *super* speedy," she said as if this were a breakthrough of some kind. Mckenna and Nissa waited for the punchline.

"Which means," she continued, "that most of the older files have already been, like, put in."

They continued to gape at her.

"Oh! Sorry—in the computer, I mean!"

Lucy showed them to a desk cooped up in the back corner of the room; hidden behind mountains of folders was the same ugly beige metal box with a glossy dark screen that Andre had in his office.

"I've never used one before!" Nissa said.

"It stores all your records?" Mckenna asked.

"Some. We're working on backing things up. There are computers in, like, every department but this one. But I'm literally *the worst* with technology. Jason's great, though . . . He's a total genius. Maybe I should call him? To see if he can help you girls out, of course . . ."

"Of course," Mckenna said, grinning at Nissa.

Some twenty minutes later, it was Jason to the rescue—apparently, he was "in the neighbourhood anyway."

"My hero!" Lucy said, putting a hand to her heart. Jason—tall, fair-haired, with just the right amount of freckles—responded with cheeks the colour of Nissa's left sock.

Mckenna watched as Jason's fingers swept the keyboard, entering who knew what and making dates, places, and names appear out of thin air.

"1977, right?"

"Yes," Mckenna said, leaning closer to the screen.

"Port of Boston?"

"Boston, yes."

"The third of August?"

"Yes!" Nissa shouted from across the room; she had just returned from checking up on John and Brigit. "So . . . is my name on the passenger list?"

"Checking . . ."

"You've got this, Jase!" Lucy said, squeezing his shoulders.

"Found you," Jason said, his ears and cheeks now a perfect match. Lucy, Mckenna, and Nissa leaned over Jason's shoulder to get a closer look at the screen.

PORT OF DEPARTURE AND SAILING DATE: *Dublin, Ireland; July 21st, 1977*

PORT OF ENTRY AND ARRIVAL DATE: *Boston, Massachusetts; August 3rd, 1977*

NAME AND AGE OF IMMIGRANT: *Nissa Febland; three years old*

SEX: *Female*

COUNTRY OF CITIZENSHIP OR LAST COUNTRY OF RESIDENCE: *Unknown*

PARENTS: *Unknown*

NAME AND ADDRESS OF RELATIVE IN FORMER

COUNTRY: *Arethusa Febland*

BIRTHPLACE: *Unknown*

INTENDED FINAL DESTINATION: *Boston, Massachusetts*

PHYSICAL DESCRIPTION: *Hair—blond; Eyes—blue*

The colour drained from Nissa's face.

"It doesn't say where I was born? Who my parents were?"

Jason shook his head.

"But I have family."

"Apparently so," Jason said, unfazed.

"And it says their full name?" Mckenna asked.

"Yep, there it is—Arethusa Febland."

Mckenna continued to watch Nissa intently, then put a hand on her shoulder. "You have someone related to you somewhere, Nissa. And we know now that your ship came from Ireland. And we know your last name! That's something, isn't it?"

"It's not all that surprising, really," Jason said. "Boston's always been a major port city. And since the Great Irish Famine in the 1840s, Irish families have been the largest immigrant group in Boston. Actually, I'm pretty sure Massachusetts is the most Irish American state."

"So, I'm also Irish?"

"Not necessarily. Dublin is also a major port city, so it's possible you're from somewhere nearby, like England or Scotland, but your vessel left from Dublin."

"Jase, you know *everything*," Lucy said with admiration.

Jason shrugged. "My grandparents are Irish immigrants—they never let me forget it."

Nissa was quiet all the way to the State House. She hardly reacted when John began his apricot rant again, sparing the front desk clerk no details.

"You alright?" Mckenna asked Nissa quietly as John called out his daughter's fax number for the entire floor to hear.

"I have a living relative," she said, staring down at the white marble tile, "and she never came for me . . . or wanted me to stay. For all I know, she's the one who sent me here."

Mckenna didn't know what to say to this. "We don't know what happened. There has to be more to it."

Nissa said nothing.

"What I don't understand is," Mckenna continued stubbornly, "how is it possible that the passenger list doesn't include your place of birth? So strange . . . but we'll do some digging, okay?"

"No, that's fine," Nissa said. "I'm fine."

Mckenna didn't press her.

Mckenna almost felt normal that day—like just another tourist, traipsing around Boston with who must've looked to others like her sister and her grandparents. Though, she couldn't shake the feeling that she was being closely watched.

They stopped for lunch near the harbour, Mckenna's favourite spot thus far: A massive blue marina filled with boats, ships, and yachts stretched out for hundreds of acres across the Massachusetts Bay; behind them, the city skyline hovered like titans guarding the portal to their homeland.

"It's been lovely, but we best be off," Brigit said, squeezing Mckenna and Nissa against her chest.

John tapped them on the heads. "Couldn't have done it without you." He slapped a bill on the table and leaned in. "My treat. A thank-you for putting up with this one." He tilted his head towards Brigit.

Chuckling, Mckenna and Nissa thanked him.

"Do you want us to call you a cab to the airport?" Nissa offered.

"Oh, no need, luv! Our ship's waiting for us just there." She gestured behind her, where hundreds of travellers were waiting to board a large grey vessel.

No way, Mckenna thought. "Um, Brigit . . . Your cruise wouldn't happen to be bringing you back home to Limerick, now would it?"

"Well of course not. What a silly question!"

Mckenna knew it would have been too good to be true.

"Ships from Boston nearly always go straight to Dublin," Brigit said.

Mckenna and Nissa exchanged incredulous looks.

"Bleedin' Dublin," John muttered.

"Oh, shut up, John. Be grateful I'm not dragging you on a plane. You see, he's afraid of flying . . ."

"I'm not afraid of nothing! You girls don't listen to her . . ."

"Well, see," Mckenna began before they could start another public spat, "we're actually looking for a way there."

"To Dublin, luv?"

"Yeah. I . . . uh—"

"She's reuniting with her mother!" Nissa said importantly.

Mckenna glanced at her in surprise.

"Oh, that's wonderful! Isn't that something, John?

"It's important, is what it is. You know, a mam can take the place of all others, but their place is one no one else can take."

Mckenna smiled at this.

"Do you think you could help?" Nissa asked hopefully. Mckenna had to admit that she had a way of gaining sympathy from others.

"Maybe we can explain you two are joining us last minute! Do you have passports?" Brigit asked.

"No . . ."

"Oh. Then I'm afraid I don't know that we can . . ."

Mckenna wracked her brain. Could they sneak on board somehow? She looked down at their small carry-ons—there was no way they could squeeze inside either of those. Could they pass off as staff? No, surely, they would have to show identification . . .

Any hope of getting onto that ship disappeared as quickly as it had come.

They accompanied John and Brigit to the port, thanked them for lunch, and were just about to bid them a last good-bye when Mckenna stopped short.

In a flash, she was overcome by a cyclone of anxious thoughts she didn't recognize. An enigmatic fear had sprung from nowhere, as spontaneously as the euphoric feeling that overcame her when Nissa reunited with her bracelet.

This time, she was feeling someone else's nerves.

But where had the fear come from? What was it a fear *of?* She closed her eyes, attempting to narrow her focus on the reason behind this upsurge of emotion.

She was anxious about . . . about . . .

About being a total screw-up.

There it was. The thought came and went, and she knew now that the fear she was experiencing was of messing up—specifically, of being fired. She began inhaling and exhaling rapidly.

"What's wrong with her, Brigit?" John said, peering at Mckenna's ghostly complexion.

Mckenna looked around, scanning the crowd until she found the source of her sudden fit. *Aha*, she nearly shouted aloud when she spotted the scrawny, scared-looking ship attendant inspecting passports as passengers boarded. She closed her eyes once more.

It's his first day on the job. Mckenna couldn't explain how she knew this. She also knew that something had already gone terribly wrong today, and he would do anything to avoid another incident.

Mckenna cracked a smile, and her eyes flew open. She knew what to do—but she needed John and Brigit's cooperation.

"Let's do it," John said after Mckenna told them her idea. Brigit, albeit worried, wanted to help, too.

And so the unlikely foursome arrived in front of the ship attendant, determined as can be.

"Good day, ladies, ma'am, and sir!" the attendant said with a broad smile.

"That's Admiral to you, son," John shot back. Mckenna fought to keep her composure.

"Of course, uh, Admiral. May I have your names, please?"

"Callaghan—family of four," John said.

"Callaghan . . . Callaghan . . ." he muttered to himself,

skimming through his list. "Hmm . . . I'm sorry, sir—Admiral—but it appears I have just two passengers down under that name."

"Oh, that's how it *appears,* yeah? Well if that's how it *appears,* then I'll just leave my two daughters—"

"He means granddaughters, of course."

"—in America with the rest of you eejits."

Mckenna felt her—or rather the attendant's—chest tighten. *Good. Keep at it, John . . .*

"And while I'm at it, I'll go ahead and throw another thousand worthless American dollars out the bleedin' window." John faced Mckenna and Nissa and threw up his arms. "Girls, you're going to have to stay in America, if that's okay with you, 'cause apparently this man's list's as concrete as the tablets of the covenant."

The attendant's stress levels must have peaked because Mckenna felt the need to burst into tears. She decided to use this to her advantage and let her eyes well up.

The attendant looked distraught. "I-I'm so sorry, sir—"

"*Admiral,* Jesus Christ, do you even listen?" John bellowed, his voice carrying far enough to gain concerned looks from passengers standing way in the back of the line.

The attendant was visibly shaking now.

"This guy has it out for us foreigners! Who do I have to talk to about your hostile attitude?"

"Please, Admiral, you and your family can go on ahead! Here's the key to your room; unfortunately, there's nothing I can do about the size—"

"Nothing you can do—?"

"Oh, pity, but that'll have to do, won't it? Thank you, young man," Brigit said, and steered John away.

"And the Oscar goes to . . ." Mckenna whispered in Nissa's ear as she and her "family" embarked on a vessel that, by some miracle, was leading them straight to Ireland.

She decided not to question it.

As the waves rocked gently beneath her, she grasped the cold metal rail and leaned forward, staring out until the port, high-rises, and—somewhere way beyond—Abredonia Woods vanished from sight.

"She's travelling," the High Priestess said, her eyes lighting up. Today, the stone stopped at a spot in the Atlantic Ocean, close to the Massachusetts coastline.

"Your protégé followed through quickly," Pravadi said, impressed.

"Actually, this wasn't their doing."

Pravadi lifted an eyebrow. "Then how?"

"There are other forces at work that share our desire to unite the girl with her mother, with different motives, of course," the High Priestess said, scoffing. "But if it will speed things up, then so be it."

"Are you speaking of 'the good people'?"

"Don't be so superstitious, Pravadi. You won't burst into flames if you don't call them that."

"I'd rather not take the chance," she said sternly. "Speaking of—where do they stand on the Scrolls?"

"It's proving difficult. They don't share our point of view."

"No," said Pravadi. Her eyes were closed now, and she was focusing. "Perhaps not all of them."

Mckenna couldn't quite believe it. She was on a ship to Ireland accompanied by someone she had met just a few days ago, who happened to share that same innate feeling that she didn't belong, and that the answers she sought were far beyond the confines of her small town.

"It's strange, isn't it? But it also doesn't feel so strange, does it? Kind of like eating a good mouldy cheese," Nissa said in a low voice late that night as they lay on their pullout bed—which had taken the ship attendees over an hour to squeeze into John and Brigit's tiny, two-person cabin. Mckenna was growing accustomed to Nissa's outlandish comments. In fact, she found them refreshing. Nissa seemed in better spirits now that their plan was in motion.

"Can I ask you something?" Nissa said over Brigit's soft snores. "What exactly happened that day at school? On the field."

Mckenna hesitated. She was afraid this question would surface. The last thing she wanted was to frighten Nissa away, even though she didn't seem the type to scare easily.

"I . . . don't really know. I can't explain it right now, but I promise I will when I know."

Nissa nodded. "I know you will."

"But what I can tell you is that I just found something out about myself, something that doesn't make much sense to me yet. And the only person I think who'll be able to help me understand is my mother—whoever she is. I know that doesn't make much sense . . ."

"That's okay," Nissa said lightly. "You don't have to talk about it right now. I guess I wouldn't know how to explain what I'm searching for either."

Really, where had this girl come from?

"I just have to ask, though . . ."

Mckenna's chest tightened.

"Is it anything . . . bad? Like, something that could get you—us—into trouble?"

Mckenna swallowed. Seán *had* implied that people *may* be after her, but she couldn't say for certain—so why worry her? She couldn't have Nissa turn back now . . . She liked having her around.

"No. Not that I know of." That was sort of the truth.

The days passed swiftly aboard the ship. Mckenna spent most of her days out on the upper deck gazing out into the open water, hoping to spot a whale, shark or—

"Mermaid!" Nissa yelled out one afternoon after hours of watching the dancing waves. She swore she saw what looked like a dolphin with hair.

"Did we eat lunch?" Mckenna asked, unfazed.

"Oh. No, I don't think so."

They soon realized they had been sitting around doing nothing but swaying and staring for over three hours. No wonder Nissa was beginning to see things. Meals on the ship weren't exactly luxurious the way she imagined they were on typical cruise ships, not that Mckenna was complaining—she could eat pasta, pot pies, and potatoes every day of the week (she *was* half Irish).

"Did you girls think we'd be dining with the captain over candlelight?"

John explained they were on an ocean liner—more of a passenger-cargo vessel made for longer voyages, simply to get from point A to point B; cruises were much pricier, designed for vacationing and stopping at various ports along the way. While that would have been quite the splendid detour, Mckenna was glad they were headed directly to Ireland and would arrive in just a few more days.

"I don't mean to, you know, put a damper on our, uh, escapade?" Nissa whispered in Mckenna's ear the following evening during a game of *Crazy Eights* with John and Brigit, who were arguing over whose turn it was. "And I'm all for adventure, but do we have any sort of plan? And what will we do when we run out of money . . .?"

"We've been lucky so far," Mckenna whispered back, picking up a card for the fourth time in a row on her turn. "We'll figure it out."

"Oh, it's your turn, is it?" John hit the table.

"Mine now," Brigit said. "So, where is it your mam lives, luv?"

Mckenna hesitated, then looked round at Nissa, who nodded. "Some place in the north. Ballycastle."

"Oh, 'north' like Northern Ireland!" John interrupted. "And that's right on the north-eastern coast, not far from Belfast. I'm not sure how you'd get there from Dublin," he said, shaking his head.

"Are there any trains we could take?"

John let out a snort. "Trains! Nah, not all the way up there, not now. You'll need a car or a lift there. Won't be easy to find someone willing to head into that political war zone."

Mckenna heard Nissa gulp. "War zone?"

John leaned in. "You don't know? Been going on for ages. What are they teaching in school these days?"

Mckenna shook her head. "We really mostly focus on American history." Something she always resented.

"So, so wait, what about this war zone?" Nissa said, her eyes widened to twice their normal size.

"Back when I was teaching, I was asked to be a guest lecturer at Queen's College in Belfast. Was nearly ten years ago—1981, and the riots, the violence . . ." He looked away, his pale blue eyes remembering. "Lots of baggage there, let me tell you. See, Protestants were loyal to the United Kingdom, and Catholics wanted nothing to do with those holier-than-thou, land-grabbing Brits. They wanted Ireland to be *one* republic. But 'The Troubles' started back in the late sixties—a time of civil rights movements. Peace, love, Lennon and all that. Well, at the time, the Catholics living in Northern Ireland were fed up with being discriminated against—they felt the policies were mostly there to protect the Protestants—the loyalists. And so they marched in protest. But it got ugly fast. The British Army got involved, of course, trying to end it all, but it led to riots, then more riots over the years. From the looks of it, the situation's not improving. There are still bombings from both sides . . ."

"*That's* where we're going?" Nissa squeaked, rounding on Mckenna.

What had she gotten them into?

For three days straight, Mckenna thought about this not-so-minor setback. She had assumed there would be some kind of bus route or train she could catch—and that bombs weren't going off on street corners. How could she have not thought to research before making such a bold move? She hated herself for being so *impetuous*—what Seán often called her. At the very least, things might have proved easier if she could drive. Why couldn't she have gone for her license last year when Andre insisted?

On their last night at sea, Mckenna excused herself from dinner (fried tilapia and lima beans) and sauntered off to the upper deck.

Staring up at the veil of darkness, she spotted three stars amid the otherwise foggy ether. They winked at her from the abyss, like they wanted to let her in on a secret they'd been sharing amongst them.

"I don't know what I'm doing," she whispered to them. "I'm gonna need more of your help. If that's okay . . ." Whose help? She wasn't sure. But she knew she was getting some from someone, somewhere.

A loud crashing wave made her jump, and she tore her eyes away, just for a moment, from her silver companions. When she glanced back up in hopes of one last glow or glisten, there was nothing above her but black.

VII

The Magnificently Strange Newgrange

Dublin, Ireland

Mckenna was woken at the crack of dawn by the captain's announcement blaring over the speakers. They were ahead of schedule by a few hours, and the ship was docked at Alexandra Quay, about two kilometres from Dublin's city centre.

Filled with adrenaline, Mckenna kicked off the covers and shook Nissa awake. She was amazed she'd come this far. Her mind wandered to Seán and how thrilled he would be to know his daughter had set foot in his university town.

Back on the west side of the Atlantic, Seán was just hanging up the phone with his travel agent, Dina. He was certain she knew people in very high places—this was not the first time she was able to pull off the impossible. A few years back, when their flight got cancelled during a layover in Atlanta, she managed to get them on another plane within the hour—in first class, no less. Seán was fairly certain Dina's sauciness could get her whatever she wanted.

"Why the devil are you looking to fly there at this ungodly hour, and without your husband?" she had shouted through the receiver some thirty minutes ago, her voice hoarse, Seán guessed, from smoking a full pack of cigarettes in one sitting.

"*Partner,* Dina—not husband. Remember, gay marriage laws and all that?"

"That still a thing? Bunch of backwards-thinking bastards." Seán heard her strike something, and then blow out (smoke, no doubt). "You didn't answer my question."

"Business trip," he lied.

"Don't do that," she said dully. "As if I don't know. You draw for a living, no one's sending you nowhere. Something happen? Don't you go screwing up your relationship, now. He's too good for you."

"Can you book me the flight or not, Dina?"

"Of course I can book you the flight, who do you think you're talking to? Hang on."

He waited less than two minutes before Dina picked up the line again. "Okay, get going, fast—it leaves in two hours. Gave myself double commission, so you're welcome."

Which brought him here, at his doorstep, with Andre begging him to come to his senses. "You're going on a wild goose chase! It makes no sense to go after her; we need to stay put in case she tries to reach out. We don't know that she went to Avebury Henge—you think she'd go that far?"

"Our kid? Without question."

Andre let out a deep sigh. "Seán, even if you did find her, you know that not even you can talk Mckenna out of this."

Spoken like a true lawyer, Seán thought. He had heard all his arguments, all week long. "I'll never forgive myself if something happens to her, Andre."

Andre leaned back against the front door, somber-looking. Seán knew his mind was wandering, analyzing, remembering.

Andre crossed his arms over his chest and looked at his partner. "What happened?" Seán knew he was referring to their relationship. "We've always been on the same side."

"This is different," Seán said in a low voice.

"Why? How could you think it's okay to leave like this?" Seán could tell he meant leave *him* like this.

"Because you don't know Abby. She's trouble. And Mckenna's so damn stubborn that she won't stop until she finds her."

"And you think if you stop her, you can make this all go away. Mckenna's gifts and everything that comes with them."

"It's better this way. You need to trust me."

"I want to, I do, but I just don't think I'm ever going to agree to fighting this. There's no denying who she is, Seán. We need to be there for her, not hunt her down and drag her back home where she'll live on, miserable."

"But she'll be *safe,* you see."

"No, I *don't* see. It's one thing wanting to keep Mckenna out of danger her whole life, but another thing entirely acting like we didn't just find out she's . . . like her mother."

Seán scoffed at this.

"This is who she is, and we have to deal with it, support her. I'm sorry if I fail to see how propelling someone against their nature is right. And for *you* to think that's right, of all people . . ."

Seán felt as though he'd been flattened by a bus. "You're serious?" he said quietly. "So that's what this is about, is it? You think this is like trying to force the 'gay' away?"

"This is no different."

Seán was at a complete loss for words. Incredulous, he mumbled, "I'm going to miss my flight."

Once they disembarked, Mckenna, Nissa, John, and Brigit huddled near the docks.

"Watch yourselves," John said gravely. "Northern Ireland is no place for two young girls."

"If you need absolutely anything, you call this number," Brigit said, handing Nissa a piece of paper.

"We'll do that! Thank you for everything, Brigit. And John, we couldn't have done it without you."

"Yeah, you have mad acting skills," Mckenna said. She couldn't help it—she would miss their company.

"There's lots you don't know about me," John said, winking. "I was quite the theatre performer in me day."

Mckenna smiled, wishing she could sit around and listen to all of John's life stories. In return, he ruffled her and Nissa's hair and handed them a hundred-pound note. They tried to refuse it, but he wouldn't take no for an answer. This must be what it felt like to have grandparents.

"Be careful, luvs!" Brigit said, embracing Nissa first, and then Mckenna, whom she held onto a little longer. "I do hope you find your mam. Just remember this: She may not be what you'd expect, but that's *okay,* okay? Because family's family, and you stick with 'em, end of story. Unless they're serial killers, of course!"

With a final wave and a "Don't trust any loyalists!" from John, the cab drove off, and Mckenna and Nissa found themselves completely on their own, standing among hurried passersby in Ireland's most populated metropolitan city.

Now would be a good time to show up, little wren.

And now she was relying entirely on a bird. A freaking bird.

Since John's charming little anecdote about Belfast, Mckenna had been trying to justify to herself charging into said battleground wielding nothing but a crumpled-up note from someone who lived there over seventeen years ago. John had made it quite clear that heading to Northern Ireland was at their own risk, but she had come this far. There was no way she would abandon this quest now, however arbitrary it felt.

She halted in her tracks, and put out an arm in front of Nissa. There it was again, that feeling that someone was watching.

"What's going on?"

Mckenna looked around. Nothing. "I think with all of John's stories, I'm just feeling a little jumpy," she lied.

"Oh, there's no use worrying about that now—we'll be okay. Can I walk now . . .?"

They headed down the quay where the ship had docked, their backpacks stuffed with all the food they could grab from the ship, and walked along a seemingly endless dark, narrow river. The water became more still as they moved away from the port and walked on towards what was gradually appearing to be a real city. Commercial buildings lined both sides of the river—salmon facades and Georgian-style brownstones making up pubs, restaurants, and hotels—and running across the water joining the two ends of town were a series of short pedestrian bridges. It would have been a charming sight if it weren't for what John said of the cultural divide between the city's north and south side—the north, supposedly, being more underprivileged. She saw the bridges not as connectors, but as symbols of the socio-economic gap that still existed.

"It smells," Nissa said, snapping Mckenna out of it. "Do you think it's the river? I just spotted a ton of trash down there. Those poor fish . . ."

While Nissa went on about city folk carelessly dumping waste into our natural water sources, Mckenna spotted a purple and yellow double-decker tour bus, which sparked an idea.

"Hold that thought," Mckenna said, interrupting Nissa at the words *waste management*. "What if there were tours to Northern Ireland? I mean, it's a long shot, but it's all I've got."

"That might work! There must be a tourist information centre around."

With a goal in mind, they walked deeper into the city, more or less following the crowd and stopping anyone who looked like a local for directions.

Mckenna was beginning to see why Seán boasted so much about this place. While John indeed had a point—Dublin was certainly overcrowded—it had a lot of character; winding cobblestone roads led to trendy shops, bars, and restaurants built in standout architecture, one of Seán's favourite things about the city; they passed homes with coloured doors and roofs that looked like doll houses; and Mckenna was fascinated with the fact that though it was mid-morning, the streets were packed with people, from the working-class and retirees to loud and obnoxious tourists.

Tourists. Mckenna stopped when she heard what sounded like a North American accent. She turned on her heel and spotted a small group of twenty-somethings lining up outside of a cafe.

"Hello, 'scuse me," Nissa said, tapping the curly-haired one on the shoulder. "Do you happen to know if there's a tourist office around?"

"Guys—a fellow American!" he shouted, hitting his friends on the arm. "Yeah, there's one just down the street," he said, looking triumphant at having been able to help with directions.

Mckenna muttered a "thanks" and speed-walked over; as she suspected, there were no tour busses going past the northern border.

"Northern Ireland tours aren't exactly in high demand these days, I'm afraid," said the information clerk at the tourist office, an unsmiling man who grimaced when he heard of their destination.

"Well, do you know any other way we can get there?"

"By car . . . or plane," he said, shrugging. Mckenna rolled her eyes, muttering "Seriously?" under her breath. Nissa elbowed her.

The man's face tightened. "You know, you Americans are as tactless as everyone says," he nearly shouted, and then threw a map in their face. "Next, please!"

"Here's a thought . . ." Nissa said softly as they exited the tourist office. "Maybe don't roll your eyes *in front* of people?"

"But how much more useless could someone get?" Mckenna said through gritted teeth. "I'll never understand how dimwits like this one manage to land customer service jobs."

"Geez, crabby Kenna. He was only trying to help."

"Well, he didn't. Oh, a *car!* WHY DIDN'T I THINK OF THAT? Must've left my keys in the Jag."

They collapsed at a bistro table in the middle of the crowded sidewalk. Feeling particularly irritated, and now hungry, Mckenna called a nearby waiter to them and ordered a large brunch for two.

"Shouldn't we be a little more careful with our budget—?" Nissa offered up.

"I'm hungry," Mckenna snapped, but this wasn't the real cause of her frustration; Mckenna had been so preoccupied with making sense of her abilities and going after her mother that she had failed to research, plan. She had taken advantage of a kind and vulnerable person who was now relying on Mckenna for something—anything—that would make this unfledged, ill-conceived journey worthwhile.

Her mind racing and insides rolling like the Irish Sea, she mumbled a "Need some water" and shot up from her chair.

"Argh!" a deep voice yelled behind her. Mckenna spun around—she had backed up hard into some guy's knee, which he was holding onto as he hopped around in pain.

"Oops . . ."

"Are you okay?" Nissa stepped around the table.

Mckenna's victim looked up and threw a polite smile at the two of them, as if to say, "I'll survive", and brushed a strand of dark brown hair away from his face, revealing a set of green-grey eyes and the look of someone who was trying to mask their pain. He looked to be in his early twenties and was smartly dressed in a burgundy blazer and blue jeans, like he was off to a work meeting.

"It was an accident," she said stupidly, wiping her palms on her pants. "You were, like, hovering over me—I didn't see you." She was blathering, she knew.

"I sure hope it was an accident," he said with a grin, his accent similar to Seán's. "I was coming around to tell you that you're at my table."

"What—you own it?" Mckenna blurted out. She wondered when she would stop sounding so rude.

The young man smirked. "No, thank goodness, or I'd have you for trespassing."

Nissa laughed, but Mckenna, who was mad with hunger, was in no mood. "Look, we just ordered, so—"

"Wonderful, so did I," he said, and pulled up a chair beside them. "I'm starved."

"What d'you think you're doing?"

"Claiming my rightful seat—I ordered just before you did. But forgive me, I didn't know the no-toilet rule. I should've expected my table to be robbed right from under me." He pointed at the cardigan draped over the chair.

Wow, I'm rude and blind.

Nissa let out another laugh but stopped abruptly when she saw Mckenna's don't-I-feel-like-an-idiot expression.

"I'm being rude," he said, looking from Mckenna to Nissa. "No worries, I'll leave you to your lunch when the waiter's found me."

"No, *we're* the rude ones," Nissa said, offering him a genuine smile. "Plus, Irish hospitality and all that. When in Rome! Well, like, Ireland, but you know . . ."

"Oh, you're getting mixed up with Highland hospitality. Us Irish folk? Not as courteous as you'd think," he joked.

He's being nice, Mckenna thought. *Why am I such an ass?* Deciding to joke back, she said, "Something we agree on. Maybe it's a Dubliner thing, but my dad can also be kind of a jerk." God, she'd forgot how terrible she was at conversing with people.

He grinned, his eyes squinted slightly in surprise; Mckenna noticed a trace of mischief in them as they narrowed. "So you've got some Irish in you—wouldn't have guessed it. Forgive my error in judgement." He bowed his head in a mock-royal manner. "I'm Cillian," he said, holding out his hand.

Nissa took it and introduced herself and Mckenna. The latter, not used to such pleasantries, merely nodded and offered a half-smile. Lucky Nissa was there to be human for both of them. It was then that Mckenna realized she still hadn't apologized to him.

"Sorry for, um . . ." She pointed to his knee. But he brushed it off, admitting arriving at his work meeting with a slight limp would make him look tough.

"What do you do?" Nissa asked. Mckenna couldn't help but feel envious at Nissa's ease in talking to others.

"I'm a youth delegate for Dublin. And because of an issue involving the North and South, delegates from all over Ireland are getting together for a series of conferences for—well, it's sort of complicated."

Mckenna, who was slowly gaining a better understanding of the crisis in Northern Ireland, was genuinely interested now. "The North, as in Northern Ireland? Is it getting worse?"

Cillian leaned in. "It's, erm, not getting better, shall we say? It's delicate. And there's much more to it. See, a gunman from the IRA—that's the Irish Republican Army—is roaming free in Dublin, but the British government, who rules Northern Ireland, wants him sent back there to face punishment. And that's actually the main thing the organizer wants to address. She's put together several conferences to get representatives all over Ireland to vote to extradite him."

A tightness formed in her chest—was it his? "But you don't agree," Mckenna thought aloud, surprising herself. Damn this intuitive thing. Would she ever see it coming?

Cillian watched her with interest. "Yeah, I'd say that's accurate. He's fighting for a cause, to unite the island of Ireland. If we ship him off, he won't get a fair trial."

Nissa cleared her throat. "So, I guess it's not a great time to take a trip there, huh?"

Cillian turned to her. "To Northern Ireland?" He chuckled. "No, not exactly. But I've got no choice but to go in a few days. The life of a delegate!"

Nissa kicked Mckenna underneath the table, and then blurted out, "We're trying to find our way there, too!"

"Really?"

"We were just *thinking* of heading there, but it's not decided," Mckenna lied. She wasn't about to divulge their plans to a complete stranger.

"Yes, it kind of is, actually," Nissa said, oblivious to Mckenna's intimation. "There's a town up there—"

"Don't remember the name," Mckenna interrupted. Nissa finally caught her drift.

"You have family there or something?"

"Just visiting," was all Mckenna said.

"Well, I'm going as far north as Belfast. That's where we're holding our last conference. If you'd like, I'd be happy to take you there."

Mckenna looked up, stunned. She looked around for her trusty little wren, wondering if it was hovering nearby.

"Thing is, I can't offer you a straight route; I have a conference today in the Boyne Valley—not far from here—a dinner tonight in Kilkenny, and then one last conference near Connemara before heading to Belfast. I'd welcome the company, of course. These things can get quite dry. But I imagine you wouldn't want to be dragged across Ireland."

"That's nice of you, but we're going to just head there ourselves." Mckenna hoped he sensed the firmness in her voice.

"But how? No trains, no tour bus . . ." Nissa said.

Cillian wrinkled his face. "I'm not sure. It's dangerous—I'd be an eejit if I encouraged two young ladies to go off alone."

Any hope Mckenna had just felt was lost. What would she do now? Wait the war out? She pictured her and Nissa sitting on the street corner, hungry and homeless, with nowhere to turn and no way back to Abredonia Woods.

Nissa nudged Mckenna on the arm and made her eyes so wide she nearly expected her to hoot.

"Can I just—sorry." Mckenna dragged Nissa away from the table and rounded on her. "No."

"Why not? A few days, then we're there!"

"What if he's a human trafficker—or worse?"

"What's worse than a human trafficker?"

"A serial killer!" A couple lunching at a nearby table shot them disapproving glances.

"Oh, come on, Kenna. You should have more faith in people."

But she didn't. People always had a motive, in every aspect of Mckenna's life. If a student struck up a conversation with her in class, it was to ask to copy her homework; if a math teacher inquired about her approach to getting the correct answer, it was due to their envy that Mckenna found it before they did; and if her sleazy neighbour was being particularly friendly one day, it was because her top button had popped without her noticing.

"Sometimes, you just don't know someone's true nature, Nissa. He's being a little too . . . altruistic? And to two complete strangers. What's in it for him?"

"Fine, valid concern! But, my pessimistic friend, you'd be surprised: Some people don't have an agenda. They're *actually* nice, if you can believe it," she said, her eyes mocking.

Mckenna opened her mouth to protest but was shushed by Nissa's tiny finger. "How about this? We make sure neither of us is alone with him, and the minute—no, the *second*—we feel uncomfortable, we signal with a code word. Look how lucky we got in Boston . . ." Mckenna thought of the little wren perched on John's shoulder and felt compelled to tell Nissa that it had nothing to do with luck. " . . . all because we were kind and trusting!" Nissa continued. "What if this is fate, just like meeting John and Brigit was?"

Maybe Nissa was right. Maybe Mckenna's cynicism was the only thing standing in the way. She sighed. "The instant something's off, we're gone. We hitchhike to Ballycastle if we have to."

"Yes, that's the *much* safer option . . ."

They headed back to their lunch table, deciding that should they sense any red flags, their code word was *nincompoop*.

Cillian's first meeting with his fellow delegates was in County Meath, about three quarters of an hour's drive north from Dublin. To pass the time while he "subjected himself to hours of fruitless small talk," Cillian suggested that Mckenna and Nissa take a tour of Newgrange, a burial tomb dating back to 3200 BC.

"That's five hundred years before the Great Pyramid of Giza," Mckenna said, fascinated. In the driver's seat, Cillian eyed her through his rear-view mirror; she looked away and remained quiet for most of the ride, staring out into the vast green landscape.

"So much flat land," Nissa said after twenty minutes or so. "That must be ideal for farming, right?" she asked as they drove by yet another farmstead.

"Oh, yeah. Wasn't always like this, though."

"What do you mean?"

"Ireland was eighty to ninety percent forest and woodlands when humans arrived about nine thousand years ago. People avoided the forests, though, out of fear, strain . . . Instead, they travelled by water. See, back then, it was land that was the divider and water the connecter."

"If they avoided the forests and woods, what happened to them all?" Nissa said thoughtfully.

"The earlier inhabitants had nothing to do with their decline, if that's what you're asking. The first settlers were Mesolithic hunters, mostly just fishing and gathering."

"How much of Ireland is forest now?"

"Around fifteen to twenty percent."

Nissa gasped.

"Yeah," Cillian muttered. "You could blame farming, industrialization, and population increase for that."

"Oh, of course," Nissa said. "I guess the forests were cleared out to cultivate food and build shelter."

Cillian nodded. "Right. People need to eat and sleep."

Mckenna's muscles tensed up at this. "Aren't people always the problem?"

Cillian met her eyes in the mirror once more.

"Not true!" Nissa said. "People are good, just unaware. With guidance, they can change."

At this, Mckenna met Cillian's gaze, and the corner of his lip lifted into a slight smile, which Mckenna took to mean they shared the same opinion on the subject—people didn't change.

A sentiment they didn't mind keeping just between them.

Cillian dropped them off at the Newgrange information centre, where they signed up for the 1:00 p.m. tour and browsed the gift shop until a small shuttle arrived to take them to the site. Their tour guide was named PJ, short for Patrick-Joseph. "The two most important Irish saints!" he announced proudly. Mckenna was beginning to spot a name trend.

They drove for a few short minutes past vast open fields, and Mckenna's mind wandered to the flat plains they had seen on the drive over from Dublin. She began to picture how it must've looked all those years ago. It was so clear in her mind: a land full of wildlife, plants, and natural vegetation; myriad herbs and low-lying shrubs, dock species, dwarf trees . . . She could've sworn in that moment she smelled the aroma of juniper.

"Here!" PJ shouted, and Mckenna and Nissa stepped off along with the other dozen passengers.

When Mckenna thought *tomb,* she imagined a slab of stone on the ground with some sort of makeshift hood protecting it, or at most a small cave roomy enough for a corpse or two, but what stood before her eyes was neither. Truthfully, she wasn't sure what to make of it.

They were standing on a green terrain in front of a massive circular mound. "Eighty-five metres in diameter, just about." PJ explained they were facing the south side, where a hobbit-sized opening was flanked by three vertical stones that an army of Hulk Hogans couldn't lift. PJ invited them to take a stroll around, but Mckenna was way ahead of him. The front half of the perimeter wall was made up of thousands, if not millions of uneven white stones, while the back half was coated entirely in turf. Mckenna made her way around the rear; from here, the tomb could've passed for an ordinary mound if it weren't for the carved kerbstones close to the earth, ringing the structure.

"Welcome to the Boyne Valley," PJ called over the chattering crowd once everyone was done exploring and gathered back around the entrance. "You're standing in front of one of the world's most ancient architectural structures and Ireland's most famous prehistoric monument. Newgrange dates back to the Neolithic period around 3200 BC. For those not so keen on math, that's over five thousand years ago."

The hairs on Mckenna's arms stood. PJ went on to explain

that Newgrange was a passage tomb where the ancient people buried their dead, though its main purpose remained a mystery to this day ("You'll understand once we go inside!"). But the extraordinary measures that were taken to build it suggested that it probably wasn't made for just anyone. Certain materials, like the granite boulders inside the tomb, derived from areas that were far away, like County Wicklow, the Mourne Mountains, and Carlingford; each of the kerbstones weighed an average of three tons, and ninety-seven ringed the tomb; they were supposedly brought in by boats from up the coast of Clogherhead about twenty kilometres to the northeast. Mckenna wasn't great with measuring distances, but she didn't have trouble believing that historians estimated that Newgrange took several generations to construct.

"See the entrance, there?" He pointed at the doorway to where the three cylindrical stones were placed in a row. "We still haven't a clue how these men—"

"Or women," Nissa uttered.

"—transported those stones, along with the other ones inside. Another mystery is all the carvings you see on them . . ."

Mckenna examined the spiral patterns etched prominently onto the grey surface; some ran in the same directions and others in opposite ones. But it was the left-hand side of the stone that caught her eye, where three spirals connected to shape a triangle.

"There are theories about their meaning. Spirals are often associated with infinity, and so some believe the triple spiral you see on the Entrance Stone represents the cycle of birth, life, and death. This ties into the theory that Newgrange was built as a sacred burial ground to transport the soul into the afterlife."

Mckenna couldn't tear her eyes away from the trinity spiral; she felt its energy surging outwards and inwards, enveloping the stone like a shield. And then in a semi-trance, she saw a bright layer slowly form around its edges. Disbelieving, she squinted, wondering whether she was imagining the stone glowing.

"That's not the amazing part," PJ said, and the glow dissipated. "Before we head inside, keep in mind that opening up there." He pointed up over the passage entrance, where a wide gap between two stone slabs rested atop the doorway. "It just so happens that *that*—we call it a roof-box—was built in perfect alignment with the sunrise on the winter solstice. You're probably all wondering what that means . . ." The group of tourists stared at him intently. "The truth is, we still don't know. But afterwards you can tell us what your take on it is."

As PJ lined them up in single file, Mckenna remarked that on the lintel stone lying horizontally above the doorway was a series of X-shaped markings—eight to be exact.

"This is hella rad, isn't it?" Nissa said.

"Mhm," Mckenna mumbled, still studying the markings. She wondered why the tour guide failed to mention them.

They filed in through the doorway and down the passage, and Mckenna was immediately surprised at how narrow it was. Either side was lined with twenty or so standing stones that reached a little below Mckenna's head (and slightly above Nissa's). Mckenna noticed they grew taller as she approached the end of the passage, which led to a square chamber spacious enough for the group to gather in.

"You can all stand around here fairly comfortably," PJ called out. "Anyone surprised?" He looked at everyone's awed expressions. "You might've noticed that the inside isn't quite what you'd expect. See, the tomb itself only actually occupies about a third of the mound's diameter."

Mckenna's mind filled with questions as her eyes darted around the room. There was something about the form of this place . . .

"You're standing in the main chamber; behind me there are three other much smaller ones. Move around, now, so everyone gets a chance to see . . ." As he explained the wonder of the domed, corbelled ceiling above them ("Not a drop of water has ever leaked through!"), Mckenna and Nissa approached the west, north, and east chamber behind PJ. In each one lay a large, chiselled basin stone, except the east recess contained two—one sitting inside the other.

"The basins you see in each chamber were used to hold the bones of the deceased," PJ said. "When the floor of the chamber was excavated between 1962 and 1975, they recovered remnants of human bones along with some offerings, something like seven marbles and some pendants and beads. Ancient mythology states that Newgrange was built in connection with the Tuatha Dé Danann—Irish for the 'people of the Goddess Danu'. Believed to be the burial place of their chief, Dagda Mór, and his three sons."

Mckenna didn't know if it was thanks to the captive tale or not, but something inside her lifted, like it was fighting to soar out of her body. Was it her soul, yearning to escape—to unite with whatever serene, ethereal presence was inviting her here and now, urging her to return to a place of peace . . .?

Mckenna's musings were interrupted as soon as she got wind of her thoughts. What had just come over her?

"And now, for what you all really came for."

Mckenna exchanged curious looks with Nissa as PJ split the group down the middle. They stood on either side of the central chamber in silence for several seconds before the lights that illuminated the chamber went out, making some of the tourists gasp.

"Now, remember the roof-box I told you to keep in mind earlier, at the front of the passage?" PJ said. "Every year at sunrise on the winter solstice—that's December 21st—"

"The shortest day of the year," Mckenna whispered to Nissa.

"—the shortest day of the year, a beam of sunlight shines through the roof-box and travels directly up the passage, illuminating the main chamber for seventeen minutes."

A dozen heads spun round to stare down the passage, as though the winter solstice had come early.

"Wouldn't leave you hanging, would I?" PJ said.

"I'm excited!" Nissa whispered, bouncing on the spot. As impressed as Mckenna was by the cosmic alignment, how much could she expect from a mere simulation?

"Ready?" PJ's voice echoed.

Something was switched on, and a beam of light shone down the centre of the passage, lighting up the chamber floor beneath them.

Whoa.

Even simulated, the effect stole Mckenna's breath away. For a moment, she imagined she was a farmer or villager who, after decades of spent energy collecting just the right materials, chiselling and lifting with all her might, and losing loved ones in the process, finally got to witness the result of her miraculous work. She revelled in these thoughts, in this moment, imagining that it was the heat from the sun hitting her. Her arm hairs spiked again, and the soaring feeling returned.

Then something strange happened. Mckenna's attention was driven just above her head, where a kind of brilliant, light-filled globe hovered in place; the thing was neither solid nor transparent—it looked to be made up of sparkling dust particles. Mckenna raised her hand to touch it, but it drifted higher still, almost mockingly.

What the . . .

One by one, small spheres of white light appeared out of thin air. There must have been about thirty of them now, floating, lifelike, around the chamber. For a second, Mckenna thought it may have been part of PJ's light show, but no one else seemed to see them—the group continued to ooh and ah over the beam of light along the chamber floor.

And in a blink, they were gone.

"But why all this?" Nissa asked PJ over the chitter-chatter.

"Ah, the very question archaeologists and historians have been trying to answer for years," PJ said dramatically. Nissa shushed the room, and the chatter stopped. "Think of the importance that was placed on this tomb, if that's indeed all it was. Was an entire community put to work just so that they could witness this wonder occur? Did the time of year have some sort of cosmic relationship to the afterlife? We might not have answers, but we can certainly marvel at the minds and wisdom of these ancient people."

Mckenna spent the bus ride back to the Newgrange information centre pondering all that she had just experienced. She played the scene over and over again, trying to find a plausible explanation for the mysterious floating lights, and when she couldn't, her mind wandered back to the tomb and the Neolithic people. She was simultaneously impressed and baffled.

So much just didn't add up.

It all just seemed so impractical—building a colossal structure, one which could withstand Ireland's famously hormonal—as Seán always put it—weather conditions for thousands of years, just to bury a couple of royals. And basing their architecture on the movement of the sun . . . fascinating. But surely, the sun wasn't the only factor; wouldn't it have been natural to study the moon and the stars, too? Mckenna knew that if one stared at them routinely, like she often did back home, they became recognizable—the time they appeared, the constellations they formed. The Neolithic people would've come to rely on them, to trust that they would return.

Wouldn't that mean there were other phenomena that occurred around the structure to mark the other solstices and equinoxes? And what about the Xs? There were eight on the roof-box—that had to have meant something.

"Your face looks weird," Nissa said after they arrived back at the front lot and saw Cillian's car roll around.

"Mm?" Mckenna looked up at her. "Just thinking."

VIII

Kyteler's Inn

"Did you enjoy that?" Cillian asked when Mckenna and Nissa slipped back into his car, their faces flushed from all the excitement.

Nissa rambled on about the tour and PJ, who was an actual archeologist, which she found "hella awesome."

"What about you, Mckenna?"

Her heart hopped at the sound of her name. "It was something," she said, thinking of the glowing stone and dancing lights.

With a glint in his eye, Cillian said, "Full of questions, isn't it?"

Mckenna's gaze returned to the sky. "Yeah." *You have no idea.*

Seán hadn't done something this impulsive in quite some time, since he'd been with Abby, in fact. But the bookmarked page was the only clue his daughter left about her whereabouts—the one place he mentioned in connection with her mother—the place where he and Abby first met.

Avebury Henge, a site containing the largest stone circle in the world.

Sporting his trusty hurling windbreaker, he stepped out of the taxi and breathed in the familiar country air of Wiltshire, England.

AVEBURY HENGE—WILTSHIRE, ENGLAND—SUMMER, 1973

Eighteen years earlier, Seán had emerged from the tour bus looking like the worst kind of tourist; on that damp, cloudy afternoon, he wore aviator sunglasses, white shorts, and a blue, white, and red tank top with the words *French me* printed across the front.

Exactly three months had passed since he had stripped down to his underwear out in the Trinity College courtyard, set his schoolbooks on fire, and taken off on his backpacking adventure. He was proud to say to anyone who would listen that he had skied the Swiss Alps, taken cooking classes with world-renowned Italian chefs, and cliff dived off the Greek islands.

England was the last stop of his European extravaganza (what he liked to call it) before it was time to head back home to his disapproving parents and two brothers, who had oh-so-responsibly spent their first summer after graduation job hunting. *They* were thinking of their futures, of course. *They* had the sense to kickstart their grown-up lives. His father's voice rang in his ears: "Where's your head? You're going to traipse around Europe living the life of Riley?" In other words, the easy life. "Your brothers did it right, they did . . ." Seán bit his tongue; the youngest, Liam, became a snot-nosed insurance broker who preyed on the old and decrepit, while Conal, the eldest, had been groomed to take over the family farm since he could crawl—and whose only friends, Seán was certain, were a flock of sheep.

But as he dragged his strappy sandals along the muddy ground, he decided now might be time to end his trip. He'd seen the best of the continent . . . and so far, England was blander than butterless mash.

Not a moment later, he changed his mind.

From where Seán stood on the edge of the outer stone circle—the site contained two smaller ones within a larger one—his gaze fell on a willowy woman, her fiery red curls being swept up by the breeze, which was odd considering he felt no wind whatsoever.

The woman's eyes found his, and his heart felt like a firecracker that had been set off. He needed to meet her, be near her. His legs, Jello-like now, managed a step towards the stone circle, but from across the crowded, open field, she held up her palm.

He stopped, confused, then watched as she formed a circle with her finger, motioning for Seán to walk the perimeter. He obliged, thinking this was a kind of test or tease. And he was into it.

Close enough now to absorb the full extent of her beauty, he marvelled at her features: Her eyes were like amber, reflecting a warm, honey glow, and bearing wisdom beyond her years, he could tell; light freckles sprinkled her small nose and cheeks; and her lips, heart-shaped and crimson-coloured, were slightly parted, restful.

He couldn't help himself. "You're going to be hard to get, aren't you?"

Her mouth didn't smile, but her kind, oval face beamed back at him. "Stone circles were once ritual sites for ancient druids. You want to speir permission to enter first."

Speir? Seán was thrown by her Scottish slang and heavy accent. He scratched his head, having missed the latter half of what she said through the thick of it.

Seeing his confused state, she slowed her speech. "Do you knock before you enter someone's home?"

"Depends who's on the other side."

She smiled a contagious smile. "Take your hand."

Instinctively, he grabbed hers. She shook her head, fighting a laugh. "I said *your* hand—" She placed his hand flat against the standing stone nearest to them. "—and now, close your eyes.

Come on," she insisted over Seán's snickers.

"Good. Remember, you're entering a place of worship," she continued. "Introduce yourself."

"I'm Seán, luv," he said, opening one eye and giving his best smouldering stare.

Shushing him, she said, "In your head. And now, ask the circle's guardians if you're welcome to enter. Politely . . ."

That voice—he wanted to wake up to its gentle rhythm every morning. It was hypnotic as hell, sparking a tingling sensation at the base of his neck. As it travelled down his body, he decided he was willing to look like a fool and more for this eccentric, alluring stranger.

As he focused, Seán felt something—a small gust of wind. It was so swift, though. Had he imagined it?

"Breathe. Harmonize your energy with the energy you feel here, in this place."

"How do I do that?"

She placed a hand on his arm. "Be present."

Seán did his best to focus on the here and now—the touch of her fingers, the sounds of the wet ground and rustling leaves, and his even breaths—until the chatter around the site dissolved.

"I think I'm ready," he whispered.

"Then you're welcome to step inside."

Seán opened his eyes, turned to her, and closed his hand around hers. She didn't fight him on it.

Together, they entered the circle.

Avebury Henge—Wiltshire, England—Present Day

Now, Seán gazed out at the magnificent formation and caught his breath. To this day, he was still taken with the sight of the standing stones, but the heaviness in his heart had nothing to do with the monument's marvel.

He stepped closer to the outer circle and stopped himself just before the invisible threshold. Unable to shake off Abby's voice inside his head, he placed a hand on the stone nearest to him and closed his eyes.

On the drive to Kilkenny, a small castle town to the south and Cillian's first scheduled overnight stop, Nissa expressed her growing fondness for Ireland and all the scenic drives they would enjoy in the coming days. Cillian admitted that this made him quite content, as he had opted to fully embrace his role of tour guide during this otherwise mundane road trip. "Though, it's a bit of an inconvenient route for me—going north to Newgrange from Dublin and then back south to Kilkenny, only to drive all the way west to Connemara and back up again to Belfast." He confessed that he had worked as a tour guide for several years during his studies in history and political science, so he knew the best routes off by heart.

"Who mapped it?" Mckenna asked.

"Naomi, the organizer. She's running for MP in Belfast—member of parliament. Makes sense for her—she's just driving south-west the whole way and then flying back to Belfast."

"And you have to go to all of them?" Mckenna wondered.

"Well, because Dublin's where Dermot Finucane—the IRA gunman—is staying currently, I've agreed to attend them all so I can help make his case."

"Still. Could've timed it better, no?"

"Mhm."

"Hey, Cillian—what's your favourite place in Ireland?" Nissa, who wasn't listening, shouted over the wind. Her nose completely outside the car window, she was fully immersed in the landscape.

"Oh, impossible to say. You've gone and reminded me, though . . ." He made a sharp right turn on a narrow street, which, frighteningly, was a two-way. "Care to stretch your legs?

It's on the way—you won't regret it, promise."

They drove down tight winding roads and soon found themselves surrounded by mountains; they were modest ones, cloaking a small round lake down the valley below. The car came to a full stop, parked halfway between the road and the grassy slope that led to the picturesque vale. It was the most serene spot Mckenna had ever laid eyes on. It looked like a private oasis, and upon looking more closely, she could see that it probably was—a white mansion sat on the green terrain adjacent to the lake, which was bordered by a white sandy beach.

"Welcome to Lough Tay," Cillian said with longing.

"Where are we?" Mckenna asked.

"County Wicklow. These are the Wicklow Mountains. They continue on in the distance, do you see? Magical, isn't it?"

Mckenna winced, like the word was now cursed.

"It's *unreal,*" Nissa said, her mouth nearly hanging open. "Do people actually live there?" She pointed down at the stately home.

"The estate belongs to the Guinness family."

"The who?" Nissa blurted out.

"Guinness . . . You know Guinness beer, right?"

Seán's favourite beer, of course.

"Oh, we're still mi—"

Mckenna stopped Nissa before she could say *minors.* "Massachusettsians," Mckenna said a bit too loudly. "So, we love our—you know, uh—Massachusetts ale." The less Cillian knew about them, the better. The truth was Mckenna was not at all unfamiliar with beer—and wine, even. She had had her first sip of wine at about twelve years old. Seán and Andre had always agreed that introducing alcohol at a young age would glorify it less, though she wasn't allowed a full glass, of course—at least not until she was sixteen. In Mckenna's case, their theory proved positive. She had yet to care for alcohol, nor its frivolous effects.

"Right," Cillian said. "Well, Guinness beer is a religion here. That home belongs to something like the great-great grandson of Arthur Guinness, the founder. A God to us all," he cracked.

"That white sand looks so out of place," Mckenna said,

scrutinizing the landscape.

Cillian laughed. "That's because it is. The family imported it. Keen eye."

She felt a twinge of satisfaction.

"See how it lines the top of the lake? Makes it look like a pint of Guinness." He winked. "It's been nicknamed Guinness Lake."

Mckenna's heart warmed, thinking of how Seán would react to such a homage. Guilt snuck into her brain and trickled down to her gut; her dads must have been furious with her. And scared. She loved them and missed them more than she could say, but what was the point of returning to a sheltered life? Her world may be uncertain now, but at least it was no longer hollow. No longer a lie.

She leaned over the fence, listening to the birds chirping in the distance, and for a moment, she forgot she wasn't alone; Cillian was leaning over the fence beside her, his shoulder inches from hers. Mckenna ignored the current that shot across her body and turned to look at Nissa, but she was nowhere in sight.

"She's a ball of energy, that one!" Cillian said, nudging his head forward. Down below, Nissa was running towards the sand like a child who had spotted a *Slip n' Slide.*

"She isn't allowed to be down there, is she?"

"Not quite."

Mckenna watched as her friend kicked off her shoes, squished her toes in the sand, and skipped towards the water to rinse them off. There was something so fitting about Nissa in nature. She looked at home amid the mountains, water, and lush greenery. Cillian was right—this place was magical . . .

Mckenna did a double take: Several minuscule blue lights materialized, zooming around Nissa like honeybees and nectar. "Uh, are there normally fireflies around here? During the day," she added, knowing full well how ridiculous she must have sounded.

Cillian raised an eyebrow. "I don't believe so, no. Err, why?"

"You don't see those tiny lights?" She pointed at Nissa's head, but they were gone. "Oh, just thought for a second I—never mind."

Cillian eyed her with curiosity. Mckenna sensed he wanted to say something, but he held back.

Probably wants to know if I'm on hallucinogens.

"This is beautiful, by the way," she said louder than she intended. "I bet all of Ireland is."

"Yeah, but this place . . ."

"It's special?" Mckenna asked, knowing that to him, it was. "Why?"

Cillian looked deep in thought. "I supposed because it's hidden—you've got to know this spot to find it. And it's sort of perfect, isn't it? How the rest of the world should be."

Mckenna considered this. "Peaceful."

He looked sideways at her. "Unharmed," he said, and Mckenna felt a twang of anger inside her that she knew emanated from Cillian. She tried to steady herself as it surged through her, and just for a moment, his feelings became hers: He was upset about the state of the world, what it was becoming . . . and he was dedicating his life to making it right.

The resentment inside her grew steadily stronger, and what followed were sharp shooting pains around her head. The pressure tripled; she wanted to fall over and lie furled on the ground forever. Unable to suppress the pain, Mckenna let out an agonizing yelp.

"You alright?" Cillian offered his hand to steady her. She grasped it just before her balance gave, and he pulled her up towards him, his right hand resting gently on the small of her back. Her pain ceased at his touch, slowly replaced by an odd fluttering feeling.

"Fine, thanks," she said once she had straightened up.

"Are you sure? Thought you'd faint for a moment, there."

She shrugged, muttering something about migraines, and then waited in silence as Nissa pranced back up the grassy slope.

They arrived in County Kilkenny by early evening. Driving in, Mckenna noticed that the small streets and charismatic storefronts had the picture-perfect quality of a postcard; and yet

Mckenna couldn't ignore a strange, unsettling feeling in the pit of her stomach.

Cillian pulled up into the back lot of the Kilford Arms Hotel, once a sixteenth-century church, located in the heart of the medieval town. Its grey stone facade and scarlet sign were welcoming but paled in comparison to the exquisite interior, decorated in walnut-coloured wood and warm brick, with some of the artisanship reclaimed from the old ornate church.

Mckenna and Nissa beat Cillian to the front desk with the hopes of justifying their impromptu visit.

"See, the three of us are travelling together—"

"But not really, it just happened—"

"As of, like, this morning."

"But not, like, *together* together—"

"So, we're hoping you have an extra room available?"

"I'm sorry, there's just the double room left reserved under Mr. Hayes," said the concierge, a scrawny, pale-faced man a little older than Mckenna. "But we can roll in a cot, if you'd like."

Another damned cot.

At this, Nissa leaned into Mckenna's ear and whispered, "Nincompoop"—their "I'm uncomfortable" code word.

Mckenna learned back at Lough Tay that Cillian was not the tame, temperate person he appeared to be. He had lots of pent-up anger inside him. But she had a strong sense from having experienced this resentment of his where it stemmed from: unadulterated passion. He was fighting for a bigger cause, and that was something Mckenna admired in a person. He was in politics, after all. That had to feel heavy on some days, especially with what was going on right now. Her mind wandered to his gentle touch and the courteous manner in which he handled her little episode.

She glanced in his direction. He was urging the concierge to check the list again carefully for an empty room. Mckenna felt his desire to ensure she and Nissa were not uncomfortable.

He really does mean to help us.

Was she being foolish? She had only just met him that morning. Maybe foolish for a normal person, she thought. Spiderman didn't ignore his "spidey sense", did he? And these deep-seated instincts were sort of like that.

And now she was comparing herself to Spiderman.

She turned to Nissa, this time the one doing the reassuring. She couldn't exactly explain to her *how* she came to trust Cillian's intentions, so she appealed to Nissa's rational mind: Mckenna recounted Seán's unplanned Euro trip, where he'd survived for three months by sleeping on strangers' couches, then proceeded to point out that if Cillian wanted to kill them, he could have done so several times by now—and even had time to dispose of their bodies.

"Geez, morbid much, Kenna? But I guess true . . ."

"I'm so sorry," Cillian said to them, looking defeated. "The man's strait-laced; he wouldn't take my bribe. Look, I'll gladly sleep on the cot. You two take the bed, of course."

Mckenna and Nissa thanked him and insisted they pay their half of the room. He was persistent at first—"I'm expensing this stay, anyway!"—but finally agreed out of respect for their "delicate egos," he joked.

"I have to be at dinner with the delegates at half six, so I'll let you settle in," he said in a hurry, handing them the room key. "Hopefully it won't be too long, but it's a charming town and quite lively in the evenings, if you want to do some exploring of your own."

But once Mckenna and Nissa greeted their cozy room and eyed the plush duvet, they resolved it would take a forklift to move them. After the horrid highway motel and child-sized cot in John and Brigit's cabin, this was damned near a royal bed chamber. They collapsed onto the bed, their bodies now one with the mattress beneath them.

Just as Nissa drifted off beside her, Mckenna's eyelids fluttered, and the tan-striped wallpaper around her faded.

She was standing in an overcrowded courtroom. It was utter chaos: A plump, red-faced bishop was on a high platform striking his gavel, and dozens of villagers in ragged clothing were howling in rage at a distraught-looking woman, whose wrists were tied with rope, seated alone on a bench below the bishop. The scene looked straight out of a movie—Mckenna knew in an instant she was witnessing a witch trial from centuries ago, likely the fourteen or fifteen hundreds.

"Order! ORDER!" the bishop bellowed, banging his gavel again, but it did little to quiet the courtroom. "The court has come to its decision." The room finally quieted, waiting in anticipation as a small, balding man handed the bishop a roll of parchment.

"The court concludes that the defendant is guilty of heresy based on the following charges."

There was an uproar: The accused cried out in sheer anguish while the villages shouted triumphantly over the bishop.

"Denying Christ and the church; cutting up living animals to use as offerings; holding illegal meetings in the church at night; making potions to manipulate feelings of love and hate, as well as inciting people to kill and afflict Christians . . ."

He continued to read the charges over the woman's wails, which intensified as the last charge echoed across the courtroom: a*cting as an accomplice to the murder of a noblewoman's many husbands.*

"The court finds the following evidence compelling enough to support the charges. Firstly, these suspicious items were discovered close to the defendant's place of residence: ointments, powders, dead men's fingernails, the fat of murdered infants, and various other abominations. Secondly, the defendant has also confessed to using witchcraft while under the magistrate's interrogation—"

"I WAS TORTURED!" the poor woman cried from the bench. "THEY MADE ME CONFESS! Please . . . please, I'm innocent," she pleaded, violent tears streaming down her face.

"Thirdly," the judge continued, unperturbed, "the defendant has been witnessed leading a coven of heretical sorcerers operating here in Kilkenny . . ."

"IT'S ALICE! ALICE WAS THE RINGLEADER—"

"ENOUGH!" The court silenced again. "Due to this undeniable evidentiary support that has been brought forth, we hereby sentence the accused, Petronella de Meath, to death by burning—"

There was another passionate outburst from the crowd, and Petronella fell to her knees.

"NO! NO, PLEASE! PLEASE! I'VE DONE NOTHING. I'VE DONE NOTHING . . . PLEASE . . . PLEASE . . ."

Mckenna's eyes flew open. She was back in the confines of her hotel room lying beside Nissa, who was dead asleep.

Mckenna sat for several minutes reliving the nightmare. It wasn't anything like the others she'd had—this time, she wasn't centre stage. She was a bystander, watching a woman get sentenced to death for a crime she didn't commit. Though, how Mckenna knew she was innocent, she couldn't say.

Did this dream have any connection with the one she'd had on her birthday? It didn't feel like the same place, and it certainly wasn't the same woman. But another dream about a witch? She didn't know what to think anymore.

And this woman was sentenced here in Kilkenny, which could explain the eerie feeling she got driving down the medieval roads.

Something was waiting for her here.

Not knowing where she was headed, Mckenna picked up her sneakers and tiptoed out of the room.

Cillian Hayes was not your typical delegate. At just twenty-one, he was the youngest of any European representative in the United Nations, even as a youth delegate. His research project entitled *Why All Humans Are Killers*, which he published in his last year at Trinity College, had gained unexpected recognition among scholars and UN ambassadors alike. He theorized that the twenty-first century would be the beginning of the end of the world unless there were *A*—drastic actions placed towards sustainable practices and climate change; or *B*—a major decline in the global population.

He would have never anticipated such a political career, or any career for that matter; Cillian was an activist at heart, convinced he would be bound to a lifetime of picketing and petitions. He had almost turned down the youth delegate position, until an envious classmate of his convinced him that only a mad idiot would turn something like that down—he could be on the inside, help create policies, make change.

But following his first year as a youth delegate, Cillian came to realize that working in politics wasn't nearly enough. No politician was ready to implement the radical changes he knew were necessary to sustain the planet's resources. All hope lost, he was ready to bow out—until the day he was approached by someone who thought his thesis genius. Someone who shared his passion for real change; she was a frightening woman, but she had a plan. Unthinkable, at first. Even evil. And based on something Cillian hadn't before then knew existed: magic.

When Cillian walked into Kyteler's Inn, his glance passed over the homely interior and lively musicians, his nose taking no note of the comforting smell of Irish pub food; all his attention went to his search for the same frightening woman that he now considered his mentor. A woman with straight, white-blonde hair and alabaster skin.

"Hayes, m'boy!" said the inn owner, Nick, a small, kind-faced man in his mid-fifties. "What's the crack?"

"Nice to see you, Nick," Cillian said, grasping his shoulder. "Not much. Have a work thing and just passing through. Have you seen—?"

"She's waiting in the back."

Cillian's legs shook as he walked by the gaping fireplace (or primitive oven) and past the archway into the back room, where the original fourteenth-century stone wall ended. She looked elegant in her long emerald overcoat and ankle-high boots. She was seated bolt upright along the upholstered bench against the lancet stained-glass windows, her right hand covering her left and her hard gaze fixed upon nothing in particular.

He took the seat across from her. "High Priestess."

Her eyes, a deep sapphire, lifted to his. "Young protégé," she said, her voice icier than he last remembered it. "I trust she's here."

"Yes. With a friend—a girl."

"A nuisance?"

"I don't think so. She seems to keep the Wise One encouraged, and I suppose that's what we want. The two managed to get on the ship without my needing to intervene. They befriended an elderly couple who helped them on. Quite lucky, if you ask me."

The High Priestess scoffed. "Luck? I've taught you nothing."

Cillian hesitated. "You're saying . . . the Good People?"

Rolling her eyes, she hissed, "Don't be superstitious. Use their *proper* name."

He was reluctant but dared not object. "I apologize. The fae—faeries. They've been guiding her?"

"The fae want what we want," she said impatiently. "For the Wise One to find her mother. Except they want it done quickly—*before* we can get the girl to complete the first Scottish Scroll. Which is why it's *crucial* we beat them to it, and why you must be there when she finds Abigail."

"Or they'll disappear . . . and the Scrolls will never be fulfilled."

"You get it now, bravo. And you know what happens after that."

Cillian nodded. "And you're sure Kilkenny is the place the first Scroll is referring to? '*A darkness within she'll ken evermore . . .*'"

"Pravadi would be insulted by your lack of faith in her visions. Yes, Kilkenny is where she saw the Wise One discovering her 'darkness within.'"

Cillian nodded again.

"Is she suspicious at all?"

"No. I've told her I've got conferences scheduled all over, so she'll never suspect a thing."

She gave a curt nod. "At Newgrange—did she reveal anything?"

"Not yet, but she's sensed something—that, I'm certain of. I just need more time . . . She doesn't open up easily. But I reckon she's seen the Good—erm, the fae, which means it won't be long before she's accessing all the planes of existence." He remembered how she'd stared down at Guinness Lake, squinting like she couldn't believe her eyes. *Are there normally fireflies around here?*

The High Priestess didn't look the least bit surprised.

"And she's intuitive, to say the least," he continued, hoping his knowledge of the Wise One would impress her. "She can feel what others around her feel; sometimes it's as if she can read my mind." Cillian thought of the pain Mckenna was suddenly overcome with back at Lough Tay when for a split second, his thoughts were in a frenzied state of anger. He knew now that around her, he had to work hard to keep his feelings—and thoughts—in check.

"Close yourself off, like I've shown you. If you give yourself away . . ."

"I won't, High Priestess."

The Priestess fingered the stone around her necklace. "So, she's an empath. Just like her mother."

"It seems so. That's all I know for the moment. Things are moving, but slowly. We've only just met today, but I can feel that she's warming up to me."

"Just gain her trust—fast. In the meantime, I'll be doing my part. And if all goes well, things will be much easier for us after Samhain."

Cillian nodded, unable to fully grasp what she was alluding to as he tried desperately not to think about what would happen to him if he failed.

Cillian had been right—the town was energetic and full of charm. The streets were jammed with the most adorable storefronts Mckenna had ever seen. Every restaurant and shop looked like it belonged in a travel magazine, with vibrant-coloured facades and flowerpots perched atop windowsills.

Then why didn't Mckenna feel welcome here?

She walked aimlessly down the road, eventually crossing the footbridge over the River Nore, which Cillian had pointed out on the way into town. She was growing fond of the soothing sound and sight of flowing water in urban landscapes.

Not far off into the distance was the thirteenth-century Kilkenny Castle. Fully lit against the darkening sky, it was a magnificent sight: a haunting, grey-stone structure, with four circular towers greeting the north, south, east, and west winds. She stopped to admire it, her arms resting on the stone rail. She'd always had an affinity for medieval castles; their gothic architecture and grandeur provoked an almost nostalgic feeling.

There was a sudden chill in the air, and a rush of cold swept across her body. She looked down at her arms—they were covered entirely in goosebumps, as though wrapped in bubble paper.

It happened in a flash. Something that felt like a set of hands seized her around her neck and thrust her body into the rail opposite her. She gripped it, looking frantically around for the culprit.

There was no one in sight.

She pulled herself off the ground, one hand still clutching the rail, the other stroking the sore spot on her neck. *What—the hell—was that?* she wondered, but she wasn't about to stick around for the answer. She darted across the bridge, which led her to a deserted street corner. And just as she stopped to catch her breath—

"Frightened you, have I?" a sour female voice hissed in her ear.

Mckenna whirled around. Once again, there was no one near where she stood. She paced around in a circle, panicking, ignoring a passerby that glanced at her like she should be committed.

Maybe I should be, she thought; she was able to feel what others were feeling, command animals to attack, see lights that weren't there, and now hear voices.

Annoyed by the nosy pedestrians, she turned onto a quiet, narrow alleyway. Empty—except for the grey figure of a woman standing in the dead centre.

Mckenna let out an anguished cry. Her spine throbbed

violently from being struck by something hard and flat. Before she could react, she was struck again, square in the back—then again, until she collapsed onto her knees, sharp pains shooting across her whole body. She wriggled around, fighting hard not to scream.

No one's touching me—this pain isn't real. This pain isn't real.

"Not fun, is it?" the figure's voice echoed. It was high and penetrating, unlike any sound Mckenna had ever heard.

And she was struck again.

Not real . . . not . . . real . . .

"Do you want me to stop?" she asked, seeming to enjoy every bit of Mckenna's agony.

"Who . . . are you?" Mckenna managed between groans.

"You don't recognize me? Well, that's disappointing."

SMACK. Mckenna let herself fall forwards onto the cobblestones. She closed her eyes against the dull pain.

"Beg and I'll stop," it urged.

If there was one thing Mckenna would never be caught doing, it was any variety of begging or pleading.

"I . . . won't," Mckenna said, her body still writhing. *SMACK.* "ARGH!" she cried, unable to suppress her screams any longer.

Another slash across her back.

"AAARGH!"

"Will that do for now?"

The pain ceased. Slowly, she straightened up and found herself inches from the figure's face.

Mckenna gasped, recognizing the dark, wide eyes, the black hair tied over her left shoulder, the pointed nose—this was the ghost of Petronella de Meath, the accused witch from the dream she'd just had.

Petronella tilted her head to one side and smiled a broken-tooth smile. "I thought I'd never see you again, me dear Mistress Alice."

IX

A Full Moon Ceremony

"I think y-you're m-mistaken," Mckenna stammered. "My name is Mckenna."

Petronella let out a shrill noise that Mckenna supposed was a laugh. "You think I'm daft? I see that you've recognized me. I may've trusted you once, but I've grown wiser since, mistress. It's been centuries, and still, *no one* thinks you innocent. Everyone knows it was you who killed yisser four husbands. It was you who was the WITCH!"

The word *witch* scratched at her insides like nails on a chalkboard.

"Look, I'm sorry . . . but I'm not Alice. I'm just a seventeen-year-old American girl—"

"You're LYING!"

Mckenna shielded her ears.

"You're always, *always* lying, Alice. Why?" She glided closer to her until they were nose-to-nose, and Mckenna felt like she had just stepped into a walk-in freezer. "Don't think I didn't see you in the courtroom that day."

And that was when it hit her. Her dream wasn't a dream at all—it was a memory. She thought back to the vision she'd had, how she stood in the back of the courtroom waiting for the final verdict. She hadn't been in her own skin then—the hair that fell below her shoulders was much fairer, but most of it was hidden beneath a scarf. Her hands, too, aged by a decade or so, were unfamiliar. And then the feeling she had . . . it couldn't be. When the court found her servant guilty, she felt an enormous sense of *relief*. She was free.

Mckenna stood there, her mouth agape.

"Remember now?"

"How? I don't understand."

"How? I'll tell you how. You were a *brutal* witch. You didn't care about anyone around you, especially not me. You wanted to punish all the Catholics for not worshipping nature like 'we all should', you'd say. And so you'd kill Christians, and you'd convince other people to kill them. And then you killed all your husbands, one by one. And I knew it, too. I knew what you were doing, but I was still loyal to you, mistress. But you—you ran and left me to die."

"But you confessed—"

"I WAS TORTURED, YOU CRUEL *BUIDSEACH!*" Petronella shrieked, making Mckenna's heart-rate double. "I was a scapegoat. The public hated yisser witchery so much they wanted someone—anyone—to blame. If I didn't confess, they were going to keep flogging me 'til death—not that it mattered in the end. On November 11, 1324, I was burned at the stake."

Mckenna still wasn't sure she understood any of this. She was supposed to have been someone else, in some other time, still retain their memories, and be alive today, in 1991 . . .?

"You don't know, do you?" Petronella said, staring deep into Mckenna's eyes.

"I don't know what?"

"What you are."

Mckenna swallowed. "Yes. I do."

"No. You don't. Not everything." A sudden horrific laugh

escaped Petronella's ghost and reverberated around the alley. It was like being stuck inside a vibrating tunnel. Once again, Mckenna pressed her hands over her ears, this time closing her eyes and wishing for the horror to stop.

Go away, Petronella! Go away . . .

The laughter grew distant.

Go away . . . GO AWAY!

"Mckenna?"

Mckenna opened her eyes to a perplexed-looking Cillian. He was standing where Petronella had appeared, holding open the door to a pub, judging from the folksy Irish music. Above his head was a hanging sign with a purplish-black cat.

"Cillian. Hi," Mckenna said, thinking she must look like a hot mess.

With one glance back inside the pub, he let the door go and walked briskly towards her. "You don't look alright. Are you?" He placed a hand on her shoulder.

"Yeah, I mean, I was just walking around. Discovering the town. It's nice," she said, her lips trembling. He wasn't buying it, she was sure; she looked seconds away from bursting into tears.

"You look cold. I can take you somewhere for a pint, if you'd like."

Mckenna considered this for a moment. Nissa was knocked out, and she wasn't the least bit tired.

"Sure," she said before she could psyche herself out of it. Anything to take her mind off what she had just experienced.

They turned onto the main street and towards the bridge—Mckenna stopped in her tracks when she reached it.

Cillian wrinkled his brow. "Something wrong?"

No biggy—almost got thrown over the edge earlier, that's all. "Not a fan of bridges," was all she could think to say.

"We'll stick to this side of town then."

Grateful he didn't press her, she let Cillian steer her to a lively pub nearby, where the sounds of an accordion, a fiddle and some pipes blared over the crowd.

"Loud for a weeknight!" she shouted as Cillian arrived at

their booth with two pints.

"Too loud?"

"Nah, it's manageable," she said, though she could hardly hear herself speak. She grabbed a glass. "Guinness?"

"Ah, see you know me already, lass." He leaned in closer. "How is it we met this morning?"

Mckenna smiled a half-smile. Cillian grinned back, and she noticed the way it lingered slightly over to one side. "Lass?"

"Adopted it from the Scots. You going to drink that?" he teased.

"I don't drink much."

"Beer isn't really drinking."

She laughed. "That's one of my dad's mottos." She took a sip off the top.

"No, no—you're just getting the foam. Go on."

She obliged, making sure she got through to the dark stuff beneath the frothy top; it was smooth and a little chocolaty, like a creamy, alcoholic treat. "Okay, that's pretty good."

"See? I don't lie." There it was, that spark of mischief in the grey of his eyes. It was trying to hang back, undetected, but Mckenna could see it as plain as day.

"What is it?" he said, taking a fairly large gulp.

"What's what?" Had she been staring?

"Something on my face? Do I have a foam Ronnie?"

"A what?"

"Moustache."

She chuckled. "No, you're good."

"Listen," he said. "There's something I've been meaning to ask you." She caught her breath, bracing herself for the worst. *He knows something. He knows I'm different.* "Why are you heading to Northern Ireland—" She let out a sigh of relief. "—with everything that's going on?"

She fought not to bite her lip, to look as though she was burying a secret. Cillian was cool and all, and she liked him, but he was a bit more difficult to read than Nissa, who was an open book. He was keeping something from her, too.

No, he didn't have to know she was searching for her mother, nor where exactly she was headed. "I want to break a story."

Cillian raised an eyebrow. "You're a journalist?"

It wasn't complete bullshit. She was always told she looked and acted much older for her age. She opted for a half-truth. "Trying to be. Everyone thinks I'm reckless for going to Northern Ireland right now, but hey, that's where the story's at . . ." She took as large a swig as Cillian had, her head buzzing and cheeks warming with every inch her Guinness dropped.

"Why didn't you say so before?"

"It's a stupid dream, I guess."

He leaned in. "Ah, but the stupid ones are the most fun, are they not?"

His closeness unsteadied her for a moment, and her body juddered slightly, the way Andre's car did in the winter.

"I'm gonna head out," she said quickly, pushing the pint away. "I'm exhausted. Um, did you want to . . ."

Cillian cleared his throat. "Nah, I'm going to hang back."

She nodded, wondering if he felt awkward about going up to the same hotel room. She should say something. He'd been so kind to her and Nissa. "I don't want you to feel weird about sleeping in your own hotel room. It's really okay if you want to—"

"Oh, not at all. The meeting just took a lot out of me. Need to unwind a bit more."

"Yeah. Makes sense." She stood up, preoccupied, for some reason, with where to place her hands. "G'night, then," she finally said, giving him an awkward wave and turning on her heel, not knowing whether he responded or bothered to wave back.

Relieved to be alone again, she hurried down the street, allowing herself time to process what had happened with Petronella de Meath. She had been in complete shock earlier, and then Cillian came along . . .

One thing at a time.

The ghost of Petronella had been so intense and disturbing, all of it still hadn't sunk in—especially the bit about Mckenna being this Alice woman. She just couldn't fathom it as reality. And why should she? How did she know it wasn't her head messing with her? There was so much she didn't comprehend about her "abilities"—it was getting near impossible to tell the real from the imaginary.

And what now, Mckenna—you're talking to dead people?

But the truth was that even as somewhat of a realist, Mckenna never rejected the existence of ghosts. The way she saw it, the universe was infinite—humans hadn't even discovered a fraction of its possibilities. While she was indeed a big fan of cold, hard facts, she was also privy to the notion of unseen forces. After all, wasn't the majority of the universe's mass made up of material that even scientists couldn't observe? What if what they called dark matter was just an amalgam of different energies, including spiritual ones?

Mckenna's mind raced with thoughts of ghosts and witches. She made a mental note to do some research on Petronella tomorrow; she remembered seeing a library along the waterfront.

Before she knew it, her feet had carried her behind the illuminated castle, down a lamp-lit footpath that wound into the woods. As she strode, Mckenna wished she'd run into a giant neon sign that said something like: *You're not nuts! This is all happening for a reason.* It was odd—sometimes she felt guided, like no matter how arbitrary her journey felt, she was headed in the right direction. Other times she felt like a fool, like she was banking on her gut and some luck.

Luck. She'd had lots of it. It began when she met Nissa, she realized—Nissa, whose faith in Mckenna she couldn't begin to comprehend. Sans her, Mckenna wondered if she'd have had the confidence to leave her dads and delve into the unknown—or had the patience to stick with John and Brigit, without whom they'd have had a park bench in Boston with their name on it. And if Nissa hadn't been around to convince her, there was no way Mckenna would've jumped into Cillian's car, purely out of trust.

Something hooted in the night. She looked up to where the full moon hung, a solitary orb glinting in the sky. She let herself get lost in the effect of its silver skin, swirling like marble.

The sound of a bell ringing brought Mckenna back down to Earth. It came from behind the trees, along with faint voices. Unable to make out what they were saying, she stepped closer and heard . . . singing?

"Earth to moon, moon to sky,
Beneath your sacred light, I am purified."

Mckenna peeked through the trees and was awestruck by the scene before her: A group of women garbed in white robes were seated around a flat slab of stone, on top of which lay a thick white candle and several chestnut-sized crystals. They each held onto a small piece of paper and had their eyes closed in concentration.

"My past pain released and intentions set free,
I openly accept the life that awaits me."

Mckenna stared mesmerized as one by one, they walked up to the candle and held their paper over the flame until the messages, whatever they were, were gathered by the oncoming breeze.

SNAP.

Seven heads turned towards Mckenna—who instinctively leaped behind the trees, cursing the stupid twig that just snapped beneath her feet.

"If you're here to observe, you're welcome," said a serene voice, but authoritative. There was a non-Irish twist to her accent; her Rs rolled lightly, and her pitch changed with each word, like a melody.

"You're also free to join."

Mckenna didn't budge. She waited a beat before sneaking another peek through the trees and was relieved to see that the gatherers had carried on with their ritual. Their hands were joined and heads bowed down—all but one: She had glowing brown skin and striking, almond-shaped eyes, which were fixed on the place where Mckenna stood. The latter sensed she was the one who'd spoken earlier.

What's her deal? Why is she staring at me?

Mckenna wasn't about to stick around to find out. She'd had enough weird for one night. She spun round and walked briskly through the woods, then fell face first into a muddy patch. Staggering forward, she ran back up the paved path and to the bridge. She stopped short. *She's gone,* Mckenna told herself. *I told her to go away.* She took a deep breath in, out, in and out again . . . then sprinted across.

Nissa shook Mckenna awake at eight o'clock the next morning. "I'm wired," she said, sipping coffee from a hotel mug.

"Where d'you get that?" Mckenna managed to say through an exuberant yawn.

"Downstairs! There's a whole spread. I now *love* traditional Irish breakfasts. Eggs, fresh bread, chutney, potatoes—"

"Shhh . . . Loud. Early."

"You can have the rest," Nissa said a notch lower, handing over her coffee. "This is my third."

Mckenna gulped some down and noticed Cillian's empty cot. "Where's Cillian?"

"He left this on his bed." She handed her a note written in a neat script.

Morning, lasses!

I'm off to my morning meetings, so I'll catch you later on.

There's a deadly full breakfast downstairs—the best in Kilkenny (and it's included).

Cillian

"I like Cillian, don't you? Funny, smart, hot . . ."

"Yep, very nice. Definitely not a serial killer—so far."

"And *hot . . .*"

Mckenna began fiddling with the contents of her bag.

"He must like to start the day early," Nissa continued. "He wasn't here when I woke up at six."

"You were up at six?"

"Well, we did sleep, like, twelve hours."

Right. Nissa had fallen asleep almost instantly. Mckenna's night, not so restful. Mckenna had been up for most of the night going over her encounter with Petronella de Meath. She had hoped Cillian hadn't heard her tossing and turning—he had crept in about an hour after she'd come to bed, at which point Mckenna pretended she was comatose.

"Yeah, I think I'm just groggy from oversleeping." She felt terrible lying to Nissa, but how could she tell her that the ghost of a fourteenth-century house servant blamed Mckenna for her horrific death and threatened to kill her, let alone how she stumbled upon a coven of witches on a late-night stroll in the woods?

"You stink a little," Nissa said, wrinkling her nose.

Recalling her fall in the mud, Mckenna lifted the covers up to her neck in an effort to hide the evidence. "I had a bad dream and I . . . tend to sweat a lot. Happens once in a while."

"Oh," Nissa said, looking concerned. "About what?"

Mckenna hesitated. "Can't remember."

It took a great deal of Nissa's nagging for Mckenna to agree to an early start, but after a much-needed long, hot shower, Nissa finally managed to drag her down to the hotel dining room to get breakfast, and she was grateful. Mckenna hadn't enjoyed such a tasty meal since Seán cooked her her birthday breakfast. Was that already over a week ago? She'd almost forgot how much she missed Seán's homemade Irish soda bread. She slathered butter over the top and bit off half the slice.

"Okay, I must know," Nissa said, doing the same. "Why does the butter here taste like *heaven?*"

It was true. The butter was nothing like American butter. It was richer and creamier, and the perfect blend of sweet and salty. It might've been the hunger pangs talking, but Mckenna decided she could easily live off of Irish-buttered soda bread alone.

After breakfast, Nissa begged Mckenna to explore the town, and so together they passed the various shops, stopping in for a look at some of the more peculiar ones; Nissa's favourite by far was a sports store with a front window lined with stuffed animals.

"But *why?*" they wondered, imagining scenarios in which the somewhat disturbing decor would attract anyone other than a toddler. Mckenna was giggling so hard as they sauntered past more shops and across a few small roads that she almost failed to notice what they were about to step foot on.

The very bridge she was deathly afraid of crossing.

"Wait!" She grabbed Nissa's arm and spun her around.

"Ouch," Nissa said, yanking her arm back. "What's wrong?"

"I, uh . . ." Mckenna scanned her surroundings for some inspiration. "I'd really like to go to the library. It's just up here." She pointed down the riverside street on which they stood—John's Quay—to a classic-style, grey-stone building that she remembered seeing the evening before.

"Oh, perfect, I finished all my books on the boat! Do you think if I took one out, they'd let me mail it back?"

Relieved, Mckenna led Nissa to the scarlet double doors, flanked by grey Roman-style columns. They entered a plain, square interior, mostly made up of grey and beige tones. Some desks overlooked the river by the tall, arched windows, and the rest of the space was filled with row upon row of bookshelves. Save for Mckenna and Nissa, the place seemed to be empty.

When Mckenna turned around, Nissa was already browsing the closest bookshelf. It was the only window she had to squeeze in some ghostly research. Eager, she searched the rows for a librarian, finally finding a lanky middle-aged woman sprawled on the floor of one of the aisles. She had thick, waist-length sandy hair and a pair of round glasses sitting on the bridge of her nose and attached to a multi-coloured string. One by one, she was sticking coloured labels on the spines of the entire bottom row of books and muttering to herself.

"11307 . . . 11308 . . . 11309 . . ."

"Sorry," Mckenna said quietly. "Do you know where—?" She was stopped mid-sentence by the librarian's index finger. Mckenna waited until she finally looked up and acknowledged her presence.

"What can I do for you?"

"I'm looking for, uh . . . information." Mckenna realized how dim that must've sounded considering where they were.

"You're going to have to be more specific."

"It's kind of a weird topic."

The librarian blinked back at her, her expression suggesting that she didn't care.

"I'd like some information on a fourteenth-century witch trial. Or maybe thirteenth . . . I'm not sure."

The librarian stared on, her long fingers now tapping on one of the hardcovers.

"And I'm pretty sure it took place here, in Kilkenny. So, I'm not sure whether to look at history books or . . ."

"We've got newspaper archives."

"Oh! Great. Uh, anything on Petronella de Meath and her mistress, Alice something . . ."

"Alice Kyteler."

Mckenna's heart jumped at the sound of the name, like it was that of a distant relative whom she hadn't heard from in ages. "Yes. Kyteler. How did you—?"

"You heard of Kyteler's Inn just over the bridge? It was Alice's home. Her servant's death was a big local story," she said, pushing herself off the floor and dusting herself off.

Kyteler's Inn. She'd heard of it, but where? If it was just over the bridge, no wonder Mckenna wasn't welcome to cross it.

"What happened to Alice?" she said as the librarian brushed past her and disappeared around the end of the aisle. Confused, Mckenna followed, trailing behind her as she speed-walked to an office round the back—shutting the door in Mckenna's face—and emerged seconds later hugging a folder against her chest and holding out a pair of latex gloves.

"Wear these. Some of these clippings are quite old."

Thrilled, Mckenna seated herself at a desk in the corner of the library and began sifting through the newspaper articles, reading the first one that caught her eye with intrigue.

NARRATIVE OF THE PROCEEDINGS

AGAINST

DAME ALICE KYTELER

FOR SORCERY.

A.D. 1324

She swore under her breath; the rest of the article was impossible to read, damaged from some sort of liquid. The following clipping was written in Irish, as was the next, and the next. Mckenna removed eight more articles from the pile before she finally found an English one, dated seventeen years ago.

GHOST OF KYTELER'S INN RETURNS

The ghost that is rumoured to haunt Kyteler's Inn was sighted yesterday at around 3:00 p.m. inside the fourteenth-century establishment.

The spirit, who had not been seen in at least seven years, has long been believed to be that of Dame Alice Kyteler—the inn's original owner.

Kyteler made her fortune as the widow of four well-to-do men, all of whom died under suspicious circumstances. Fuelled by resentment over her wickedness and accumulated riches, Kyteler's stepchildren accused her of witchcraft. She later became the first reported person in Ireland to be condemned for witchcraft and sentenced to

> *be burned.*
>
> *However, on the night before her punishment was to be carried out, Kyteler was aided by a wealthy and loyal friend and fled, letting her handmaiden, Petronella de Meath, be burned in her place on November 11, 1324. It is said that the poor maiden cried out repeatedly for Alice to save her.*
>
> *Could yesterday's ghost belong to the ill-fated Petronella de Meath? According to one of the inn's regulars, it is quite likely.*
>
> *"Oh, I never believed it was Alice's ghost," said Cormac Walsh. "I could tell it's an angry presence, and what's Alice got to be mad about? She escaped scot free."*

The rest of the article went on about the charges laid against her, which Mckenna already knew of thanks to her dream—or memory.

It had to have been Petronella, Mckenna thought. She looked at the date—from the smudged ink, she could only make out 1974, the year Mckenna was born. She squinted, trying to decipher the day, but it seemed to be written in Irish. She could make out that there were two words: *Me . . . Fó . . . and is that a nineteen or a fourteen . . .?*

"There you are!" Nissa's voice squeaked, startling her. She was holding a thick book in her hands. "I read two chapters and I already can't put it down." She held the novel up, and Mckenna read out the title *The Eye of the World*. On the cover a man and a woman were riding horses in front of a full-moon backdrop.

"I didn't know you were a fan of fantasy," Mckenna said after reading the synopsis in the inside cover.

"Oh, heck yeah. Anything that takes me away to another world," she said dramatically.

Mckenna smiled, then pointed at the article date. "Look—does that look like a four or a nine?"

"Hmm . . . pretty sure it's a four."

"Will you be taking that out?" the librarian asked, appearing beside Nissa.

"Here's the thing—we're not staying here long, but I'd *really* like to finish it," Nissa pleaded. "Do you think I can maybe mail it back to you when I'm done? I swear I will, and I'm a fast reader!"

Mckenna could tell the librarian was fighting an eye roll. "It's never been taken out, so why not, I guess," she said dully, and she turned on her heel and disappeared in her office, as though she was done with human interaction for the day.

When they returned to the hotel room, they found another note from Cillian:

> *If you're back, feel free to join me for lunch in the pub downstairs.*
>
> *I'll be there until about 2:00.*
>
> *Glad you're enjoying the town!*
>
> *Cillian*

Mckenna and Nissa took Cillian up on his offer and met him in the pub's restaurant section, where he sat in a leather booth, sipping a cappuccino. They had a pleasant lunch; Cillian insisted they try the Guinness stew and potato pie. Mckenna had eaten these traditional Irish meals tons of times at home, but Cillian was right—this really was something special. He swore that the ingredients in the US ("not for anything") tasted nothing like they did in Ireland. "The cheese, for instance, here isn't pasteurized, so it doesn't sit all heavy in your stomach." Nissa said she was all for eating more naturally. She was even considering becoming vegetarian.

"It's wonderful for the planet," Cillian encouraged. "Do you know how much energy—how much *water* it takes to raise livestock? Something like fifty gallons a day, for a cow at least. Also, imagine the plastic wasted packing all that meat. Our land and waters will be completely done for."

Mckenna had no idea. "Why doesn't anyone talk about this?"

"Because there isn't enough awareness!" Nissa shouted, turning heads.

Cillian looked bitter. "Because people like the easy way out. They look for immediate solutions, not long-term ones. Farmers know how much they consume: I've spoken to dozens to support my research, but they won't admit to the damage it's causing. The industry's far too ginormous. But it's logic, isn't it? Recycling's great, but if we keep abusing resources the way we are—with the global population increasing so fast—the damage we do will be irreversible."

They sat for another half hour discussing things like plastic use and waste reduction, and Mckenna was actively engaged, a rarity for her when it came to conversation.

Just as she was beginning to trust Cillian, her sixth sense—if that was indeed what it was—kicked in, detecting a struggle inside of him. He was fighting hard to conceal something . . . and it was working.

Perhaps it was for the best and she should get to know people without swimming around in their heads. Everyone was going through something, right?

God, I have such trust issues.

When Mckenna tuned back in to the conversation, Cillian was asking if she and Nissa were enjoying this impromptu, more scenic route to Northern Ireland. Nissa responded by putting a small hand theatrically to her chest and professing her love for Ireland, especially Kilkenny, as it was the "cutest town in the world."

Mckenna felt differently, thanks to Petronella. Nonetheless, she wasn't lying when she disclosed she did feel affection for Ireland, beginning with its people (the live ones); she thought of John and Brigit, of course, and each of the friendly shop owners she and Nissa had encountered on their stroll through town. She added that as grateful as she was to be sightseeing, she was eager to reach her destination.

"I was talking to the concierge this morning, and he said Ballycastle was *beautiful*," Nissa blurted. Mckenna's spoon fell to the floor with a clatter.

"You trusted *me,* though," Nissa said when Mckenna scolded her for telling Cillian their destination. They returned to a tidy room with chocolates on their pillows, which Nissa was already unwrapping.

"You're different," Mckenna said. "I knew I could trust you completely from the start, and my first impressions are usually spot on."

Nissa beamed. "Look at you, showing affection," she said, squeezing Mckenna's cheek. Mckenna slapped her hand away, fighting a laugh.

"I'm serious, though. I know he's being nice, but we always have to be on our guard."

"What is it with you wanting to keep your mom a big secret?"

Because she was some kind of mystic witch person who was forced to go into hiding to protect her from God knows who.

"Because it's personal, that's all."

"And there's nothing you're not telling me, right?"

Mckenna hesitated. "No. Of course not."

Nissa scrutinized her. "Fine. But you know, it's like you said—we would've been dead and buried by now. So maybe you're keeping your guard up around him for different reasons."

"What's that supposed to mean?"

"It means you're so focused on closing yourself off that you're missing out. Or you would've missed out if *I* hadn't offered to help John and Brigit . . . and if I had let you chicken out when Cillian offered us a lift."

Mckenna knew all this to be true, but until now, she didn't think Nissa was bothered by her introvertedness.

"It may not seem like it to you, but I'm *trying,* okay? I risked everything to come here—I left my family behind. It's easy to tell others to take chances when you have nothing to lose."

Nissa stared back at her, undeniable hurt in her eyes.

Mckenna instantly regretted her words. She wouldn't soon forget the devastation on Nissa's face as she stalked out of the room, book in hand, passing by a confused-looking Cillian on the way out the door.

"I, um, came to tell you both that we'll have to stay one more night. I've got a meeting to . . ." He paused. "Everything alright?"

He stopped mid-doorstep. Mckenna noticed his eyes were particularly green tonight.

"Yeah. Just a difference of opinion."

"Ah." He closed the door gently behind him. "Well, that can happen."

"We've never had an argument before," Mckenna said, realizing it as the words escaped her.

"Well, then it was bound to happen. Friends fight, and that's a good thing. Means you both care."

"What are you gonna say next—a best friend is like a four-leaf clover . . ."

" . . . hard to find and lucky to have," they both said in unison.

Mckenna chuckled. "One of my dads says that all the time."

"*One* of your dads . . .?"

Mckenna wanted to bite her tongue. What was it about Cillian that made her feel so vulnerable?

She nodded, looking away. Cillian smiled. "You don't have to feel shy with me about it. Love is love, right?"

Mckenna's face flushed. Before now, Nissa had been the only other person who made her feel that having two dads was completely normal. She had told her during one of their talks out on the ship deck, and her reaction was not what Mckenna had expected: "As hard as it must be not having a mom, you're lucky to have grown up with two loving parents. Even if it's not considered 'normal.'"

Nissa's kindness made Mckenna think that perhaps she was right—she needed to give others the benefit of the doubt.

And in thanks, she'd driven Nissa away.

"You alright?" Cillian said, watching her.

"Why are you being so nice to two complete strangers?" Mckenna said, hearing the note of accusation in her voice. She was sure he did, too, but this was something Mckenna had been wondering ever since their first encounter at the Dublin bistro.

Cillian paused, squinting slightly. His gaze drifted past her for a moment. He looked to be choosing his words carefully. His eyes settled back on Mckenna's. "Because if someone hadn't helped *me* when I needed it most, I wouldn't be where I am today."

Mckenna wondered if he was referring to his career. "So, you're paying it forward, huh?"

"Something like that." He smirked, and Mckenna's insides did a kind of cartwheel. He then excused himself, saying he had one last dinner obligation, and as he opened the door to leave, he turned around to say, *"Slán go fóill."*

Mckenna tilted her head.

He grinned. "Means bye for now." And he swung the door closed.

"Wait!" she called out just before the thud. He cracked it open and peered inside.

"I have a weird question."

His eyes filled with curiosity; he tilted his head. "Sure."

"What are the months of the year in Gaelic?"

Cillian scratched his head, and began to recite.

"Wait!" Mckenna shouted more loudly than she meant to. "What was that you just said?"

"*Meán Fómhair?*" he said smoothly.

"Yes. What month is that?"

"September. Why?"

Mckenna nearly let out a gasp. That meant the article was written on September 14, 1974, and according to its source, the ghost of Petronella had reappeared for the first time in seven years just the day before.

The day Mckenna was born.

X

ESME THE GOOD WITCH

As Mckenna paced the room, a whirlwind of frantic thoughts overwhelmed her. It had taken her most of the night to accept the fact that she'd seen a ghost, but once that did sink in, Mckenna still hadn't taken Petronella's claim that she was Alice all that seriously. Yes, she had dreamt the scene in the courthouse, but maybe seeing visions was one of her latent abilities she had yet to fully discover.

But now she didn't know what to think. Could it be a coincidence that Petronella de Meath had turned up on the day after Mckenna arrived in this world? Had Petronella been out to get revenge on Mckenna—or Alice, rather—since the day she was born because of what she, Alice, had done to her? That would mean Mckenna had a past life. Did she even believe in past lives?

What did it even matter what she believed in? There was no one she could turn to who could help her understand.

But maybe there is. Feeling somewhat hopeful, she left the room and headed for the bridge over the River Nore. Petronella hadn't appeared since she sent her away, just before Cillian showed up in the alleyway. She should be safe now.

As she walked through the town and stopped dead in front of the river, she wished that on the other side among the trees, the coven would be gathered there once more. She took one step forward onto the bridge.

A rush of wind knocked her off her feet, and a shrill voice screamed in her ear.

"YOU'RE DEAD, MISTRESS!"

Mckenna tried to scramble forward, but the force that was Petronella's spirit pushed her down, flat on the concrete surface.

"Petronella . . . please. Let's . . . talk."

The translucent grey embodiment of Petronella de Meath materialized before her.

"Oh, my dear mistress Alice wants to talk now? Am I frightening you, mistress? Are you afraid to die?"

Mckenna's body was hauled halfway across the bridge. She landed hard, feeling her foot roll and a muscle in it tear. She yelped in agony.

"Did that hurt? That's NOTHING!"

Mckenna closed her eyes tight, waiting for the worst to happen—but nothing did. She opened her eyes instead to a stunned Petronella, who looked as though she'd been hit with a tranquilizer dart; she was hovering about a foot from Mckenna, staring past her. Mckenna turned around as far as her aching body would let her to find the source of Petronella's distraction.

A magnificent blue light, radiant like that of a fallen angel, appeared a distance away. Mckenna felt a sense of peace and elation; she could stay in this very spot for eternity . . .

Then a kind, melodic voice spoke to her. "Make it right, Mckenna. It's time."

Mckenna turned to look back at Petronella, whose body was still hovering above her staring longingly at the end of the bridge.

Make it right . . .

Mckenna understood what she had to do. Grasping the rail, she pulled herself off the ground, feeling twinges of pain all over her right foot.

"Petronella, do you hear me? It's—it's Alice."

Petronella continued to stare ahead of her, but a twitch of her eye told Mckenna she'd heard her.

"Petronella, I am deeply, deeply sorry for what I did to you." she said, remembering how Alice had abandoned Petronella just before her death sentence. "You—you kept silent while I did all of those horrible things. You were a true friend. And I was . . . wicked."

Petronella's head started to turn towards Mckenna.

"There is no excuse for my—my cowardice, and I will have to live with that for the rest of my life, and all my lives to come," she added. "You deserve to be at peace, Petronella. You deserve to go into the light."

Mckenna wasn't sure if she was imagining it, but the greyish spectre that was Petronella's apparition was brightening.

"I called for you, mistress. But the flames . . . they caught before . . . before . . ." Tears streamed down her now-corporeal face, her cheeks flushing pink. Mckenna watched stunned as the rest of her ghostly form came to life in front of her. Petronella didn't seem to notice; she cried and cried, until her weeping echoed up and down the bridge.

Something in Mckenna shattered. Her heart sank into her gut and soon she, too, was shedding uncontrollable tears. Was Alice still a part of her? Whose remorse was she feeling: hers or Alice's?

How could she have caused such suffering?

But I didn't. I would never do this, Mckenna decided. *I'm not Alice.*

Slowly, she reached for Petronella's hand. "I can't change what Alice did back then, Petronella. But I can help you now, as Mckenna. You can be free of the hurt you've been carrying with you all these centuries. Do you want to be free?"

Petronella's dark eyes met hers, and for the first time, Mckenna saw her as the wounded woman she was back in the courtroom.

Petronella nodded, and Mckenna pulled her into an embrace. "You can let go, Petronella." She held her close, her eyes shut tight as she wished for Petronella's soul to find peace.

When she opened her eyes, she was standing alone on a deserted bridge. Petronella was gone.

At the end of the bridge stood the woman from last night's gathering, tall and poised, her eyes so striking that Mckenna couldn't tear hers away. Clutching the rail, Mckenna dragged her sprained ankle behind her, but as she neared the woman, Mckenna could think of nothing to say. The pain was growing unbearable now. The world around her spun, fading . . . fading . . .

Until she saw nothing but black.

"Have you still not learned the basics," the High Priestess said as Nick walked away with hers and Cillian's drink orders. "At this stage, it should be no harder than spell casting."

"I'm nearly there, High Priestess. It's just long distances that I have trouble—"

"You're lucky my seer sent me here," she said, stone-faced. "Or you would've been forced to astral travel to me."

Or she could have a bloody phone number like everyone else. "I'm working on it, Priestess."

"And are you working on what we're here for?"

"Yes. I've urged her to explore the town, and it's possible something's happened—she looked distraught yesterday when I found her, here in fact, just in the alley. She wouldn't tell me a thing, though, which I suppose means it's something out of the ordinary. Which is a good sign—"

"All I hear is mere speculation. 'It's possible.' You 'suppose.' If it's not fact, it's nothing."

"Yes, Priestess."

"And what do you mean 'here'? In *this* alley?" She nodded at the pub's entrance.

"Yes. Does that mean anything?"

"I sensed that female spirit roaming here yesterday. Her energy is lower than it's ever been."

Cillian shivered involuntarily. "Do you think it has something to do with the '*darkness within*?'"

"It might." She looked like she'd stumbled on buried treasure. Her gaze hardened again. "But none of it matters if she is unable to lock a connection with her mother. It's crucial she is confident in her abilities. Help her find it—do what you must." She leaned in close. "Make her feel the magic in her veins."

"Of course." Cillian had no inkling as to how to make that happen. "Though, she might've already found her."

"What in the name of the Goddess are you talking about?"

"She thinks Abigail is in Ballycastle," Cillian said triumphantly."

"Are you certain?" The word *certain* weighed on Cillian like a millstone.

"I—well, she's doing all she can to get there."

"But you're not certain." Her voice turned venomous fast. Cillian felt his skin prickle.

"I'm not, High Priestess. But, see, neither is the Wise One. So, how can I be—"

"Because if you'd done your research, you'd ken that that's where Abigail fled from in the first place. So, my dear protégé, tell me: As the most wanted mystic on this Earth, would you damn yourself by returning to where there's a high chance you'd be found?"

Nick returned with their drinks, and Cillian straightened up. "Prey have hidden in plain sight since the dawn of time to evade their predators, have they not? If you're asking if I'd do the same, my answer would have to be yes." He held in his breath.

The High Priestess pondered this for what felt to Cillian like a fortnight. "Camouflage," she finally said.

Cillian nodded, a little uncertain. "And with the protection spell she's cast, it's not as though she can be spotted, so why not go back to where she feels most at home?"

She held her chin up. "Very well." He breathed a little easier. "In the event that you're wrong, which we ken is likely," Cillian fought hard to keep from throwing his drink in her face, "I'll be carrying out a plan of my own. Get her there. And don't lose her."

"I won't, High Priestess. What are you planning exactly—?"

"Just get her there. If there is any change, you will be the first to ken."

Cillian gulped, knowing full well she did not mean this as a courtesy.

Mckenna awoke to a damp, squishy surface beneath her. She was lying on the grass beside the flat slab of stone where a ritual candle and crystals were placed. She made to sit up, expecting to feel her ankle throbbing painfully, but it didn't.

"All better?"

Emerging from behind her was the woman from the ceremony and the bridge. Carefully, she knelt beside Mckenna, placed her arm around her neck, and propped her up against the nearest tree trunk.

"Yes," Mckenna said, confused. "What happened to my ankle?"

"It's sprained," the woman said.

"Right. So why don't I feel anything? Did you give me a sedative or something?"

"Just cypress oil, some frankincense, and a wee bit of reiki."

Some what, what, and a wee bit of what?

She held up two small, blue glass bottles. "Cypress is an essential oil that reduces inflammation and increases circulation, and frankincense helps reduce the bruising. Reiki is a form of energy healing."

Mckenna stared blankly back at her. Her brain was so full of questions, she didn't know where to start.

"You must have a lot of questions."

Ding ding ding.

"My name is Esme. You stumbled upon my coven, did you not?"

So she did recognize Mckenna. "Yes, I'm sorry about that—"

"What ever for?"

Mckenna shrugged.

"What you witnessed was a full moon ceremony—a time to release that which no longer serves us, let go of a part of ourselves that we've outgrown, and welcome in the new. Our moon travels a twenty-eight to thirty-day cycle each month, see. And the full moon represents the most powerful point in the cycle—the starting of death, of something new. An opportunity to meditate on dreams and manifest goals."

Mckenna wasn't sure she fully grasped the concept—or the accent—but she nodded anyway, fascinated.

"You, yourself, are capable of manifesting whatever it is you want much more easily than others. So you must be careful which energy you choose to put out there into the universe, Mckenna."

Mckenna started. "How do you know who I am?"

Esme sat cross-legged on the ground and faced her. "You ken you possess abilities," she stated pointedly. "But you don't ken the full extent of it."

"My dads hid it from me. I didn't know a thing before my seventeenth birthday."

"They did well to protect you, *boireannach glic.*"

"Protect me from *what?*"

"Now is not the time to say," she said with empathy.

Mckenna's frustration grew. "Why not? Why doesn't anyone want to tell me the truth? How am I supposed to understand what's going on with me, how to use these abilities?"

"There is a time for everything. And your intuition is stronger than you ken. You must always follow it. Do you see how you helped Petronella? And no one showed you how."

"The blue light. Did you . . .?"

"I conjured it, yes. And you will come to learn how to, too, *boireannach glic.*"

Mckenna paused to gather herself. "What does that mean?"

Esme smiled, like she had been waiting for the question to arise. "It's Scottish Gaelic for Wise One."

Mckenna listened anxiously.

"But it's not the first time you hear this term, is it, *boireannach glic?*"

"My mom called me a Wise One in her parting note to my dad. But I haven't been able to find a reference to it anywhere. Can you tell me what it means? Please," she added, her eyes pleading.

Esme's penetrating gaze nearly put Mckenna in a trance.

"A Wise One has lived many lives as a witch before this one, and carries the burden of these past existences with them into their next life, and every life after that."

Alice, Mckenna thought.

"Yes, you were Alice Kyteler, and you must live with what you've done. Petronella has been waiting for you here in Kilkenny during every one of your lives. She must have reappeared just when you incarnated again." That explained the article. "But you mustn't regret the past. What's important is that you've made it right, and you've learned from it."

"So, those dreams . . . they really were memories?"

Esme nodded.

"I . . . I was evil."

"Your soul has evolved since. You are not the same person you were."

But there's evil inside me.

"We all have light and shadow in us, *boireannach glic.*"

Mckenna sat there speechless for some time until Esme placed a hand on her knee, bringing her back to the present. "I leave you with this," she said. "Be attentive to the meaning of your dreams, and be cannie who you trust."

"Sorry, be what?" Mckenna said, not catching the slang, which she assumed, by now, was Scottish.

"Careful."

"Because people are hunting me." It wasn't a question. But Esme was already making her way towards the footpath.

"Wait," Mckenna called out. "What if I have more questions?"

"I have faith we'll cross paths again." And then before she continued on, she said cryptically, "The harvest moon will occur on the same night as the autumnal equinox. A very rare occasion that won't happen again for another nineteen years."

2010. Did she know *everything?*

Avebury Henge—Wiltshire, England

It had been three days since Seán arrived in Wiltshire, and every day, he'd spent hours skulking around the stone circle, hoping he would spot his daughter across the monument.

And every day, Seán had been disappointed.

Andre had been right. He was on a wild goose chase; he was no different from his own daughter, who was just as naive as he was to think that by following some gut instinct, she would run into someone who didn't want to be found.

One more hour, he promised himself. One more hour and he would call Andre to apologize for lashing out at him and tell him he was coming home. Mckenna was strong; he should've trusted her to take care of herself. To come home when she was ready.

Fifty-five minutes later, Seán was seated cross-legged in the centre of the stone circle. He checked his watch—the monument was closing in five minutes. How had he let it come this far? Crestfallen, he buried his face in his hands.

"I hope you asked permission to enter beforehand," said an ethereal voice.

A voice that Seán hadn't heard in seventeen years.

XI

The Three Legs of Man

Mckenna couldn't believe that a mere week ago she was traipsing around Boston without any clue as to how she was going to pull off voyaging to a faraway continent. Sailing with John and Brigit felt like a lifetime ago, and seeing Nissa in the schoolyard, eons.

Nissa hadn't spoken a word to Mckenna all morning. When Mckenna returned to the hotel room from her encounter with Esme the night before, Nissa was turned over on her side, unmoving. Though, Mckenna had a strong sense she'd heard her come in.

Cillian elected himself tour guide during their four-hour drive to Connemara, educating them on Irish history whenever the opportunity arose (and when it didn't) and pointing out quirky facts about the passing towns. A couple of hours into their drive, Mckenna's heart warmed when he announced they were a few kilometres past County Limerick—home of John and Brigit, and according to Cillian, where Irish coffee was invented ("Bless them!"). She glanced at Nissa, who continued to stare out at the grazing white sheep along the country road.

"What's all this?" Mckenna asked, stifling a yawn. Stirring awake after a good hour-long nap, she looked out to a lot less greenery than she'd remembered. They were driving through a vast landscape of grey stone that looked as though it had been smashed into bedrock with Thor's hammer.

"We're passing through the Burren, part of County Clare. Its name comes from the Irish word *bhoireann,* meaning a stony place. Mad, isn't it?"

"You're, like, a walking encyclopedia," Mckenna joked. Cillian let out a hearty chuckle.

"But what *is* it?" Nissa said, gaping around her. Nissa may have not been speaking to *her,* but at least she had ended her silent protest.

"A natural phenomenon. All this you see on the surface is limestone. Took about twenty million years to form. There's no landscape like this anywhere."

"Looks sort of dead, though," Mckenna thought aloud.

"Quite the opposite," Cillian said. "The Burren is home to seventy percent of Ireland's native plants, plus lots of small animals you wouldn't see anywhere else."

"Like what?" Nissa said.

"Pigmy shrews, bank voles, pine martens . . ."

"You're making those up," Mckenna said with a grin.

"I swear on my mum," he said, his hand to his heart. "And that's not counting the hundred species of birds."

"The land must be protected, right? For there to be so many different kinds of wildlife," Nissa said.

"Oh, without question. Notice how quiet it is here?" he said, bringing the car to a full stop. "Far from the savage hands of humankind . . ."

Nissa laughed, but Mckenna remained thoughtful. She agreed that some things were better left untouched.

"Our conference is in the main town, Clifden, but it'll be about another two hours. Should we stop to have a bite or do you want to power through? We'd get there just before noon—"

"Power through," Mckenna and Nissa said in unison. Their eyes met fleetingly in the rear-view mirror.

The drive was spectacular. After the Burren, Cillian slowed down as they drove past views so majestic, for a moment she was convinced it was all a reverie. Even then, she wasn't so sure she could dream up the panorama before her: A lake of mystic topaz stood silent and still beneath smooth mountains, gradient green as though stroked by a paint brush. Beckoned by a light wind, the water drifted ever gently, almost shily towards the bordering hills. Not a sound emanated from the elements. It was a space for thinkers and observers. No one else deserved to be in its presence.

"We've now entered Connemara," Cillian said.

Mckenna sat speechless, and Nissa's head was now completely out the back window.

"That was my reaction, too," he said. "And you haven't seen half of it. We're not far from the Inagh Valley—it's a gem here in Connemara. But we're almost at the inn, so . . ."

"Detour!" Nissa shouted, crawling back into her seat.

Cillian looked sideways at Mckenna. "You okay with that, Mckenna?"

"I don't mind taking the scenic route."

They drove another little bit, passing more glorious green mounds and small lakes, or *loughs*. The Connemara landscape was ever changing. Every other minute was like entering a portal to another mystic land.

But none was quite like the Inagh Valley.

Cillian slowed down beside some particularly rowdy sheep, and Mckenna caught her breath. It was a vista fit for a harlequin romance, an otherworldly place of peace and wonder. Across the water, a cluster of mountains (called *bens,* Cillian told them), more of them this time and much grander, framed the edge of the lough. They appeared to be sparkling.

"That's quartz up there on the bens," Cillian said, confirming Mckenna's suspicion. "There are twelve of them." He turned the ignition off, stepped out of the car, and opened the back door for Nissa.

"This feels . . . magical," Nissa said.

She was right, and not just due to its bewitching effect. As isolated as the area was, Mckenna got the distinct feeling that it was home to many creatures, the same way the Burren was.

"Oh, but it is. There's lots of folklore associated with the Inagh Valley. It's said to be home to faeries and goblins."

Faeries and goblins?

"Oh, I *love* faeries!" Nissa said with longing.

"It's just folklore, though," Mckenna said uncertainly—she wasn't certain of anything these days.

"Yes—and no. Our nans and granddads believe them to be real, without question, but that's because they were raised with tales of good and bad faeries, faery queens, leprechauns—stories that have 'happened' to neighbours, friends, friends of friends. Nowadays, faeries are more of a superstition."

"What d'you mean?" Mckenna asked.

"Well, doesn't really matter if you believe in them or not. See, faeries in Ireland have a reputation of being . . . unforgiving. But as long as you show them respect, they'll do the same."

"What happens if you don't?" Nissa said, looking worried.

Cillian chuckled darkly. "It's not something you leave to chance."

Like a true guide, Cillian gave Mckenna and Nissa some time to roam and soak in their surroundings. Sure Nissa was still avoiding her, Mckenna hung back as the former went off on her own and took a seat by the water's edge.

"Lass, if there's any place in the world you can make up with someone, it's here," Cillian said, appearing beside her.

Mckenna let out a long, drawn-out breath and joined Nissa on the ground. "Did you ever think you'd get to witness a place like this?"

Nissa looked ahead in silence.

"I didn't," Mckenna said. "My dad said he'd never come back. Too many bad memories . . ."

Still, she said nothing.

"Nissa, I have no idea why I said what I said. I was being defensive—I didn't mean a word of it. I'm sorry."

Nissa finally turned to face her. "I know that."

"You do?"

"Of course. I just didn't know whether you'd swallow your pride and say it."

"My pride? I—I'm not—"

"It's okay." Nissa smiled. "You did, and that's what counts."

Mckenna felt her face flush.

"What you said made me think, though. You were right."

"Oh, no, Nissa, I mean it. Forget what I said—"

"What I mean is, I realize that leaving was not as hard for me as it was for you. There's no one waiting around for me. And I should've understood that. I'm going around acting like this is a vacation. But you, you have a real life-changing thing you're after. And here I was, offering to help old folks find their way around and chatting up a complete stranger over lunch . . ."

"But *those* are the things that helped us along. John and Brigit were our ticket to Ireland, and Cillian, he's taking us right to our destination. If it weren't for you, I'd have run back home by now."

"Oh, we both know that's not true. You're way too stubborn."

Mckenna opened her mouth to protest, but Nissa broke her off. "Anyway, I was thinking about what you said . . . so I went back to the library, 'cause the librarian seemed to know her inventory backwards and forwards. I thought I'd ask if she ever came across my last name, Febland. Figured any bit of information would help, right?"

Mckenna leaned forward. "Yeah, of course. And?"

"She said, 'There's an English name if I've heard one.'"

Mckenna gave a short laugh, thinking of the librarian's apathetic face. "So, your parents could be from England. That's something! I wonder how she would know that without a second thought, though."

"That's what I said. She said from what she knew, Febland was a rare surname, and she'd only heard it once . . ."

Mckenna couldn't handle the suspense. "Where?"

Nissa began rearranging the rocks on the ground. "There was a couple . . . Simon Fage and Annie Febland. The newspapers made them known as Febland and Fage—'The Free Felons.'"

Mckenna's heart sank.

"They ran a nation-wide drug trafficking ring."

"Come on, that means nothing," Mckenna said, shaking her head. "Doesn't mean it's them."

"It could be, though. They were most, um, active throughout the late sixties and seventies."

"Nissa, seriously—this British Bonnie and Clyde, they're not your parents, okay?"

"They disappeared after 1977."

Right after Nissa was shipped to America. *Shit.*

"It's okay. Really," Nissa said, a slight smile forming; though forced, Mckenna wondered how she possibly could after learning this bit of information.

"I want you to feel like you can tell me anything. You're here for me, and I wanna be here for you." She couldn't imagine Nissa having to deal with this news on her own.

And just as Nissa nodded and flashed a more genuine smile, Mckenna saw them once more—the bright green, firefly-like creatures whizzing around Nissa's torso.

"Do you—do you see this?"

Nissa's puzzled expression told her she didn't. "See what?"

"The—" she started to say until one dashed past her, nearly colliding with the bridge of her nose. She spun around, determined to keep sight of it.

"Are you okay . . .?"

Mckenna had never jumped up so quickly. She chased the speck of light down the lakeshore for several hundred yards, until it stopped short near a bush bordering the water. She watched closely as the thing, about one inch in length, hovered over it.

Mckenna now knew what it felt like to be a moth mesmerized by a mysterious glow, one so divine she couldn't help but reach out . . .

Her body jolted, and the landscape around her began to spin

in place. Then, it was as though she had dropped from several stories high onto the ground, but somehow she landed without impact, like a parachute steadying her landing. The scent of juniper and lavender hit her nose.

She peered around to find herself in what looked like a children's storybook. The sky was mist-free and a clear, Mediterranean blue, and she was standing in the midst of bushy, moss-covered trees, their trunks wide enough to house a small family; wild flowers of some exotic species Mckenna didn't recognize; and a narrow stream, winding its way down a rocky hill. Several small fish hopped joyfully in and out of the water, following the current.

Hopping fish . . .?

"Take off your shoes," said a cheery voice. For a moment, Mckenna thought it was Nissa, but instead, she turned to face a tall, slender woman, her features fair and delicate. Mckenna admired the thick, wavy braid that fell over her left shoulder and passed just below her waist. The woman smiled and lifted her flowing, pale pink dress to reveal her bare feet.

Half mesmerized, half mystified, Mckenna kicked off her shoes, and she was immediately grateful that she had—it was like standing in a pile of feathers.

"Um, who are you? And where am I?"

She beamed. "Me name's Niamh," she said in a honeyed voice. "And *you're* the one who followed *me*."

"You're the firefly? I mean, the flying creature thing . . ."

Niamh grinned. "We're the fae—or what your kind like to call faeries."

Mckenna might've been able to deal with empathic abilities, tenacious birds, even a little telekinesis, but faeries?

"I can see you need time to let that sink in. But it might help to know that you've actually seen us before."

She was right—back at Lough Tay. "I've seen you around my friend, Nissa. But she doesn't see you."

Niamh's eyes glinted. "She's not meant to."

Mckenna gulped, wondering if she was summoned because she was in some kind of trouble. She remembered Cillian's warning about faeries and their unforgiving nature. Had she done anything to anger them?

"Quite the opposite," Niamh said.

Mckenna's froze. *Niamh can read my thoughts.*

And you can read mine, Niamh's voice said inside Mckenna's head.

How . . . am I doing this? Mckenna thought.

All humans are inherently telepathic. They've just stopped listening to their impulses.

What do you mean by stopped?

In another time, humans only communicated through thoughts. People were open with each other and communicated freely with other spiritual realms—angels, deceased loved ones, so-called 'mythical' creatures. And because of this transparency, the fear of death did not exist.

Mckenna tried processing it all. *Okay, but why are you telling* me?

Because you're on the verge of learning your fate, and you won't succeed if you don't embrace your gifts. You're more gifted than most—it's important you don't let fear stop you from developing those gifts.

If she was referring to Petronella, then yes, she was deathly afraid of her. She never wanted to see another ghost in this lifetime.

That's the sort of thinking that will sabotage all our futures, Niamh said.

Mckenna had forgotten she was being eavesdropped on. *What do you mean by all our futures?*

It's not me place to tell. It's time for you to go back now.

Wait—I have so many questions!

And you'll get your answers, but you can't stay. Time works differently here, and Nissa will be wondering where you are.

Just one thing, please. How can I help Nissa?

Niamh looked thoughtful. *Griffons are majestic creatures, aren't they? You never know what treasures they hold.*

Before Mckenna could form a coherent thought, she was whisked off her feet and found herself once again at the water's edge, sprawled on the ground beside the bush.

"Mckenna!" Nissa called out before she spotted her. "What are you doing on the ground?"

"I—uh, was I here this whole time?"

"Huh?" Nissa pulled her off the ground. "You ran off out of nowhere, and then I saw you head over here, so I followed."

"And I . . . didn't go anywhere?"

"No . . ." Nissa looked at her like she'd developed chickenpox. "You okay? Where are your shoes?"

Mckenna looked down at her feet and gasped. They were, in fact, naked among the damp, unkempt grass.

Oh, come on.

"Kenna, what happened?"

What could she possibly say that would make any of this sound sensible? "When we were talking, a wasp landed on my elbow, and I'm allergic, so I freaked and made a run for it." And then tossed her shoes in the lake?

"Oh, no! Did you manage to shake it off?"

"Yeah—at first—but it, uh, flew into the back of my shoe. So, I removed it and threw it in the water," she said, cringing at her own ludicrous story.

"Where's your other shoe?"

Right. "I'm not sure . . . The wasp was still buzzing around me, so I took my other shoe off and tried to swat it. Then, uh, I think I might've passed out briefly." Ridden with guilt, Mckenna added, "But I don't think it got me. I'm fine."

Only Nissa would trust such an implausible tale.

Mckenna did her best to avoid dirt or sharp pebbles as she walked gingerly back towards the car alongside Nissa, who was inspecting the ground for her. From a distance, she saw Cillian leaning against his car, a cigarette hanging from his mouth.

He looked up, and swiftly tossed it into the bin at the edge of the road. "Thought you'd swum up to Man's Island or something," he said, motioning to a small islet in the centre of the lake. "Where're your shoes?"

Clifden was a quaint and colourful town situated at the foot of the twelve bens. Notwithstanding its small size, it was still the largest town in the Connemara region. "It's considered the capital, but it's not, really," Cillian added.

"I'm starving," Nissa said, rubbing her belly. Mckenna scanned the small street for a place to eat and did a double take when she saw blue sign with yellow block letters that spelled out *Griffin's Bar.*

Griffons are majestic creatures, aren't they?

"How about there?" Mckenna said louder than she intended. Seeing Nissa's and Cillian's startled faces, she cleared her throat and added, "Looks good, right?"

Griffin's Bar might've given off a truck stop vibe on the outside, but inside it was a typical Irish pub with lots of oak and snug bench seating. They were waited on by a lanky woman with a friendly face, whose inquisitiveness Mckenna found a touch irritating. ("You poor dear, where are your shoes? They find you on the side of the road, then?") She was in no mood to disclose her, Nissa's, and Cillian's complex relationship. Cillian agreed; leaning in slightly, he whispered to Mckenna, "Just going to start telling people you're hitchhikers . . ." She hit him on the arm. Smirking, he excused himself from the table.

Nissa, on the other hand, didn't seem to mind the socializing. Mckenna could tell she enjoyed chatting with locals every chance she got; she had a natural warmth about her that harmonized effortlessly with theirs.

"You're such a dear," the server said after Nissa complimented her green pendant. "It's made of Connemara marble—one of the rarest marbles in the world. And your charm is absolutely lovely!" She grasped Nissa's charm between her bony fingers and squinted at it. "You're Manx, then? I don't reckon I hear an accent—you must've spent loads of time in America!"

Mckenna snapped her gaze towards the server. Nissa choked on her water.

"I'm what?" she said through violent coughs.

The server stared from Mckenna's perplexed expression to Nissa's. "Manx—from the Isle of Man, of course. You've got the Latin motto engraved on the back."

Mckenna remembered glancing at the obscure words the day she found Nissa's bracelet.

"Are you sure?" Nissa said.

"Oh, yes. Me granddad's Manx—and proud of it. 'Whithersoever you throw it, it will stand,' he'd say. It refers to the Isle of Man's coat of arms: three standing legs connecting from the centre. Odd symbol of choice now that I say it aloud . . ."

Mckenna, on the other hand, thought the symbol made perfect sense.

Her friend's eyes welled up. Indeed, griffons did hold great treasures. She squeezed Nissa's hand. *Thank you, Niamh.* She turned her gaze towards the window, half-expecting the faery to be peering through it, winking and prideful. She wasn't, but Mckenna found herself staring out at something just as unlikely.

There, perched on the windowsill, were her trusty pair of Converse sneakers.

XII

The White Horse's Vision

Avebury Henge—Wiltshire, England

Seán was convinced he was dreaming. How long had he been out here, alone with his anxious thoughts, his head seething with the fear of losing his daughter? The ghost before him had to be just that—an apparition. A hallucination.

"I'm not a ghost, Seán," Abby said tenderly. She had always been able to do that—know what he was thinking. She crouched in front of him so his eyes met hers, a distinct honey-brown, like Mckenna's.

"It's really you," were the only words his brain was able to lump together. Abby smiled a smile he hadn't allowed himself to dream about in many years. Her lips hardly stretched or parted; it was the light in her eyes that did all the work, making her whole being glow with a divine luminescence—the kind you only read about in folktales.

"How did you know I was here, Abby?"

"You ken better than to ask *me* something like that."

"I didn't think you were alive," said Seán, the pent-up anger from the last seventeen years surfacing.

"For a good reason, Seán." His heart jolted at the sound of his name. "You've both been safe all this time."

"You abandoned us. There's more reason in a bag of Taytos."

"You'd be dead," she said pointedly, "and Mckenna and I, we would've been prisoners up until she came of age."

"But you won't tell me why, will you? And what use they have for both of you—or who *they* are," he said with a clenched jaw.

Abby lifted her hand to his cheek, her expression melancholic.

Seán slapped her hand away. "Always so cryptic. She's out looking for you, you know. Your *daughter.*" He stood and began pacing around the centre of the circle, then stopped and placed his hands on his hips. "I thought this would be the first place she'd look. I told her we met here."

"Have you told her where we lived?"

"No, never—" He stopped himself, suddenly remembering the note. "The note you left me. Christ, I haven't read that in—seventeen years! Always kept it in my wallet but . . . I completely forgot that you mentioned . . . You think she went to Ballycastle?"

"Yes," Abby said calmly. "But it's okay. She'll soon find nothing, and she'll return to both of you. She just needs some time."

Both of you. She knew about Andre—of course she did. Guilt ate away at him; today marked a week since he stormed out on him.

"No. We'll go looking for her. Both of us."

Her eyes smiled again. "She can't ken about me. You understand, Seán?"

Seán furrowed his brow. "I won't lie to her again, Abby. And she won't believe me, she's got mad instincts; she knows you're alive somehow. And if you won't come, then I'll go myself and bring her home—"

"If you do that, she'll resent you for it. You ken our daughter; she's got to follow her gut. It's better you leave her be."

Seán stared back at the former love of his life, not knowing whether he wanted to pull her towards him or walk out on her, the same way she had him.

She held out her hand. "Come. Let's talk, Seán."

Every cell that made up his corporeal body was telling him not to. He could feel them tightening, resisting. *She abandoned you and your daughter. She's trouble. She always has been . . .*

But beneath the skin and bones, his soul was shattering. He needed to touch her, to follow her, to find out as much as he possibly could about what really happened seventeen years ago.

"Okay," he said, and dropped his hand into hers.

"Not surprised you haven't heard of it," Cillian said when they asked where the Isle of Man was. They discovered it was a small island in the Irish Sea between Ireland, Scotland, and England. It was self-governing, so it was technically not part of the United Kingdom—but it was still a British Crown dependency. *Wonder what happened there,* Mckenna thought.

"Kind of an odd place, if you ask me. And *why* do you ask?"

Nissa and Mckenna exchanged glances. The former still appeared shocked from the revelation.

"Just curious. We heard that nice server mention it," Mckenna said.

"She was a weird one, wasn't she? A bit annoying, really."

They arrived at a grand-looking hotel, its facade old and ornate, set amid acres of secluded woodland. Around the front courtyard, prim yet convivial gardens overlooked a calm bay, bens blanketing the edge. "Ballinakill Bay," Cillian said. "The hotel was once a manor, now converted into a five-star hotel. Georgian architecture, of course, which means it was built around the seventeen or early eighteen hundreds. You can see by the symmetry . . ."

They dropped their bags off in their room, a large Victorian-style chamber adorned with antique objects, paintings, and what Mckenna imagined were the finest linens in all of Ireland.

Mckenna looked down at her shoes and thanked Niamh silently for coming through at the last second; she couldn't imagine walking inside a place like this dragging her muddy, bare feet.

Though, she had no business walking into a place like this at all.

"Oh, no worries, this is a business expense," Cillian said, waving away Mckenna's offer to stay at a bed and breakfast in town. He leaned in: "And, *really* . . . I'm not a terribly elegant guy. What'll I do with a full suite to myself?"

Mckenna hesitated. It just wasn't right to accept. This was a work trip, and she and Nissa were an imposition.

Then why did she feel the exact opposite? Like Cillian wanted nothing more than for Mckenna to stay?

"If you're sure you're cool with it, then we're cool," she heard herself say. Nissa, still quiet and looking solemn, merely nodded.

"Brilliant! I've got a conference in a bit. You should come."

Mckenna raised an eyebrow.

"Not *in* the actual meeting, of course—that'd be dull as dried fruit. It's being held at Kylemore Abbey, an Irish landmark. Thought you'd like to see it."

Mckenna felt yet another urge inside her that wasn't her own. In Cillian was a strong desire for Mckenna to go with him.

She looked round at Nissa, who muttered, "I think I'd like to hang back. Maybe lie down for a bit."

Mckenna couldn't leave her. Not now, in her sullen state. "I'll stay with you—"

"No, no. Go." Nissa needed to be alone. It didn't take an empath to understand that.

"Is she okay, you reckon?" Cillian said, opening up the passenger-side car door.

"She will be. She just needs time to . . . cope."

"Anything I can do, lass?"

Mckenna's heart gave a jolt at the word *lass*. "You mean other than be our chauffeur, tour guide—"

"Ah, but I've got selfish reasons for doing such things."

"Like sociopathic, serial-killer reasons?"

"Christ, you guessed it." His eyes lingered on hers a moment too long—he nearly ran over a family of sheep, who let out a series of angry *baas* as the car swerved.

"Stupid livestock . . ." he muttered, glaring into his rear-view mirror.

"So," Mckenna said, swallowing. "What are these self-ish reasons?"

He kept his eyes on the road. "It's been nice, you know." Mckenna watched him, her body temperature rising. "It's not often I get to visit my top spots in all of Ireland. It's helped to get my mind off the state of things."

Not exactly the response she was anticipating.

They reached yet another Irish treasure that made Mckenna muse on how Seán could have left this exquisite country behind all those years ago. The area was cloaked by woodland and grassy mounds, and set into the face of the highest one, its reflec-tion mirrored in the shimmering lake, stood an intricate, castle-like monastery. Mckenna gathered the gothic-style structure was Kylemore Abbey.

They pulled up in the visitor's parking lot, and like verbal diarrhea, Cillian divulged the abbey's whole history, from its erection in the late 1860s, to its tragic love story, to its Victorian walled garden that attracted visitors from all over.

"I'm running a little late, so I'm going to head inside," Cillian said, his voice a touch shaky. *Why is he so nervous? Am I making him nervous?* Mckenna could feel his body tense up like it was her own.

"The grounds are really something," he continued. "If you go down this way—" He pointed down the concrete path that wound into the woods. "—you'll walk past the little church. And the view of the lakeside is just . . ." He trailed off.

"I'm sold," she said, hoping she'd put him a little out of his misery.

"I'll join you as soon as I can," he said, placing a light hand on her shoulder before letting himself through the double doors. Her eyes trailed down to the spot on her shoulder, wondering whether the fluttering in her chest reflected her own feelings or Cillian's.

Being an empath was puzzling.

Mckenna followed Cillian's directions down towards the church, which she wasn't too keen on visiting. The Catholic Church was one of the reasons her dads had never been able to get married. And she would never respect an institution that denounced anyone for living an honest life. So instead, she stopped at a clearing and gazed out towards the lake, wondering what sort of sea life lingered in the depths.

As though in response, a single ripple formed in the centre of the water. On a regular day, she wouldn't have thought twice about it. But today was not like most days.

More ripples, the wind now hurling the water in circles like an underwater cyclone. Or was it the wind's doing at all?

It wasn't. Something began to rise out from under the lake: It was a rounded hump of some sort, like the back of an animal. A goose? Swan, perhaps? No, this creature was much larger, for the ripples were now as wide as Cillian's car.

Mckenna was on the edge of the lake now, watching as the thing rose higher, until what emerged was the body of a white horse.

Her mane was long and wavy, and her coat glistened against the dark surface like a lone star at nightfall. She was smaller than an adult but larger than a foal. Mckenna stood stunned as the regal-looking creature scraped her hoof on the water's surface, as though solid, and began galloping to and fro.

Mckenna sensed that the horse was exhilarated, like she'd been waiting years to surface. She watched her for some time, somehow unperturbed by physics being defied before her, until the creature returned her gaze.

Mckenna had always been one to reject the idea of hypnosis. She believed anyone with the teensiest bit of willpower could resist suggestion. But the equine's all-pervading stare did something to her that made her abandon this once-ironclad faith. Upon meeting her cobalt eyes, Mckenna felt her mind withdrawing from her body, as though she were drifting into a peaceful sleep.

Eachna was the horse's name, though Mckenna could not say how she came to know this. In fact, Mckenna swore she knew *everything* in that moment. Her perception was no longer skewed like that of the ignorant human. It was clearer than it had ever been. Inside Eachna's glowing eyes was the very same terrain she stood on, but no longer beautiful and pristine.

She blinked, and then she was in it: The thousands of trees that sheltered the mountainside looked like they'd been chewed up and spit out, the lake water had turned a yellowish brown, and floating at the surface, dozens of species of fish lay dead. Up in the sky, a thick layer of smog replaced the cloudy mist. She fell into a fit of coughs, for the odour of the rotted trees and dead sea life was too much to bear.

Eachna appeared beside her, beckoning Mckenna to mount, bareback. And so she did. If there was any chance she could be led away from here, wherever *here* was, wherever this horse had transported her, she would take it. Hoofs grazing the water, together they rode towards the centre of the lake, where the maelstrom from which Eachna had emerged awaited them.

In the depths, the vortex swallowed them in one swift motion; it was as though her body was being sucked into a colossal vacuum. She and Eachna spun round and round in a swirl of cool air, and the next second, Mckenna found herself surrounded again by the lush greenery, Kylemore Abbey visible beyond the trees.

And she was very, very wet. *Couldn't have transported me back on land?* The water was still again, now, and the horse nowhere in sight.

Fighting to tread the frigid waters, Mckenna swam in circles, scanning the lake. "Eachna?"

Nothing.

"Eachna!"

Something was coming. A faint voice shouted in the distance. She called back, "EACHNA!"

"Mckenna! Mckenna, what the Jaysus are you doing?"

It was Cillian. Humiliated, she swam towards the shore, wondering how on Earth she was going to explain herself now.

She reached the shallows, set her feet down and began walking, trying her damndest to look casual—like taking a cold swim had been her intention all along.

"Water's g-g-great," she said, unable to keep her teeth from chattering.

"Are you completely mad?" He grasped both her arms and rubbed them up and down, as though this would miraculously generate heat through her sopping clothes.

"I guess I . . . fell in." What else could she say? That she was lured to the depths by a white horse who, incidentally, transmitted some sort of vision to her of—Mckenna wasn't sure *what* she had just witnessed. Had she crossed over to a parallel realm or into another time? Was what she saw what this place would become—what the world would ultimately become?

Cillian's expression was a cross between confusion and concern. "Go on, lass, let's get you changed quickly." Pulling her in slightly, he steered her back on the path back to Kylemore Abbey. Her body trembled from what she deemed were early symptoms of hypothermia, but her face felt as hot as fresh baked potato pie.

"I swear, I saw it racing around!"

Mckenna's head spun around at the word *racing*. She caught sight of two men trimming some fir trees along the water.

"It's a bleedin' myth, you eejit," said the other, looking irritated.

"Not from where I was standing. And the last sighting was seven years ago, remember?"

"Do you know what they're talking about?" Mckenna whispered.

"You wouldn't believe it if I told you," Cillian said.

Mckenna scoffed. "Trust me, I'm pretty open-minded."

Cillian cast a sideways glance at her. "This lake's known as Pollacappul Lough. It comes from the Gaelic *pol a capall,* which translates to *Place of the Horse.*"

Mckenna had to keep her mouth from falling open.

"There's a legend of a white horse that's said to rise from the lake every seven years. And that man's claimed he just saw it." He chuckled.

"Do you believe him?"

"I'm rather open-minded," he said with a grin. "You were around the water—or, rather, in it. You see anything?"

Mckenna shook her head and waved his question away, as though it were the most preposterous thing in the world.

XIII

THE PARTY ON FAERY HILL

Cillian was awoken that night by a soulful apparition of the High Priestess, whose astral self appeared content.

"Well?"

"She's seen it, yes," he whispered, glancing over at the open doorway that led to the girls' cot. He tiptoed over and closed it, carefully. When he turned around, it was the first time Cillian saw the High Priestess smile.

"You're certain?"

"Yes, she was shouting the horse's name. High Priestess, that's everything on the first Scottish Scroll. She's gone to Newgrange—"

"Her soul's beginnings, she need discover," she recited.

"She's been to Kilkenny. Has your seer seen anything?"

"Yes. Pravadi saw Petronella de Meath pay our wee Wise One a visit. She now kens of her past life as Alice Kyteler. Of her evil nature, unforgivable sins. *A darkness within she'll ken e'ermore,"* she continued, her eyes mad with triumph.

"And here, in Connemara, the white horse has shown her

what will become of our world," Cillian said, reminding himself this was all for the greater good.

"But 'tis the horse's vision of Earth Mother—" She paused, like she wanted to savour the moment. *"—that lights her path to days of yore."*

Cillian knew the first Scottish Scroll only too well, but hearing the words spoken made his body quiver.

"We've only just begun. Do what you must now. Pravadi predicts she can be swayed, but it will take much effort. As for me, I'm not one for working hard; I'd rather work smart. But if you can manage it, the last bit will be a breeze. As for Abigail, keep trying. Keep pushing. If the Wise One doesn't find her by All Hallows' Eve, I do this my way," she warned.

"Priestess, if I may . . . the plan would be put at risk if we force her against her will—"

But in a trice, the High Priestess was gone.

Cillian realized he was sweating—copiously. Careful to step lightly, he walked over to the bar counter and guzzled two full glasses of icy water, lost in thought.

He wanted to move on with the plan as much as the High Priestess did—for the good of the planet—but he knew that if Mckenna didn't find Abigail before Halloween, the High Priestess would take matters into her own hands; if Mckenna fought her destiny, the Priestess would force her against her will, then kill Mckenna and her mother without a second thought.

Cillian had to get through to her.

He jumped at the sight of Mckenna's silhouette in the doorway. Even in the darkened room, he couldn't mistake her presence. Her figure shapely, her hair cascading over her shoulder, and since today, her skin infused with the mind-numbing scent of juniper and lavender.

And the vibrations her body emitted, they were magnetic. Her energy field extended well over five feet around her, certainly drawing in anyone crossing her path. Surely, she was unaware of this.

She had so much to learn.

"Oh, sorry. I didn't know you were up—uh, I mean, *here*."

Christ. He slid coolly behind the counter. "I had, erm, a nightmare. I'm all out of sorts." His mind wandered to his astral encounter.

"Me too," she said, her eyes squinting the way they so often did. She was reading him.

"You all right, lass?" He stepped round the counter and moved towards her, hoping, knowing that by nearing his racing heart to hers, he would divert her attention from his thoughts. Though, he still wasn't sure if she could pick up on those. She could certainly sense his feelings . . .

Something inside him awakened, like the white horse after a seven-year-long slumber, and whatever it was began to race just as wildly. He inched closer, hearing Mckenna's breathing deepen. Her hand clung to the doorway, as though her knees would give out if she let go. He felt like his might, too. Was she feeling this because *he* was? Empaths must be emotional wrecks.

He studied her as she tried to penetrate his mind. Such power she didn't yet know she had. He imagined her ill fate if he failed to sway her, have her see reason. All he needed was to have her understand the bigger picture.

"Why are you so afraid?" she said, looking up at him. Cillian stepped back, nearly tripping over himself; he hadn't been keeping his feelings in check. Her eyes were like Tiger's Eye gemstones—all-knowing. He couldn't tear his own away from their golden-brown lustre.

"What do you mean?" He kept his voice scarcely above a whisper.

"I-I can't explain it."

He waited for her to let her guard down, open up to him. Her lips parted for a moment, and then met again.

"You can tell me," he said, now standing a safe distance away.

She stood in the dark, unmoving, for several long minutes.

"Cillian?"

He hadn't realized how weak his heart was until now. "Yeah, lass?"

"There are things about me that . . . that . . ."

His heart was pounding so madly now, it rang like a bass drum in his ears.

There was a crashing sound, like shattered glass. Mckenna whipped around, and Cillian followed her into the next room, flicking the light on. Nissa was sprawled on the floor amid shards of clear glass, weeping.

Cillian's jaw tightened. *Perfect fecking timing.*

"Nissa!" Mckenna cried, running to her side.

"Watch the glass," Cillian said, putting his arm up to stop her. Leaning carefully over Nissa, he helped her back onto the mattress.

Mckenna gasped. "Nissa, you're bleeding."

"I-I rolled over and kn-kn-knocked over m-my water glass," Nissa stammered in between wails.

"It's okay, we'll bandage that up. See? You're okay. Why are you crying . . .?" There was a tenderness in Mckenna's voice when she spoke to her, like that of an older sister. He watched her eyes soften, the fire in them gone. There was only warmth there; in that moment, Cillian realized Mckenna could never be turned, not with Nissa around to look after. She inspired the good in Mckenna, and she always would.

Slowly, he backed out of the room— "I'll ring the front desk for a medical kit." —and made his way to the elevator, knowing full well what he needed to do.

That morning, Nissa looked to be in much better spirits. While Cillian checked them out of their room, she confessed to Mckenna what happened in her sleep: She'd dreamt of arriving in the Isle of Man and finding her parents dressed as bandits, having a big bash with all of Nissa's other long-lost relatives. That was when she woke up startled, knocked over her water glass, and rolled over onto the floor.

"But early this morning, I had *another* dream," Nissa said, her eyes glistening with hope. "A voice was telling me to come back home—my real home." She said this as though the voice were real, but Mckenna was afraid of what might be waiting for Nissa if she did indeed go back. What if there was no family waiting for her there at all? No records of any kind?

The drive to Belfast was silent, to say the least. Nissa was knocked out almost immediately, and Mckenna, who hadn't slept a wink, dozed on and off during the full four and a half-hour drive (hopefully sparing them from any loud snores). It was amazing the distance they could cover in just a few hours—all the way from the West Coast to the north-eastern part of the island.

She would be lying if she said sleeping the whole way wasn't what she intended. She'd been avoiding eye contact with Cillian all morning. Their middle-of-the-night encounter was . . . heavy. She had to physically keep herself from moving to him, from touching him, and she couldn't comprehend why she felt such a pull. Were they even her urges, or his?

The image of his body close to hers entered her mind as she slipped in and out of cat naps, cruising by fields and farmsteads, until—

"We're here," Mckenna heard Cillian's voice say over the rock song playing on the car radio.

"But I still haven't found what I'm looking for . . ."

Tell me about it, Mckenna thought as she climbed out of the car, her shoes hitting muddy ground, and stretched out her throbbing legs. Then squinty-eyed and groggy, she walked gingerly across an unkempt front yard alongside Nissa, who was nearly prancing.

Are we lost? Mckenna wondered as they reached the entrance of what looked to be someone's home: It was a three-storey cottage, ivy vines covering most of the brown brick, and potted plants placed along the edges of the wraparound porch. What struck Mckenna the most was the glossy black front door, a jarring colour for such an otherwise friendly façade.

The door swung open just as Cillian grasped the large brass

knocker. Before them stood an elderly woman, about as small as Nissa, spatula in hand and hairnet fitted around her large ginger bun.

"Inside, inside, it's Baltic out here!" the woman, who Mckenna gathered was the bed and breakfast owner, shouted over the howl of a spontaneous wind. They entered, and Mckenna was greeted by the smell of pumpkin and nutmeg and a kitchen that she knew Seán and Andre would have adored: The cupboards were stained a dusty green, and the flooring was a mosaic of various patterns and earthly tones. But Mckenna's favourite feature was the peculiarly shaped rack (made of antlers?), from which about a dozen copper pots hung low over the kitchen island.

"You're Mr. Hayes?" the woman said to Cillian as she forced his jacket off, then turned to Mckenna and Nissa for theirs. "And guests?"

"Please, Cillian's fine. Pleasure, Ms. Beattie. It's nice to put a face to the name. And yes—my friends, erm, surprised me on my trip. Is that . . .?"

"Yes, they're wee girls, they'll fit just fine."

Mckenna knew Nissa was wondering the same thing—where, pray tell, would they be *fitting*?

"Have the other delegates arrived?"

"Ages ago." She waved his question away. "Go on, sit by the windy in there." She pointed past the slim archway leading to the adjacent room. "I'll make your tea."

Before Mckenna knew it, she, Nissa, Cillian, and Ms. Beattie were sipping black tea around the living area—which was just as quaint, with a flood of natural light, wall-to-wall carpeting, and eclectic furniture, probably circa 1950. They sat quietly for several long minutes. Why did Mckenna get the sense that Ms. Beattie was keeping an eye on them?

"Ms. Beattie, I've been wondering something," Nissa said, evidently unable to resist breaking the silence. Ms. Beattie glanced up from her teacup, looking a tad cross. "Is there a reason your door's painted black?

"Of course, there's a reason! There's a reason you've got pink hair, I bet."

Nissa chuckled.

"Black's for protection. Repels all the untrusty folk, you see?"

At that, Cillian placed his tea down with a clatter. "Thank you for the tea, Ms. Beattie, but it's been a long drive. Would you mind terribly showing us to our rooms?"

Abby steered Seán to a small café a few minutes' walk from the Avebury monument, where they sat by the bay window covered in hanging plants.

Seán looked out at the now-pounding rain. "This place hasn't changed."

"You recognize it."

Seán looked at her incredulously. "You mad? Course I do! We'd stay 'til closing."

"And this is where—" they said simultaneously. He knew that she meant to utter the same words: *This is where I instantly fell in love with you.* Seán looked into the eyes of the woman who both mesmerized and infuriated him. She had always been the calming, nurturing person who sat before him, but there was a change in her, one he couldn't quite pinpoint.

"You're different," he finally said.

She smiled. "I've found peace. It was right for me to leave."

"And the people who were after you . . . they think you're dead?"

Abby hesitated. "I can't be sure. That's why I remain hidden."

"Isn't it risky, then? For you to be out in the open like this . . . with me?"

She placed her hand on his. "I appreciate the concern, Seán, but there's no one on this Earth that's capable of finding me—not unless I mean for them to." She winked.

He looked doubtfully back at her.

"I promise."

She was referring to a spell of some sort, he was sure. He

thought it best not to ask too many details. After all, he'd left that dark part of his past behind.

"I just need to know one thing." He pulled his hand back and wrapped it around his coffee mug. "Is Mckenna in any sort of danger?"

"You needn't worry about Mckenna. She's intuitive, and she'll only get stronger."

"You wouldn't know, though, would you?" He scoffed. "With you being in hiding."

She blinked, then smiled.

He continued to eye her. "You've been checking in, haven't you? In your own *special* ways."

"I have."

Seán sighed. "It's just—sometimes, she's . . ." He couldn't bring himself to say it.

"You're referring to the darkness inside of her."

Seán wasn't all that surprised she knew what he couldn't say.

She continued. "It's a part of her, Seán. Not to mention she's of age now, which means she's feeling the effects of a Wise One more than ever."

"You've called her that before—a Wise One."

Abby tilted her head, looking uncertain. "You still don't know what she is."

"You know I don't, you never explained it to me. You said it was better I didn't know." How could she not remember?

She nodded. "And it is. Just ken that she's carried many burdens with her over many lives. But you raised her to be good, so you must trust that she is."

He sipped the last of his coffee and stared down at the bottom of his mug. "I've still got to find her, Abby. I'm lying to her just being here—again. She's searching the world for you." He looked up at her. "We should find her together."

She sighed, looking remorseful. "In time. But for now, she can't ken about me. It's not the right time."

"Ah, another vague explanation. Like your bleedin' letter."

"I'm sorry, Seán, but it's best. The less you ken, the better."

Mckenna dashed up the B&B's three full flights of stairs, skipping every other step, and burst into her and Nissa's double room waving two pamphlets above her head: one labelled *Isle of Man Ferries* and the other *Ballycastle Beaches.*

"Nissa! I went down to ask Ms. Beattie if there's a way to get to Ballycastle and—are you here?"

"I can't hear you, the fan's on!" Nissa's voice shouted from the bathroom.

"Okay, well I have something to show you when you get out," she said, unable to contain her giddiness. Among her mound of tour pamphlets, Ms. Beattie had found a bus leaving for Ballycastle the next morning and ferries sailing to the Isle of Man day and night.

They were *so* close. She couldn't wait to tell her.

She tossed the pamphlets on their smaller-than-standard double bed, where Nissa had laid her favourite floral sweater and the book she had checked out of the Kilkenny library, *The Eye of the World.* Mckenna picked it up; it was hefty, but Nissa still managed to finish all 784 pages. Fluffing up the pillow behind her, she flipped the book open and began skimming it absent-mindedly, until her eyes fell on two words that up to this point she hadn't been able to find in any other publication: *Wise One.*

She gasped.

"What did you want to show me?" Nissa said, swinging open the bathroom door, a towel wrapped around her small head. "Oh, you're reading it! It's good, right? I really have to find a way to mail it back . . ."

Mckenna looked up at her. "Just picked it up, actually. What's it about?" she said, trying not to appear stunned.

"It's *so* good." Nissa jumped atop the high mattress. "It's a bit hard to explain. It's a fantasy, and the main characters are channelers; they can access a natural power source from the four elements—you know, earth, air, fire, and water—and also a fifth one, spirit."

"And what's, um, a Wise One?" She gestured at the page.

"Oh, well these channelers are supposed to become Wise Ones, which are, like, spiritual leaders. But if you're gonna read it, I don't want to say too much."

"I doubt I'll read it. Does sound interesting, though."

"Yeah, it really is. And the Wise Ones are Dreamwalkers, so they're able to dream of the future and project themselves into other peoples' dreams." She hopped off the bed, removed the towel from her hair, and disappeared into the bathroom.

Mckenna's thoughts unravelled over the dull noise of the blow-dryer. Had the author made up all that about Wise Ones, or was it based on myth, or perhaps existing research? Was becoming a spiritual leader part of a Wise One's path? Did Mckenna really have the ability to have premonitions and manifest herself into people's dreams?

"Well?" Nissa said, emerging from the bathroom, her wispy hair still damp on the ends. "You were gonna show me something."

Of course, she'd almost forgot. Mckenna held out the Isle of Man and Ballycastle pamphlets.

Nissa's face glowed. "Oh!"

It turned out all of the delegates from the border regions and around Northern Ireland were staying in the neighbourhood. Along with Naomi, the organizer, and one of Ireland's political party leaders, two representatives were lodging at Ms. Beattie's; four were at a smaller inn half a block down; and the remaining six a little further up the road.

Mckenna met the foursome when she, Nissa, and Cillian were called down for dinner with the guests that evening. Ms. Beattie insisted that with the state that Belfast was in, it was too dangerous for anyone to be out and about. Mckenna, however, felt it might have been safer to hang out in the street riots than around this table; it took all of five minutes for the delegates to enter into a spat about the circumstances surrounding the Irish Republican Army jailbreaker, Dermot Finucane, which she recalled Cillian explaining back in Dublin.

"Look," began Luke Doyle, the youth delegate for County Donegal. "I think Ireland should stand united, too—and I get that that's what Finucane was fighting for, but the IRA are extremists—"

"Stop there, Doyle." Tara Quinn, who was the County Sligo youth delegate, put up her hand. "He's fighting for a cause—a cause we all believe in—and *you loyalists* want to jail him for it," she spat at Naomi. "Not to mention, your lot murdered Dermot's brother! If it were me . . ."

"The man's a terrorist," said Naomi, a leggy, striking woman whom Cillian suavely introduced as Belfast's future MP.

"If we hand him over, he'll be beaten to death by prison guards, and you know it," Cillian retorted. Mckenna followed his gaze up and down Naomi's slender physique.

"Maybe he should be," Naomi said, her lips pursed and eyes fierce. Cillian dropped his knife, which hit his dish with a clatter. Tara spat out her wine. Naomi didn't waver. "He's been roaming free since 1983. We all have political incentives, but I use my tongue when I want to address them, not my gun."

"*Please,* you don't have a bleedin' gun . . ." Luke said, taking a swig of beer.

"It's like Thatcher said," Naomi continued. "Dermot's freedom gives terrorists the idea that they can do whatever they please, then run off down South without consequence." Mckenna had heard Seán's ramblings about Margaret Thatcher, the former UK Prime Minister. Suffice to say, he was not a fan.

"Yeah, collecting welfare cheques that *we* pay for . . ." said Luke.

"What about his comrade, James Clarke?' Tara asked.

Mckenna could tell Naomi was trying to keep her composure. "He's roaming free, too."

"Fine, and?" Cillian said, placing his glass down a little too firmly. Mckenna felt Cillian's frustration rise. "Are we to just hand people over to the British whenever they throw a tantrum?"

Naomi's eyes narrowed. "You sound like one of them—an

IRA supporter."

"If you're asking me if I want to end this segregation, then maybe I am a supporter, yeah."

"You're a terrorist, then?" Luke shouted, standing up. "Because it's the same thing—"

"I'd rethink that statement, Doyle."

"Enough." The room silenced as Devin O'Connor, leader of the Progressive Democrats, spoke for the first time since the debate ensued. "Mr. Hayes, the notion that such savagery should be considered a political statement is sickening. It must end."

"Mr. O'Connor, with all due respect, loyalists have just as much blood on their hands—"

"We will reconvene this discussion at our conference in the morning, when all of the delegates will be present. For now, we eat. And then later, we drink." He was referring to the cocktail party Cillian told them about earlier, a kind of meet and greet for the delegates.

She didn't know what made her do it, but Mckenna couldn't get herself to move past such a troubling topic. She cleared her throat. "I'm sorry but . . . I have a question." All six heads, including Nissa's and Cillian's, turned towards her. "The violence, the bombings, the shootings from the past, like, twenty years, comes down to Catholicism versus Protestantism, right?" she said, remembering John's stories of Northern Ireland.

Naomi was the one who responded. "It began that way, but this is not a religious conflict. This is about one part of Ireland who wants to remain part of the United Kingdom, and nationalists who want to be independent and have a united Ireland."

"But aren't Irish nationalists Catholics and loyalists Protestants? You're saying this guerilla war isn't sparked by religion, by opposing beliefs—but isn't this, on some level, about a Catholic minority within a group of Protestants who feel their government isn't accepting of their faith?"

"Well, it's clear whose side you're on—"

"Oh, I think both sides are total idiots, actually." Despite the gasps and looks of horror, Mckenna continued. "They both went too far. Practice the faith you want—who cares. Some want to separate because of it? Fine. None of it will matter when we're all swallowed up by cyclones and forest fires, anyway."

The group exploded with laughter, except Cillian, who stared at Mckenna as though she had just materialized through a puff of smoke. Nissa, on the other hand, looked like Christmas had arrived early. "I think what Mckenna's trying to say is that, um," she began apologetically, "the idea of fighting over religion is sort of trifling when you consider the more urgent environmental challenges we're facing."

"Oh. You're activists." Naomi's undertone made Mckenna want to hurl her plate across the table.

"Journalists," Mckenna snarled through gritted teeth. Nissa began to nod frantically.

Mr. O'Connor intervened. "I, for one, appreciate your tenacity and passion on the topic, Miss . . .?" Naomi rolled her eyes.

"O'Dwyer."

"And Febland!" Nissa squealed.

"You're both Mr. Hayes's guests, are you not? You must join us for a cocktail, then."

"Oh, that's okay—"

"Nonsense. I insist."

"That was . . . unexpected. But brilliant," Cillian whispered in the stairwell a half-hour later. "What made you say those things?"

Mckenna shrugged. She didn't actually know. Throughout dinner she'd been wondering if what she blurted aloud was her own take on the matter or if it stemmed from either Nissa's or Cillian's sentiments. She was starting to feel like she had no control over what she was thinking or saying.

"I'm just . . . I don't know. I guess the idea that these are the kinds of things we're fighting about pisses me off." Which was true.

"I one hundred percent agree with you, lass."

"Yeah?"

"Yeah."

They stood near the banister for a moment. This was the first time they'd been alone since the night before.

"I think you've got a natural leader in you. You understand what's important. What the world needs."

It happened again: an acute tingling sensation that began in the tips of her toes and travelled upwards towards her thigh, goosebumps swiftly forming. Her legs weakening, she leaned farther back until the base of her spine hit the wooden handrail.

"I'm gonna go change," she managed to say, and darted up the stairs.

Mckenna hadn't spent much time playing dress-up like lots of the other girls growing up, though Andre had graciously volunteered to participate on more than one occasion. So when Ms. Beattie summoned her and Nissa to her sewing room that evening, inviting them to sift through her old clothes to wear at tonight's cocktail party, Mckenna wasn't mentally prepared for the girlish squeals and over-the-top runway show that frolicking about in dresses apparently involved. She couldn't remember a time her stomach hurt so much from laughing.

It was all thanks to Nissa, of course, who made it apparent to anyone who would listen that she had nothing to wear for the evening. "All those important people around, Kenna! I am not showing up like *this.*"

It turned out Ms. Beatie had quite a bit of style in her younger days. Nissa looked sweet in a floor-length, dusty rose skirt, which she paired with a puffy-sleeved white blouse, and Mckenna wore a wraparound wool dress, in a forest green that she found suited her colouring quite well.

It was a clear night, and warm for late September. The cocktail party was held under a massive white tent, perched in an open field atop a hill; fairy lights hung along the roof and sides, and tealights illuminated tall, round tables that were scattered about, draped in white linens.

Cillian, who had walked over with them, was quick to snag a table—nicking a couple of champagne flutes from a passing waiter along the way—but was pulled away by some delegates within minutes of their arrival. Mckenna and Nissa didn't mind a bit; it was the perfect time to hash out their travel plans to the Isle of Man and Ballycastle.

"Who knows if I'll find any records there! But I just have this strong feeling that I'm supposed to," Nissa said, guzzling down the rest of her champagne. "I don't know how to explain it. I sound like a total loon—this was *good,* by the way."

"It really is," Mckenna said, polishing hers off, too, and in a blink, their empty flutes were swapped for full ones. "And if anyone's a 'loon', it's me. I'm just sorta . . . going with it. Is that crazy?"

"Completely."

Halfway through their second glass, they recounted their journey: how they came to meet, how they ventured to and around Ireland by placing blind faith in complete strangers, how they discovered bits of their past along the way.

"Speaking of strangers . . ." Nissa slurred slightly, using air quotes around the word *strangers.* "Cillian."

Mckenna's face flushed. "What about him?"

"It's just been so easy. Convenient . . ."

Mckenna had thought about this a number of times. She wasn't even sure if she trusted him, but the pull she felt towards him, and the feelings she was able to read into, they were like a giant, murky cloud, obscuring any sound judgment she had. Around him, her intuitive gift vanished in a puff of smoke.

"It's kind of nuts, I know. Do you trust him?"

Nissa stared past Mckenna, swirling her champagne around. "I mean, yeah. I think Irish people are just more hospitable. I just can't help but wonder . . ."

"Wonder what?"

"Do you believe in magic?"

Mckenna choked on her drink. "I'm . . . not sure. Why?"

"Because all of this makes me think everything really does happen for a reason. Like if you stay positive, if you have faith, everything will work out in a beautiful way. And that's magic, isn't it?"

Mckenna smiled, wishing she had Nissa's optimism. "Yeah. Maybe."

"This is INSANITY!" someone yelled drunkenly at a neighbouring table.

"Would you keep your voice down?"

"If I'd known we were on a faery hill, I'd have never come!"

"Wind your neck in!"

Mckenna and Nissa glanced over at the two men having the spat, then back at each other with intrigue. Trying to appear casual, they hopped over to join them.

"What's a faery hill?" Nissa said, poking her nose between their heads.

The one who had been shouting, a plump, bearded man sporting a checkered vest and a bowtie, turned to her gravely. "Oh, you poor American. I'll tell you! All over Ireland, there are mounds that look like regular hills, but underneath them live the wee folk—what some call the wee ones, or you can call them the fair folk, the good people, the fae . . ."

"Get on with it," said his bony-faced friend.

" . . . and you *never* climb a faery hill without permission."

"Why not?" Nissa asked, placing her head between her palms, her elbows nearly knocking over a couple of flutes.

"Don't listen to him," his friend said. "You can do what you bloody well please."

"Catch yourself on! You've a death wish, do you?"

Rolling his eyes, his friend moved to another table. The bearded man hung back and got in closer, his expression filled with dread. "Bad things happen to people who disrespect the wee folk."

"Like what?" Nissa said.

"When I first moved to Belfast, me flatmate brought me to see the faery hills, but he warned me, he did, not to get too close 'cause of what happened to his grandad. The poor old bloke was spouting off about faeries being make-believe, only existing in stories. Said nothing would happen if he walked over to a faery hill and kicked it."

Nissa gasped. "What happened?"

"Your man went over to it, as promised, and kicked it while his friends watched. And when he did, he fainted on the spot and rolled down the hill, unconscious."

"Maybe he just tripped—"

"Just wait. That's nothing!" He leaned in closer. "The next morning, your man woke up paralyzed from the waist down."

Mckenna thought of Niamh, the faery from the Inagh Valley, and couldn't imagine her harming any living being, let alone an innocent elderly man.

"No way," Nissa said, also disbelieving, and then fired more questions at him. Mckenna felt sick, like discussing this was disrespectful to Niamh, and also confused; what if Niamh were capable of hurting others? Was she manipulating Mckenna, only to get closer to her, to hurt her in some way?

Letting out a long sigh, she backed away from the table, stepping out of the tent and under the full moon.

It was much larger than any moon she'd ever seen; a brilliant sunset orange, it cast a warm glow over the grounds.

"Nothing quite like it, right?"

Mckenna's body jolted at the sound of Cillian's voice. And then she remembered what Esme said back in the woods. "Is it the harvest moon . . .?"

"It is, but not just any. Tonight's the—"

"Autumnal equinox," she finished, Esme's soothing voice echoing in her mind: *The harvest moon will occur on the same night as the autumnal equinox. A very rare occasion that won't happen again for another nineteen years.*

"How do you know that?"

"Ms. Beattie mentioned it . . ." Mckenna said, knowing Cillian wouldn't buy it.

"Ms. Beattie. Right." Cillian raised his eyebrows, then stared up, leaning his body back slightly. "Pulls you in, doesn't it?"

It did. It was a colossal lodestone, and she a speck of iron. "Does it mean anything?"

"The harvest moon? Loads of things. It dates back centuries. To the Celts, the harvest moon marked the time before Samhain, which is Halloween. They'd gather crops, dance, drink, celebrate their blessings. I remember every year when it'd happen, my mum would take my brother and me to the park. She'd give us a push every time we'd say something we were thankful for."

"That's really nice. I didn't know you had a brother."

Cillian gave a half nod. Mckenna didn't press on.

"It's also a time for creating change," Cillian continued. "To look in, sort through your strengths, your weaknesses. Find where you want to see change, and ready yourself."

"For what?"

"For that change to come."

Goosebumps ran up Mckenna's arms, then it was as though a lightning bolt had struck her. A surge of energy flowed through her body and inside her bloodstream. It'd been there all along, it just hadn't been awakened. Her heart thumped so hard and fast, it made her ears ache; and her chest, it felt like it was seconds from cracking open. She wasn't sure what was happening, but she could feel it was a *need* energy. She had to do something . . . she had to do something right now.

Esme's message. If there was a time to embrace who she was, it was here, under the harvest moon.

"I have to go," she blurted, then hurried across to the edge of the tent, snatching three votive candles in her path, and ran down the hill and into the trees. She stopped at a small clearing, where the moon hung over the surrounding trees. And there, in the centre, sat a small tree stump, only too perfect for the occasion. She placed the votives on it, pleased, though not surprised, that the flames didn't get blown out by the breeze.

Not knowing what exactly to do, she followed her intuition; she kneeled on the ground, staring at the fire dancing wildly, and allowed herself to take in a slow, deep breath.

"To whoever's listening, my name is Mckenna O'Dwyer." Her voice echoed through the trees. "I've felt like half a person all my life. And now with all this, these abilities, these people that are suddenly a part of my life, I'm starting to feel like . . . like I have an identity. They've helped me get to know myself a little better, and I'm grateful.

"I'm here because I accept who I am; I was born a Wise One." The leaves rustled around her. "I don't know what that means yet. So, Abigail—my birth mother—if you can hear me, I'm coming to find you. I can feel how close you are . . ."

Something prompted Mckenna to open her eyes. Hovering above the candles was a golden light, like a solitary orb, growing larger and larger, until Mckenna could feel its sacred energy. Within the light, she could see the face of a female, but not in great detail. She didn't need to, though, for she knew this woman was loving, all-knowing, forgiving; she accepted everyone and scorned no one; she was the one the world turned to through times of grief; she was the mother of all living beings.

Mckenna wanted to speak to her, to reach her somehow. She inhaled, praying for her to step out onto the earth and take Mckenna by the hand, to guide her towards her rightful path. But instead of flesh and bone she felt a breath enter her body, and her heartbeat slowed, as though in rhythm with the trees, flowers, and pebbles under her feet.

She was in rhythm with the universe.

Cillian smiled at the moving scene before him, and at the dazzling light of Mother Gaia, then slowly retreated. *She's embracing her magic. Shouldn't be long now.*

He emerged from the trees and spotted Nissa back in the tent chatting away with Rune, a fleabag delegate whose gaze appeared to be penetrating Nissa's blouse.

The timing was perfect. He made his way over to them.

"Rune, maybe that's one too many, yeah?"

Rune gave a short laugh. "What's too many? I'm still standing, aren't I?"

"Sure, sure. Would you mind if I borrowed Nissa, here, for

a moment?" He clapped him on the back, and Rune stumbled slightly.

"Super great party," Nissa said, following Cillian to the shrimp table. "Where's Mckenna?"

"That's what I was just coming to ask you," he said, feigning puzzlement. "To tell you the truth, I'm a little worried."

"What for?"

"She was saying some funny things earlier. Things about herself—dunno if it was the champagne or . . . never mind. I could just be imagining things."

Nissa sobered up quickly. "What sort of things?"

"Something about who she really is? A secret . . . and that she didn't need us anymore. Honestly, she wasn't making very much sense. Has she told you anything?"

A gloom was cast over Nissa's face. "No, nothing. Where did she go?"

Something foreign and yet also familiar coursed through her, and Mckenna felt like this was the true beginning of her journey. Like she was now closer than ever to finding her mother. She had power within her. She just had to trust it.

Slowly, she brought her awareness back to the present moment. To the earth she stood on, to every cell that made up her body, to every imperfect thought . . .

A twig snapped. It was Nissa, her brow furrowed, standing at the edge of the clearing.

"Nissa. Hey," she said stupidly, jumping to her feet.

"Watcha doing?"

"Sitting here . . . needed a bit of quiet, you know?" What was she doing here? How did she find her?

"Don't lie, please." The disappointment in Nissa's voice made Mckenna's throat swell. How much had she heard? "You're hiding something."

Mckenna couldn't think up a proper response. "What? No,

I . . ." What had came over her suddenly?

"You were out late that first night in Kilkenny, and you've been acting super weird since. I didn't ask, figuring you'd let me know if there was something—"

"There's nothing to tell, Nissa," she insisted, hating herself.

"What kind of person invites a stranger to cross the world with them, and then doesn't tell them the full story?"

"It's not—I—"

"Who's your mom? Who are you?"

Mckenna froze. What could she say? Her mom was a kind of sorceress? That Mckenna had abilities, saw angry ghosts and had dreams of witches being burned? Oh, and she could talk to animals, see faeries, could sometimes feel others' emotions, and, possibly, move things with her mind? All of it would frighten her to death, make her rethink this whole voyage, their entire friendship.

"And what's a Wise One?"

She *had* heard everything. "The truth is, I really don't know."

"Well, was this a ritual? Are you, like . . . a witch?"

I might be. She wanted to say it, to tell her everything. But she thought of how adamant Seán was about keeping Mckenna away from Abby's world, about how her mom had left them for their safety, though safe from what or whom, she couldn't say. There was something huge coming and with it, the potential for great danger.

And all this time she'd put Nissa in danger.

"You're really gonna stand there and say nothing? I've told you everything about me and my crappy life." Nissa's voice was shaking now. "Kenna, you're my *only* friend."

"Maybe . . . maybe I shouldn't be." She nearly choked on the words, and her heart sank into her stomach. She had to lie, she had to let her go. She never should've dragged her into this; this was *her* journey, her path. She didn't know what threats awaited her, but they wouldn't be Nissa's to face.

A thought entered her brain, and suddenly, Nissa's worries became clear: Nissa was afraid Mckenna was lying about who she was—and that she didn't need her anymore.

"The truth is I have been lying to you. About lots of things. I'm not who you think I am. I'm not good, I never was. I just needed help getting here. But now with all the Isle of Man stuff, you're just . . . slowing me down. You don't need to follow me anymore."

If Nissa wasn't utterly crushed a moment ago, she was now. "I won't anymore, then. Good luck," she muttered between tears, then took off into the night.

XIV

Lessons in Ballycastle

Mckenna stood desolate in the woods as Nissa's footsteps faded, mortified at what she'd just done. She didn't know how long she stood there, staring at the spot where her best friend walked out of her life, likely for good, not daring to move for fear she might collapse onto her knees. Above, the sky lit up and thunder boomed in warning; still, she stayed unmoving, the rain hitting her like water dumped from a pail. Soaked head to toe, she finally dragged her feet back up the hill, the party noise growing louder with each step.

"A journalist? Come off it."

"Well, she's still studying."

At the sounds of Cillian's and Naomi's voices, she slipped under the tent, stopping behind some disorderly delegates toasting rounds of drinks.

"No wonder. A group of intelligent, educated adults discussing real-life matters, and then *she* jumps in like a wild dog offering no insight whatsoever into the matter."

"She's got no experience in politics, Naomi. She's a kid."

A kid? Mckenna balled up her fists, her nails nearly puncturing her skin.

"You remember when you used to be passionate about what you did, before you got to know all the rules?"

"The passion, I remember . . ."

Mckenna peeked over one of the shorter delegates' shoulders and spotted Naomi's body inches from Cillian's, her fingers entwined in his.

She had the urge to leave for Ballycastle right then and there. She was but an hour away—why should she wait for some tour bus the next morning?

Because you have literally no other way of getting there, she thought miserably. And so ducking behind the party guests, she speed-walked back to the B&B under the falling rain, where she was relieved to find Nissa asleep on the living room sofa. Mckenna thought to wake her, but decided it was perhaps best that for tonight, she had some space.

Yep, morning, she thought. *Everything will be better by morning.*

Mckenna awoke at 6:00 a.m. to find all of Nissa's things gone. Skipping two steps at a time, she ran down to the kitchen, where Ms. Beattie was already serving breakfast to some early risers.

"Your small friend left at the crack of dawn to catch the first ferry to the Isle of Man, I'm afraid. Didn't she tell you?"

Tears stung her eyes, and she wiped them before they fell. Mckenna knew this was for the best, but she'd be lying if she said a small part of her didn't believe things would (magically?) fix themselves, that she'd wake up and by breakfast time, they'd be laughing at how ridiculous their spat was. "Our first fight," they'd say, then they'd be on their way to Ballycastle together, and from there, to the Isle of Man, where her sixth sense could guide them to find the answers she sought . . .

"Have a wee bite before you go," Ms. Beattie insisted when she caught Mckenna sneaking out the front door at half past six. Mckenna thanked her for the stay and delicious food and blamed her early tour bus for her quick departure.

"I left your dress hanging back in your sewing room. Thank you for letting me borrow it, Ms. Beattie."

"What for? Take it, I've certainly no use for it." Feeling it'd be rude to refuse, she nodded and thanked her again. She managed to roll it up tight, the way Andre had taught her, and stuff it in at the bottom of her bag.

She got to Ballycastle, County Antrim within the hour, with very little money left in the wad of cash she'd "borrowed" from her dads, half of which she'd given to Nissa to hold onto. She could afford a couple of nights in a hostel, maybe, but soon, she'd have to improvise.

Mckenna learned from the driver, a lanky, stern-looking man named Mortimer, that Ballycastle was home to about four thousand residents, the majority of whom were Catholic, and that violent incidents happened almost daily between the Irish Republican Army and the loyalists. As the sea came into view, Mckenna peered out at the waves rolling into the rocks below.

A war—here? *Unfathomable.*

Mortimer took a roundabout and slowed near a modern white building, *The Marine Hotel,* and explained that it was bombed in 1979 by the IRA, along with four other hotels in towns across Northern Ireland. "City folk who don't know better still come up here for Giant's Causeway, the sea and such, but nothing more. Not safe nowhere, right now," he added. Mckenna's eyes darted around the nearly empty tour bus, where one young couple sat, terror-stricken. "Should've listened to your mam," she overheard the man say.

The bus veered into town, where people were as sparse as hairs on an old man's head. "It's best you don't wander too far," Mortimer said as he parked the bus. "It's not safe for lone travellers, you see."

Mckenna stepped out onto a slope in the colourful town centre, tasting salt in the air. Sure enough, after exploring the small, noiseless streets, her promenade led her to the teal waters of the marina that opened up to the vast ocean. She felt lonelier than she'd ever been; how would she go on without Nissa? She was her little spark of hope—an always-upbeat ball of energy that carried her through the day, that reassured her she wasn't just a foolish teenager following a hunch.

And Cillian. Had she imagined what they had, or had she been too quick to judge, to take what he said to Naomi out of context? She suddenly wished she could call her dads—they would have been so proud that she finally came to them seeking love advice. But calling them would only amount to dreadful guilt. She needed to keep going, to find answers.

"Where are you, Abby?" she wondered aloud.

A familiar *chirp* echoed inside her ear. She snapped her head around and caught sight of a small bird—no, a wren—perched on a magazine stand. Hardly daring to believe her eyes, she loomed nearer, examining its tiger-striped feathers.

"You're the same little guy, aren't you?"

The wren chirped excitedly, nicked at the magazine beneath its large feet, and flew off.

This is weird as hell, she thought. And just when she didn't think it could get any weirder, something caught her eye: On the bottom right corner of the magazine were the words *Magic by Chance. Healing crystals, herbs, oils, and more—for all your holistic needs. Magic* was written in large purple letters.

Not a coincidence, said a small, hopeful voice in her head, which sounded quite a bit like Nissa's. Full of adrenaline, she ripped the cover off and asked anyone in sight the shop's whereabouts. Most hadn't heard of it, but a kind old lady finally pointed her in the right direction.

"You better be onto something, Wrenny," she muttered, spotting the shop window in a kind of back alley, somewhere she would've never thought to look.

The perfect location for someone who didn't want to be found.

Her hand trembling, Mckenna pushed open the door, setting off the tinkling of wooden wind chimes, and entered a room about the size of her bedroom. In an instant, the familiar scent of sandalwood, which Seán so often burned, filled her nose; wall-to-wall shelves were packed with all sorts of pretty and strange objects: crystals of various shapes and sizes, women's jewellery, plants and herbs, books, tarot cards, incense sticks, candles, and instruments she'd never seen. Fascinated, she looked round for a worker, but there was no one in sight.

Meoooooow.

Mckenna jumped as a cat with mixed chocolate and caramel patches stared up at her from the Moroccan-style rug.

"It's nice to meet you, too. Where's your human hiding, missy?"

Meow, she responded, then pranced over and brushed up against Mckenna's leg.

"How do you know she's a she?"

Mckenna's eyes darted around the small room and landed on a sharp-faced woman with spiky grey hair. She was standing at the very top of a ladder, stacking the highest shelf with heavy-looking brass bowls. Had she been there the whole time?

"I, um, just guessed." Actually, she'd known the cat was female the moment she meowed. "I've never seen her pattern before," she said awkwardly, stroking the cat's chin.

"She's a tortoiseshell. You don't commonly see them around."

"What's her name?"

"Caireen." She eyed Mckenna suspiciously, then began climbing down the ladder. "Can I help you with something?"

"Yeah, actually. I'm looking for someone. Abby—Abigail Douglas?"

At the last step, she froze. "Is that a question?"

Mckenna laughed nervously. "No, sorry. That's her name. Do you . . . know her?"

"Can't say I do."

And just like that, any spark of hope Mckenna had left went out. "Oh."

"What's it matter to you?" She walked over to the cashier counter and retrieved a bag of cat treats from behind it; a split second later, more cats—tabby, ginger, black, grey—emerged from every direction. Mckenna counted eight, plus Caireen.

"Whoa."

"They get that a lot," she said, hand-feeding each one. Amazed at how still they sat waiting to be fed, Mckenna said, "Geez. They're so disciplined. Do they do any tricks? Like, play dead?" She chuckled.

Like a trip of fainting goats, all nine cats fell flat against the floors and countertop. Mckenna gasped—did she just have them do that?

For the first time since she arrived, the woman looked at Mckenna with real interest. "Who did you say you were?"

"My name's Mckenna. I'm Abby's daughter."

Eyes wide with curiosity, the woman nodded once, then pointed at the bulletin board behind her, where a single tarot card was pinned: *Death*.

Mckenna gulped.

"I do a proper reading every day, and every day, my cards are spot on. Today, it was the death card that came out." Seeing Mckenna's face, she added, "It means great change; something is ending and another thing's beginning. All day long, I couldn't imagine what this meant for me. But it wasn't meant for me, was it? I welcome you, Wise One."

Mckenna realized she hadn't let out a breath since she read the card. She exhaled, relieved that this frightening woman wasn't going to curse her or something. "You . . . know who I am?"

"I do. And your mother."

"You said—"

"Can't be too careful these days. Besides, it's true that I don't know her, just know *of* her." She clapped her hands loudly, releasing the cats from their trance and sending them scurrying off to their hiding places. "Come back tonight at half eight."

"Me? Or the cats . . ."

"You, of course."

"Right," she said, nearly tripping over Caireen, who was licking her shoe. Mckenna kneeled to pet her. *Sorry, missy . . .*

"Will my mom be here?" But when she looked up, the woman was gone.

It was a long day. Mckenna spent most of it walking along the shore, watching the skies for any sign of Wrenny, and admiring the sea views—or was it the ocean? Where the Atlantic bordered the Irish Sea, she wasn't sure.

Feeling like trapeze performers were swinging around in her stomach, she returned to the shop at 8:30 p.m. sharp. With a deep breath, she pushed open the door.

It couldn't be . . .

"Esme."

Esme smiled in the way her eyes could. "Dear *boireannach glic.*"

Question after question flew into Mckenna's head. But she merely stood there, her vocal cords severed, it seemed, from her body.

"Walk with me. We have much to catch up on."

Mckenna followed Esme behind the cash counter and up a narrow flight of stairs. They entered a modest, open-concept apartment. It was Zen-like, decorated in creams and silvers, with splashes of soft pastels.

"Make yourself at home." Esme gestured towards the rose velvet sofa. Everything looked so prim. Mckenna removed her shoes and sat, unsure where to rest her hands.

"You don't have to worry about the fabric, it's not delicate at all. Velvet's very animal-friendly, in fact."

Mckenna nodded. "Oh? That's good." She was nervous, and it must've shown because Esme smiled, excused herself, and returned moments later with two steaming cups of tea. "Always calms my nerves. I often meditate with it, in fact."

She took a small sip, the jasmine flavour wrapping around her soul like a blanket. "Do you live here?"

"Aye."

"And . . . is it your shop?"

Esme nodded.

"But Kilkenny . . . and now here. What are the chances—?"

"Nothing's been left to chance, *boireannach glic*. Despite the name of my shop . . ."

Mckenna couldn't wrap her head around it. "I just saw the bird and . . ."

"It was speaking to you, wasn't it?"

"I think so." This was lunacy. "Wait, why were you in Kilkenny? And did you know I'd come here?"

"I was asked to fill in for an old friend. Her mum was sick, and she asked for help leading her apprentices while she was away. I said no, at first—my shop, my customers needed me. But my guide spoke to me, assuring me I was needed in Kilkenny more."

"Guide?"

"Spirit guide."

Right, questions later. "That night, when you said, 'I have faith we'll cross paths again', did you know I'd come here?"

"I was hoping, yes. Your mum felt connected to Ballycastle, and so I knew that deep inside, you'd feel the need to come here, too."

"Is my mom here now?" This was really all she cared to know. She watched Esme's smile fade, and her eyes fill with sorrow.

"Alas, your mum's not been back here since she left seventeen years ago."

Mckenna's heart shattered inside her chest. Breathlessly, she said, "In Kilkenny, you said that my intuition was strong, that I should trust it. Well I did, so how the hell can that be true if she's not even *here?*" Her face hot with fury, she stood up, feeling the need to pace.

"It's hard to believe right now, but this is where you're supposed to be. You're too angry, too hurt to face her now. You need time to heal and understand, to learn. That's why you're here in this moment. Trust in divine timing."

None of this made sense. "Learn? Couldn't I learn whatever it is I'm supposed to learn back in Kilkenny? What's the point in coming all this way? I don't need a beach vacation."

"After Kilkenny, it was important for you to journey here the way you did; a traveller's destination is not a place, but a change in their awareness."

Mckenna was in no mood to decode anything. "This is too

much. This is too . . ."

A small, damp nose rubbed against her foot. *Hi, Caireen.*

"Just tell me this, please," she said, stroking Caireen's chin. "Is my mom alive?"

Esme stared deep into her. There was something about her eyes, like portals to another plane. "You ken the answer to that."

She was right. Mckenna could hardly explain it, but ever since her birthday, it was like she'd awoken from a zombie-like state, called by a voice to seek out answers, find her truth. The voice, she'd always known, was her mother's.

"If I stay, I need to know everything," she demanded. "I want to know who my mother really is and what happened right before she had me. I want to learn how to control my powers, and I want to know once and for all what it means to be a Wise One."

"That doesn't seem like a terribly unreasonable request."

Mckenna did a double take. "Really?"

"You have my word your questions will be answered. And now, I need yours." Mckenna waited for the catch. "You're to learn a lesson a day, and after each one, you're free to ask me one question."

Mckenna didn't have to think twice. "Deal."

"I'm glad. Now, I'm sure it's been a tiring day. You're, of course, free to bade here—" *Stay?* "—as long as you'd like." She pointed at an ajar door behind them. "It's a cot, but it's comfier than it looks, I promise you that."

Mckenna still sometimes had trouble deciphering Esme's speech, but she was getting the hang of it. With a last bid good night, Esme turned in.

The cot was all made up and the bedsheets, still warm from the drier, had a hint of lavender scent. Esme must've hoped Mckenna would *bade* here.

She didn't know whether she should owe it to the toasty sheets or Caireen's soothing purrs, but it was the best night's sleep Mckenna had had in a long while.

Mckenna awoke the next morning to the smell of fresh-brewed coffee, French toast and eggs—and a 5:00 a.m. alarm.

"Blessed morning," a vibrant Esme said, placing a full cup on the table in front of her. Mckenna seized it, not daring to expose her pre-coffee voice. "Did you sleep sound?"

Mckenna took one enormous gulp. "Very. Thank you for making me stay."

"I didn't make you, I hope." She served Mckenna two eggs with a side of French toast, blueberries, and English cream. Nissa's face would have lit up at this spread. "I thought to make it an American breakfast for you. I'm not too fond of the gypsy bread meself, but it seems to have come out well enough."

"Gypsy bread? We call it French toast at home."

"French? I don't see what's French about that."

"What do you normally have for breakfast?"

"Oh, I'm satisfied with a scone and chutney, maybe some fruit. And a cup of tea, of course."

Mckenna couldn't imagine starting a morning without coffee.

"You think you need coffee to function, but you might surprise yourself."

"Okay, how do you—?"

"Ah, after our first lesson," she said with a wink, then got up. "I'll meet you doonby when you've finished up. Have a shower, if you like—oh, and best dress warmly."

Mckenna assumed *doonby* meant *downstairs.*

After a much-needed shower, Mckenna made her way down to the shop, where Esme and her spiky-haired employee were sticking price tags on incense burners. The latter finally introduced herself as Dierdre, the store manager. When Mckenna shook her hand, she felt a stab of pain around her chest.

"Is she alright? Dierdre," she asked as they entered Esme's tiny car, which looked more like a toy than a vehicle.

"She's suffered more than most," was all Esme said. "You sensed her hurting."

"Her heart . . . it feels shattered. She's pretty good at putting up walls, though, because she was as cold as ice yesterday."

"Some are better at hiding their feelings than others." She immediately thought of Cillian, and the feeling that he'd been hiding something from her since the day they met. "Now, we have two stops to make today."

They drove about five minutes past the town and stopped in the middle of a small street. Wondering what couldn't wait until human waking hours, Mckenna sauntered behind Esme, trying to pick up her feet as they walked down the road for several minutes, and onto a paved path that twisted into a field dotted with trees. The sound of trickling water met her ears.

"This way," Esme said, parting branches from a cluster of oaks. Mckenna ducked underneath, letting a twig tug at her hair. They stepped into a smaller clearing, where more trees dwelled, and a stream ran between undergrowth. There, a woman with long, silver hair and about middle-aged was kneeling, her hands flat on the ground, eyelids closed and fluttering, like she was dreaming.

"Let's sit," Esme whispered as she lowered her body to the grass, crossing her legs.

Mckenna followed suit. "Who is that?"

"Her name is Bianca. She's a woman in my coven. Her son isn't well; she comes here every morning at dawn."

"What is she doing?"

"She's connecting with the earth's energy."

The woman lifted her hands from the ground and began picking small wildflowers from a nearby shrub. Mckenna noticed her lips moving.

"Now, she's thanking nature for her sacrifice."

The woman's eyes were closed again as she spoke, holding the flowers to her chest. She then lifted them to her nose and breathed in their scent, the expression on her face serene, grateful. As though meant for her, a gust of wind swept her hair off her shoulders. She stood up and tossed the flowers into the stream.

"Why did she throw them?"

"The loving and healing energy she raised from the ground they grow on is now out in flow, with her intentions tied to them."

Mckenna nodded in understanding. "To help her son."

Esme smiled. "Aye. Wherever the flowers may end up, the energy attached to them has now gone with them. The flowers might get picked up, eaten by an animal, or decompose, affecting other life. Life which continues to carry on and affect more life."

"It's like energy never dies."

Esme's eyes sparkled. "Do you know what that is?"

Mckenna shook her head.

"Magic."

Mckenna felt fully awake after that, keen for whatever Esme had in store for her next. They drove twenty minutes out, passing fields and farmsteads (really, how many did this island have?), and pulled into a public parking lot.

A sulphury scent filled the air, carried by a chill breeze. Pulled by the rushing sound of waves, Mckenna walked to the road's end. Far below, the sea whispered its calming notes, both melodic and fierce, as though longing to impart wisdom to the land and sky. "I hadn't realized we drove so high up."

"Beautiful, isn't it? Come, we've got a wee trek. Hope you're wearing comfortable shoes."

She followed Esme about a mile down a red dirt path, which gradually wound downwards to the water's edge.

"Where are we?" Mckenna said as a rocky landmass came into view.

"Below, where you see the rock formation—that's the Giant's Causeway."

As they drew nearer, Mckenna did a double take at the dramatic sight before her: At the foot of the cliffs lay uneven hills of thousands upon thousands of interlocked black rocks in the shape of hexagons. Like a three-dimensional jigsaw puzzle, the pieces fit together flawlessly. Esme urged Mckenna to walk around the site. She did, stepping up and down from stone to stone.

How could they have formed so perfectly? And why were

they all at different heights? How were they floating on the sea?

That was when she realized . . .

"Esme, these aren't rocks, are they? These are columns."

"Indeed. Forty thousand columns beneath the sea—basalt columns, meaning they're formed from lava. Some as tall as thirty-nine feet. All of this was the result of a volcanic eruption some fifty million years ago, during the Tertiary period—but of course, there's also an Irish legend that explains it all." Mckenna smiled at this. "A Scottish giant, Benandonner, challenged an Irish giant, Fionn MacCool, to a fight. Being very proud, Fionn accepted and built a causeway across the North Channel to Scotland for the two to battle. But when Fionn saw the size of Benandonner, he ran back to Ireland and had his wife disguise him as a baby.

"The funny bit is, when Benandonner saw the size of the baby, he thought, 'if the baby's that big, can't imagine his dad!' So, he bolted back to Scotland, destroying the causeway along the way. Across the sea to the Scottish isle of Staffa, there are the same columns, made of the same basalt."

"So, which story is true?" If faeries and ghosts existed, why not giants?

"Which do you believe?"

Mckenna took a moment. "Before my birthday, I would've thought, well if it's backed by science, then that's the explanation. But now . . . I don't know what's true."

"You know, something like seven species of seabirds have made this area their home. And the rocks, they host exotic plants you scarcely find anywhere else. Extraordinary, isn't it?"

Mckenna wasn't sure what Esme was getting at.

"What do you think now? Without overthinking it."

"If I don't think too much about it, I'd say a volcano erupted, and this was the result." Then a thought occurred to her. "Death and rebirth?"

"Precisely. The cycle of nature. Cause and effect. The interconnectedness of all things. Think about what would happen if we cut down all the trees. The creatures that feed off them would die, and eventually, humans would lack oxygen and die, as well.

Like every living being, whatever is done to nature, nature will react—sometimes in positive ways, like this causeway, and sometimes in not-so-positive ways. So, I ask you this, *boireannach glic:* What is the lesson here?"

"I think . . . well, I'd say respect nature."

"Why?"

"Because it'll fight back."

"There are two more lessons. What else?"

Mckenna was usually good at being tested, but Esme's all-knowingness was a *touch* more intimidating than Mr. Heathley's delusional theories. "I think . . . maintaining balance in general. Like, Newton's law: For every action, there's an equal and opposite reaction. So, I guess, consider your actions carefully?"

"You guess?"

"Sorry—I'm sure."

"You're right. And the last, I'll tell you meself." Mckenna sighed in relief. "The truth is often what requires the least thought." Esme winked.

"Does that mean there were no giants?"

Esme tilted her head back. "Oh, indeed, there were," she said. Her brain slightly spinning, Mckenna watched her hop from column to column, like she was playing a solo game of hopscotch.

Mckenna didn't want to seem ungrateful, so she waited until they sat for lunch to ask the question that was gnawing at her insides. "Who's my mom? What happened the year she was pregnant with me?"

"I reckon that's a two-part question," Esme said, taking a sip of her white tea.

Mckenna's legs rattled with impatience. "Please."

"You get one after each lesson."

Mckenna considered her words carefully. "Who is my mother?"

Esme locked eyes with her. "Your mum and I grew up together. We were neighbours in Aberdeen—on the East Coast of Scotland—since we were nine years of age. She, another one of our neighbours, and I, we'd run and play together in the forest, oh, nearly every day. And then one afternoon, we had company; we were paid a visit by the fae folk."

"Faeries."

"Faeries adore children, did you know? Because they're brutally honest, fun-loving, open to possibilities, and don't question their existence—no cynicism."

Mckenna smiled, thinking that sounded an awful lot like Nissa.

"Every time we'd go out and play," Esme continued, "the fae folk appeared to us. We trusted them, and they grew to trust us. They began to tell us things, dark things that would become of our Earth if humankind continued to abuse."

"Abuse . . .?"

"Our planet. They told us the three of us were special, and we would grow up to be strong women who would help spread empathy across the world. Over time, we came to be like sisters, your mother, our friend and I—"

"Who's your friend?"

"Her name was Maeve."

"Oh, I'm sorry," Mckenna said, feeling thoughtless.

"That's alright." Esme smiled, then continued. "As teenagers, we began educating ourselves on the environment, such as ecological conservation and sustainable practices. Now, I teach Environmental Science at the University of Ulster." Mckenna drew back, impressed. "In the meanwhile, we never lost touch with the fae. They taught us how to tap into our spirituality, access other realms, and use magic we would have never imagined existed—magic that anyone can access. Though, one of us, they said, was already gifted with it."

"My mother."

"They told Abby she was an incarnated elemental. Not to worry, we hadn't a clue what it meant either at the time," she added, seeing Mckenna's puzzled expression. "An elemental is a spiritual being connected with one of the four elements of the Earth, such as faeries and gnomes, salamanders, sylphs, undines . . ."

"What are—wait, gnomes?"

"Another day," Esme said as casually as if they were discussing fashion trends.

"You're telling me my mom was, like, a faery in her past life, and she came back as a human in this one?"

"She'd chosen to, yes. But that's not for me to explain."

Mckenna sat there, mouth agape.

"In our late teens, we agreed we'd share the message of the faeries with those with the same environmental interests as us—who could help us in our cause to make humankind aware of the danger our planet was in. We began holding gatherings, teaching others what the faeries taught us."

"What does spiritual training have to do with the environment?"

Esme smiled again. "Just about everything. But let's stick to the topic of your mum for now." She took another sip of her tea. "During the gatherings, Abigail and Maeve began to clash. They each wanted to lead, but their views on how best to do that were no longer in harmony. Your mum soon reached a point where she needed some time away. She took a trip to England."

"Where she met my dad." Mckenna was starting to see the whole picture now.

"Once she'd fallen for your dad, that was it for her. She said she had found her true calling. They moved to Ballycastle and bought a home, not so far from the Giant's Causeway; it was her favourite place to be. Can you guess why?"

Mckenna could. "She could see Scotland from across the sea."

Esme nodded. "She wrote to me every week, saying she would continue our cause here. Not long after, she was pregnant with you, and about three months in, she stopped writing."

"Do you know why?"

"I do. But it's not me place to say."

"Please. I need to know—"

"And you will. You will hear it from the person who ought to tell you, at the time when it ought to be told."

Mckenna's sleep that night was interrupted by disturbing dreams involving her mother, shrunken and faery-like, flying around Abredonia Woods, pointing and laughing at Mckenna as she ran frantically through the trees, searching for her.

"We fear what we don't understand," Esme offered the following day as they strolled through a neighbouring town, which seemed even smaller than Ballycastle. It was brisk and cloudy, but Esme insisted that lesson two be out here.

Mckenna halted when they reached a country road fit for a Grimm storybook cover: Two rows of longstanding birch trees lined an undulated lane, their warped branches leaning inwards to form a natural arch.

"Eerie," Mckenna muttered.

"Quite," Esme agreed. "Do you sense anything peculiar?"

Mckenna glanced down the lane and shivered; the spidery limbs gave off a maleficent vibe. "Just a little creeped out, I think."

Esme nodded, then beckoned Mckenna to follow her a little ways down the road, where they stood in the shadows beneath the foggy ether.

"Is there a tree you like?"

Not understanding the question, Mckenna said, "Um, they're all nice . . ."

Esme smiled. "Is there one you're drawn to?"

Feeling stupid, Mckenna looked up the road. Immediately, her eyes fell on a birch near the end of the lane; its trunk was curved inwards, as though bowing to the tree opposite the lane, their branches entwined.

"That one."

"Lovely," said Esme. "Let's leave that for now. What you're going to do is close your eyes, breathe in deeply," she said, demonstrating taking in a long breath, "and release." Mckenna did as she was told, feeling a touch calmer with every breath.

"Keep your eyes closed and carry on . . . in and out . . . from your belly. Feel it rising and dropping. Good. Now, which part of your body comes to mind when I ask where you feel your emotions are coming from the most?" Mckenna's hand shot to her stomach like a horseshoe magnet. "That's good, *boireannach glic*. That means for you, your sacral chakra is your centre."

Mckenna was about to ask what on Earth a chakra was, but Esme continued. "A chakra is where our energy flows from, a kind of power point—the challenge is to keep them unblocked. We have seven: the root chakra," —Esme placed her hand around the base of her spine—"the sacral chakra, where you've placed your hand," —she slipped her hand to her front, just below her navel—"the solar plexus chakra, around your abdomen; the heart chakra; the throat chakra; the third eye chakra,"—she placed two fingers on her forehead, between her eyes—"and the crown chakra." She lay her hand flat atop her head.

"Now, keep your hand on your centre, and open it."

Mckenna's eyes shot open. "How do I do that?"

"Take note of what's happening in your body. What you're feeling. Then picture yourself doing a good cleaning. There's no one way," she added as Mckenna raised an eyebrow. "'Flow follows focus,' they say."

With no clue as to who *they* were, she closed her eyes again, her hand pressed against her sacral chakra. She imagined it as a goblet, brim-full of doubts and worries about her mom, Nissa, even Cillian. How was it that her relationships all ended in abandonment? She took another deep breath and imagined pouring the contents of the goblet out.

"I think I'm centred now," she said, feeling a slight warmth in her belly.

"'Think?'"

"I mean, I'm centred now."

Esme nodded. "Next, you're going to ground yourself. Some prefer to ground first, but I don't see how I'm to ground if I'm not centred. It's best you take off your shoes."

Why did everyone want her to take off her shoes?

She followed Esme off the road, onto the grass, and beside the tree she'd pointed out earlier—which, standing this close, came across as having legs and a face.

"Close your eyes, and feel what's beneath your feet. The supple earth, wet leaves, twigs and pebbles . . ." Esme began slowly, allowing Mckenna time between each word to absorb it to its fullest. "Imagine yourself a tree that's just been planted. You're given a new home, new life. Years pass, and your roots grow longer, wider, until they begin to spread, and you begin to grow taller. You don't stop growing until you reach the lowermost cloud in the sky."

Esme had a way of injecting power into every syllable, as though her breath was charging them with intention. As she guided her, Mckenna felt a connectedness to the earth similar to what she'd felt under the harvest moon. The soles of her feet were rooted to the ground, and the top of her head grazed the mist above them. Because she and all of humankind, they were part of it all; they were once mere organisms, formed entirely by the Earth's elements, and billions of years later, here they still were, in a more evolved form. But at their very core, they *were* the Earth.

"We are the Earth," Mckenna whispered into the wind.

"Go on," Esme said softly.

"We're the water, the plants, the mountains . . . We're the same. But we forgot."

"And how did you come to know this?"

"I—I listened."

Her eyelids fluttered open. Esme was smiling. "And so you did."

Mckenna felt triumphant. "Can I ask my question?"

"Soon enough, we're not quite finished. Centre and ground, please."

She did as she was told. Taking three long breaths, she focused on her sacral chakra, greeting its newly cleansed state, and grounded herself, from earth to sky.

"Pay attention to your surroundings. Feel my energy, that of the tree nearest to you, and anything else that's giving off any sort of vibrations."

All at once, a feeling of gloom was cast over the road like a dark, ominous cloud. She opened her eyes and saw nothing.

"Something's here, but I don't know what exactly . . ."

"Your fear is blocking you."

Mckenna didn't doubt that. "There's . . . there's a spirit here. But I can't—I mean, I don't want to see . . ." She winced as she pictured the terrifying ghost of Petronella.

"What you're sensing is a low-energy spirit. They vibrate at a low frequency, whereas evolved spirits vibrate at a high frequency—much higher than humans, which is why they don't live in our plane of existence."

"So, when we do see them, it means they're low energies?"

"Not always. If a loved one that's passed appears at your side, they more than likely slowed down their vibration so they could communicate with you. But a low-energy spirit never evolved, which means they've not much light in them. They're not evil, per se, but they may be tricksters, they could be sticking around for revenge, or desperate to accomplish something they hadn't gotten around to before. Make you think of anyone?"

How could it not? "Can't you conjure that blue light again to make her, you know, move on?"

"I've attempted more than once to help her cross over. And look, you've just sensed the spirit's female." Mckenna hadn't realized she'd said *her.* "You're right. She's known as the Grey Lady, and she appears at dusk most days, gliding along the road. I'm afraid nobody knows who she is."

"I can't tell either, but I don't think she means any harm." Mckenna was still reluctant to see her, but she could sense the Grey Lady meant not to disturb anyone, nor be disturbed. "I just can't help thinking she's sad. I feel such . . . despair."

"You're not the first to sense that, *boireannach glic.* Let's leave her be." In silence, they ambled back up the road.

Over the next few weeks, Mckenna's sessions with Esme got more thorough but also more trying. Every morning, Mckenna practiced harnessing her powers ("Centre and ground, then focus"), and every afternoon, Esme gave her a lesson on the uses and properties of herbs and crystals. They also covered the summer and winter solstices and cycles of the moon, and one rainy afternoon, Mckenna learned about the many other dimensions and planes of existence, some of them home to faery folk, spirits, goddesses, and creatures that were widely thought to be mythical. "Like what?" Mckenna asked.

"Loads. Unicorns, dragons, sprites . . ."

"Sprites?

"Sort of like hopping fish." Hadn't Mckenna seen those somewhere . . .?

And then she remembered those funny-looking fish hopping along the stream in that storybook forest, where Niamh the faery transported her to from the Inagh Valley.

Esme continued: "Merpeople, banshees, dryads, kirnis, tanukis . . ." She lost Mckenna again at *banshees*. Though, Mckenna did recall during their voyage to Dublin Nissa claiming to have spotted a mermaid. Maybe it wasn't an illusion. And that night she found Nissa in the woods back home, there had been something crouched behind the bushes. Perhaps it hadn't been a kid playing after all.

Mckenna learned that faeries existed close to the material plane—where our physical bodies lived—which was why it wasn't as difficult for them to access. Pools of water, such as after a rainfall, could be temporary doorways into the faery realm. In fact, anything that was an in-between could be used as a doorway—between day and night, between land and water. Mckenna told Esme about Niamh, the faery she encountered at the edge of the lake in the Inagh Valley. "Ah, yes. An especially magical place."

After days of practice, Mckenna still hadn't succeeded in moving an object with her mind—she got a migraine every time she tried. Today was no different; they'd been practicing with one of Esme's amethyst crystals, which hadn't budged an inch from its position on the cashier counter.

"I don't get it, I did it without thinking back at home." She recounted the incident with the book and the time she was able to slam the door shut by merely storming towards it. Esme explained that in the beginning, telekinesis was commonly associated with mental stress, so those episodes were reactions to Mckenna's anxiety. She also explained that telekinesis was part of a psycho-energy that existed in our brains, which was once easy to tap into.

"Like telepathy, right? Niamh told me that at one time, everyone communicated through thoughts." She remembered something else Niamh had said: *You're on the verge of learning your fate, and you won't succeed if you don't embrace your gifts.* What fate was she referring to?

Back at the shop, she watched as Esme burned the end of a thick bundle of dried herbs wrapped together with string. The piney scent of juniper quickly filled the room.

"Tell me. What led you to Ballycastle?"

"It's the only place I knew my mom was connected to. I thought it'd be a good place to start. But also . . . it's hard to explain. When I read the description in Andre's encyclopedia, I just felt this pull."

"It was quite the undertaking, what with no real plan. How did you think to leave from Boston?"

Mckenna laughed. "It's crazy. There was this bird . . ." Mckenna explained all about the wren in the schoolyard: how it had landed on her windowsill, its feather blowing in and plastering itself onto a photo of her and her dads in Boston; how it had flown briefly onto John's bag, and then here in Ballycastle, onto the shop's magazine ad.

"Wrens are thought to be messengers. He helped lead you here because he was sent to do just that."

"By who?"

"The fae folk. It was important you come here. First, so you could hone your powers, learn your craft; and second, because those looking for you now cannot find you here. And you can thank your mum for that."

She knew it. There were people after her. "My mom wanted to keep me safe. I know that's why she left me and my dad. But was it because she was being chased, or because they wanted *me?*"

"Your fate and your mum's are connected. When she was

pregnant with you, the fae folk told her of an old prediction—something that piqued the interest of some radical thinkers."

"So, they wanted—want—both of us. What's the prediction? And please don't say you can't tell me . . ."

But to her surprise, Esme nodded. "I think you're ready now, *boireannach glic.*" Mckenna caught her breath, and waited. "There is a reason your mother incarnated as a human in this lifetime. She was meant to give birth to you—to 'the last living Wise One'. The fae said that together, you would act as the bridge between realms, and we would all come to live on the same vibration and communicate freely."

Mckenna let her stomach expand. "That sounds amazing. Why keep this from me?"

"Sadly, there's more to it. Our good friend, Maeve, was fascinated by what the fae had relayed to us. She wanted more—she wanted to know how such a thing could be achieved. She was consumed by the idea of utopia, spending day and night researching old prophecies, until finally, she found one that closely matched the fae's—it was written by a sixteenth century witch: *As twin flames rekindle and the last living Wise One unites with her creator, billions of souls shall expire upon this Earth. Peace shall be restored to the natural world, and all beings shall exist in perfect harmony.*"

Mckenna had difficulty processing for a moment. *Expire?* Would she cause the death of billions of souls? "I don't . . . what . . . w-when is this supposed to happen?"

"This year, on the winter solstice. There's more."

Of course there was.

"The witch wrote two texts meant to help fulfill her vision, sort of like a map. Each one outlines actions that, should you succeed in carrying them out, would bring you closer to making it come true. They are known as the Scottish Scrolls."

Mckenna's brain was rapidly numbing. "What do they say?"

"I don't ken, I'm afraid. I've searched for years, but alas, only Maeve holds their secret. And by the Goddess, I've tried talking sense into her, but she refuses to see reason. She believes in the restoration of the natural world, no matter what the cost."

Believes, present tense. So, she wasn't dead. "But how did she find out?"

"I have a theory. When she told us of her findings, Abby was distraught. She said her guides came to her in a dream, telling her that her daughter was to be named Mckenna, and that she was a Wise One. This sparked something in Maeve—she delved deep into the science of hypnosis, and learned quite fast; she could control one's perception, and she'd mastered past-life regression."

Mckenna was beginning to feel like she knew nothing at all. She heaved a sigh. "What the hell's that?"

"A way to take our minds back, to remember a different life we've lived. My theory is that she forced Abby into a session, and through one of her memories, or *yours,* Abby recited the Scrolls."

"You think Maeve could've tapped into my past-life memories before I was even born?"

"I believe so."

"So, I must have known about the Scrolls in one of my lives. Maybe when I was Alice . . ."

Esme shook her head. "Alice's time was the fourteenth century, long before the Scrolls were predicted."

Wracking her mushy brain, she tried desperately to piece everything together. "Maeve is the one searching for me, isn't she?"

Esme's eyes turned sorrowful, like she was recalling a loss. To her, Maeve *had* died. A stab of pain pierced her heart; a piece of it would always be gone, she thought, feeling the strain in her chest—in Esme's chest. "She tried to sway your mum, paint a picture of the planet's future—it would be pure, like it once was. When Abby didn't listen, Maeve changed. She could not fathom how we couldn't see the grandeur, the 'good'. She began to send threats, promising she would take you from Abby once you were born, and keep her locked up until the time came . . ."

That time was now. This year, on the winter solstice. Mckenna finally understood. "That's why my mom left us."

"Yes, but ah, your mum was cannie. She cast a protection spell, first around Ballycastle, so no foe could cross the threshold, and second, on your blood—a blend, of course, of hers and your father's."

"So that we're all protected."

"Exactly," she said, adding proudly, "The spell was so intricate, so powerful, you can't imagine; we worked for months on end. That's how she's untraceable, and why you were, too, until you came of age. It was the only way—"

"Untraceable?" Her face was hot with suppressed anger. "How am I supposed to find her, then?"

Esme smiled lightly. "She's never without her wits, your mum. Only those her spell protects are capable of finding her."

Silence fell between them. This was more than she bargained for, than she'd expected. "There's still something I don't understand."

"Go on, *boireannach glic*."

"If we reunite, won't that mean . . . all that death . . .?"

"We can't be sure. This prophecy is according to a sixteenth century witch—Elizabeth Dunlop, the Witch of Dalry. Not the fae."

"But we don't know if that's what the faeries meant, too. Maybe that's how we become 'the bridge between realms', restore peace and all that—by fulfilling the Scottish Scrolls." A thought occurred to her, and she shot to her feet. "What if the Scrolls are coming true without me even knowing it? What if it's my destiny?" She began pacing to and fro, making a handful of Esme's shop cats scatter about in their hiding places.

"We always have choice, *boireannach glic*—no destiny is written. We're all born with gifts; all we can do is harness them, and walk the path that feels the truest. Stay grounded, stay centred. Listen here." She placed a hand on her heart.

Mckenna collapsed onto the sofa, her fingers rubbing at her temples. She had known for years what her heart was yearning for, she just hadn't bothered to listen. She needed her mother.

"And your mum needs you," Esme said.

Mckenna nodded, unquestioning. "What happened to her? The witch, Elizabeth."

"She was burned at the stake in 1576."

Mckenna didn't sleep that night. She thought of what it all meant: being the bridge between realms, how being a Wise One tied into it all, where Maeve was now, what the Scottish Scrolls said. There was still so much she didn't understand, so much she needed to know.

She swung her legs off the mattress and walked over to the kitchen for a drink of water.

Meoooooooow.

Mckenna looked down to find Caireen kneading her foot. "Hey, Caireen." She kneeled to greet her, but Caireen darted for the living room and onto the coffee table.

"Whatcha doing there?" Caireen stared back and meowed again, imploring Mckenna to follow. When she reached her, Caireen leapt down and pawed at the table's bottom drawer.

"Pretty determined, huh," Mckenna whispered, then pulled the drawer open.

Strewn inside were a stack of old mystery novels, bookmarks, and a handful of family photographs. Mckenna recognized a young Seán straight away, his hair longer and wavier than she'd ever seen it. Beside him was a woman with a heart-shaped face and red hair, wild like Mckenna's. Her eyes, also familiar, were earnest and kind, but burdened. In her arms, she held a baby Mckenna, round-faced, puffy-cheeked, and fists raised like she was prepared for a round. In the background, Mckenna recognized the paisley wallpaper from the very room she'd been sleeping in.

This was their home. Mckenna fell back onto the couch, tears stinging her eyes. Caireen jumped up and nuzzled at her thigh.

"I need Nissa." She thought she'd been doing Nissa a favour keeping her away from all of this, but their time apart had left a crater in her chest. Esme was a wonderful teacher, but Nissa had been her one true friend.

Mckenna took Caireen's meow to mean, "Yes, you do." Grateful, Mckenna gave Caireen a tight squeeze, praying that Nissa was still in the Isle of Man.

XV

THE VAST IN-BETWEEN

PORT SODERICK, ISLE OF MAN
TWO WEEKS EARLIER—OCTOBER 18, 1991

Nissa was being followed.

When her ferry docked that morning at Port Soderick, she had the strangest feeling: Someone would be expecting her.

It was stupid, of course, and highly unlikely. Her mind must've dreamed it up because, Heaven knew, she was in way over her head, and she no longer had Mckenna to take charge. How did Mckenna always know what to do? She made it all look so effortless.

"Excuse me, sir! How do I get out of here?" Nissa asked one of the dock workers.

"Where you looking to be, girl?" the man said, his accent a cross between Irish and British.

"I'm not really sure. I'm looking for an orphanage, but I don't know which. Is there maybe a town nearby?" If records of her existed, she would finally discover whether the notorious Feblands she learned about, nicknamed the *Free Felons,* were in fact her parents.

"I don't know about no orphanages, girl, but the port's got shuttles going to Douglas, the capital. You'll find loads more there." This sounded like a sensible enough plan, not that she had another to go on. She glanced at the gloomy, grey overcast sky looming above her head, and that about decided it for her; she was in no mood to wander around aimlessly in the rain.

A loud cough behind her made Nissa jump. She breathed a sigh of relief when she spotted a kind-faced old lady, smiling apologetically. Offering a polite smile in return, she continued towards the shuttle.

Within ten minutes, the sky released a furious downpour, and she was let off in Douglas, where she scrambled to the nearest café for shelter. It was then that Nissa knew her instincts had been right.

She *was* being followed.

The old lady from the docks was loitering behind her, drenched from head to toe, and waving keenly in her face. Funny, had she been on the shuttle all this time?

Nissa waved back and drew nearer, thinking it impolite to ignore her, when the lady lifted a thick, wrinkly index finger and pressed it against Nissa's mouth. Too stunned to react, she merely stood there, letting the strange woman silence her like a schoolgirl.

And then the situation grew even more perplexing. Without a word, the old lady trotted out the door, pressed her face into the front window, and beckoned Nissa over. She obliged, seeing the rain had now turned into a drizzle. There was no harm in indulging an old lady; she was probably just lacking a bit of company—or her marbles.

"Hello, ma'am," Nissa said cheerfully outside the café. "I'm Nissa."

The lady nodded, then began walking ahead of her. Perhaps she was mute, Nissa thought. Bewildered, she called after her.

"Excuse me! Was there, um, something you needed from me?" The lady looked over her shoulder to throw Nissa a brief glance and once again, gestured for her to follow. Odd, she thought, but she couldn't very well leave a helpless, elderly woman to wander off on her own.

The next thing Nissa knew, she was walking for twenty minutes down a country road, trailing behind the lady like a duckling.

"Where exactly are we—?" Nissa cut herself off as she lay her eyes on what she always imagined would be her dream home. They stopped in front of a modest little cottage that looked to be a couple of centuries old, with warm red brick, copper shingles, and rustic wood shutters, which were always featured in her favourite storybooks. It was perched in the centre of a green expanse, probably larger than the soccer field in Abredonia Woods.

"Is this your home?"

The lady nodded as she stepped onto the thick lawn, then turned around to wave Nissa over.

I'm in way too deep now, Nissa thought, entering through the wood-panelled gate and into her backyard. What she walked into was something out of a faery tale: Cottony rabbits hopped around a vegetable patch, nibbling away greedily at carrots and lettuce leaves; a flock of chickens strutted about, pecking at nothing in particular; and a handful of tabby cats roamed around like guard dogs, one of which had its nose in a stream that flowed along the edge of the yard and into the woods that bordered the land.

And just when she deemed it all too perfect, sharp rays of sunlight beamed through the dark clouds, hitting her cheeks. She felt as though she was in a trance as she walked leisurely around the grounds, greeting the animals and smelling the various plants, until a hard tap on her shoulder snapped her out of it; for a second, she had forgotten she wasn't alone. The old lady was standing behind her, pointing at two steaming cups of tea on a round, cast-iron bistro table near a sunflower patch. When had she gone inside to make tea? Apparently having no choice in the matter, Nissa sat down.

"The tea will warm you up, pet."

Nissa spat out her tea. "You can talk!"

"'Course I can talk. I've still got my tongue, haven't I?"

"But why didn't you say a word this whole time?"

"There are ears everywhere," she said gravely. "And so that you didn't ask too many questions."

Nissa's expression was blank. "I just walked a mile in the rain to sit here and have tea with a stranger."

"Oh, I'm no stranger, pet. My name's Arethusa. I'm your grandmother."

Belfast, Northern Ireland

It was 3:00 a.m., and Cillian was drenched in sweat. Back in his guestroom at Ms. Beattie's, he was awoken, yet again, by the High Priestess's transparent silhouette.

"What do you mean, she's gone and LEFT?" the High Priestess's astral form bellowed, making Cillian flinch. The last thing he wanted was to tell the High Priestess he'd failed her. While he still believed in the Priestess's larger plan, he didn't want Mckenna to have to carry it out under protest. With some more time, he could sway her.

"She's gone to Ballycastle."

"I'd gathered that. Am I to thank you for your astuteness?" she said through gritted teeth. "Why aren't you *with* her? You told her you'd *bring her there*, did you not?"

"Of course, but she and her friend got into some sort of quarrel. The inn owner said they'd both left in a hurry, separately." Cillian didn't dare admit he prompted their fight. He knew Mckenna wouldn't see reason with her friend around—she made her much too soft. But he hadn't anticipated *this*.

"You do realize you can't cross the border now, not without the Wise One with you! That plan's gone to shite, thanks to you."

"What do you mean, we can't cross?"

"When you said the last time that she thinks her mother's in Ballycastle, I tried astral travelling there. It's impossible. Which means Abby has it protected. Going in by the Wise One's side would have been the only way to enter."

"But that kind of magic is . . . advanced. How is that possible?"

Her expression was envious. "It just is."

"Perhaps I can enter, High Priestess. I see the darkness inside her. And she fancies me, so—"

"Congratulations, you've got yourself a girlfriend. Did you think that'd grant you special entry? Meanwhile, she's sipping tea with her new mum, chatting about the Scottish Scrolls." Her astral face inched closer to his, and his body went rigid. "Was it too much to ask for you to *simply* guide her into fulfilling the first Scroll—"

"I have—"

"—and *remain* with her until she found our dear Abby? The rest, ah, the rest would have been child's play," she said, every word icier than the last. "Do you remember? DO YOU REMEMBER HOW IT WAS ALL SUPPOSED TO GO?" And then her face transformed into Mckenna's, pouting like a misbegotten child. Cillian rubbed his eyes, knowing what he was seeing wasn't real. Of the Priestess's many talents, it was her ability to hypnotize that frightened him most.

"I can get her back. I can get her to see what we see. I'm nearly there, let me—"

"I will let you do *nothing* else. You're a disappointment, Hayes," she spat. "We're done here. With any luck, my stone will find her the second she steps out of that town. And when she does, it's my way from here on."

"Please, if you let me, this *will* work—"

But she was already gone.

Nissa leaned back, mouth agape. "You're my grandmother?"

"I've startled you, haven't I? 'Course I have . . ."

"No, no . . . I mean, well, I'm surprised, yeah . . ." Question after question hit Nissa like a heap of falling snow, and she lay buried beneath, unmoving.

"You have questions, surely."

"My parents," were the only words she managed.

Eyes filled with sorrow, Arethusa began her story: "My daughter, Annie, met Simon at a young age. He was visiting from England, and she worked at a shop down the road. Oh, and what a beauty Annie was, like yourself. You're the spitting image."

Nissa didn't know how to react to this, so she listened on.

"Simon went in there every day, doing everything to get her attention. 'Course, it didn't take very long. He was . . . experienced. And she was, well . . . Annie. Lovely and full of heart, but as naïve as a child sitting by the chimney on Christmas Eve.

"But Simon, he was a rotten influence. Poisonous from the start, he was. They grew inseparable fast. I begged Annie to leave him, but poor, clueless girl that she was, she fell hopelessly in love. Did I mention she was young? Just sixteen at the time. Before I know it, she's moving to England with him. She'd write to me, yes, but when I started asking too many questions, she stopped. I found out Simon was involved in very *bad* business . . . drugs, I'm afraid," Arethusa added, seeing Nissa's eyes widen. "Not a year down the line, the two were wanted for drug-trafficking."

Exactly what the librarian had told her. "Annie, too?"

"Only 'cause she wouldn't leave his side. Still, she'd gotten into bad ways. They'd come back to the Isle every so often 'to see you, Mum!', Annie would say, but I knew the real reason; he had bank accounts here. See, the Isle of Man's a self-governing nation, so for Simon, a foreigner living outside of the law, this was a tax haven. I imagine this is what brought him here in the first place."

Nissa cringed, wondering if this would get any worse. It all sounded unreal, like an Al Pacino film.

"But something happened when they had you," Arethusa went on. "They started running into . . . hurdles. Things would go wrong left, right, and centre; and Annie, she started opening up to me. It turned out some of Simon's men were betraying him. He was losing loads of money, and one of them, he discovered, was working with the police. Things got so bad, Simon came to believe you were a changeling. Very superstitious man," she said, shaking her head.

From the sounds of it, this couldn't be good. "What's a changeling?"

"Oh, dear, you *are* American, aren't you? A changeling is a baby whose human soul's been swapped for a faery's."

Nissa laughed, but her grandmother showed little humour. "Wait, are you kidding?"

"No, ducky. You're not a changeling, of course, but it's not so far-fetched to assume." Before Nissa could ask what she meant by this, Arethusa continued. "I'm afraid this next bit won't be easy to hear." She placed her hand over Nissa's. "Simon, he grew angrier and, well, he became violent. Your mum—oh, she loved you so, you must know that—she wanted to protect you; she kept you here with me, but Simon's luck still hadn't changed. So, the truth is, he . . . he . . ."

"He wanted me gone."

"Annie and I were afraid of what he might do. We arranged to have us on the next ship to America."

"Us?" And then it hit her. *Arethusa Febland*. How could she not have realized it sooner? She was the foreign family member listed on the passenger list.

"Simon wouldn't let your mum out of his sight, so I snuck you away and brought you to Boston myself. I had a cousin there, and she was thrilled to take you in. But not a year after you arrived, I found out she'd died in a car accident."

Was Nissa just a walking bad luck charm? "That's how I ended up in foster care? Couldn't you have come back for me?"

Tears stung Arethusa's eyes. "I wanted nothing more, pet. The plan was always to return to the Isle to save your mum from Simon, and then we would come find you again, together. But when I returned home, Simon was here, waiting for me. He told me Annie was gone," she said, her voice shaking, "and demanded I tell him your whereabouts. Said one way or another, he'd find you, and he'd always keep an eye on me. So I couldn't risk coming and putting you in danger, you see."

Nissa swallowed the lump that had formed in her throat. "Did he—he didn't *kill* her . . .?"

Arethusa exhaled, squeezing her hand tighter.

The first tear fell, and the rest flowed like a river breaking through a dam. The walls she'd built over the years crumbled, and she was left there, in hollow skin and bones, her every fear realized. She was parentless, and her own flesh and blood a murderer.

Arethusa came around and held her granddaughter's head to her chest. Nissa didn't know how long she'd sat there, hysterical, until the dryness in her throat drove her into a fit of coughs.

"Drink up, pet. Tea soothes the soul."

Nissa let out a stifled laugh through her cries and finished off her cuppa, which was now lukewarm.

"When you found Simon here, what happened?"

"Oh, you wouldn't believe it. I was saved by three enormous dogs . . ."

A typhoon of emotions, Nissa let out another laugh. "How?"

"It's thanks to an insufferable neighbour of mine, Peter. Annoying bloke, him and his bloody dogs always stomping on my petunias . . . Well, I've since bit my tongue because his three huskies saved my life. Simon was on my porch, see, and those dogs—never minding their own business—sensed I was in trouble. Came dashing up my porch and straight for Simon's groin! He almost didn't make it out alive, I tell you. I never saw him again."

So, her mother was dead and her murderous father on the loose.

"There's something I don't understand."

"What's that, ducky?"

"Why didn't the foster system have my last name? The ship records did, I found it on the passenger list."

"Your mum did register you as 'Nissa Febland', hoping you'd

find us some day. But when I found out my cousin passed and you'd be in the foster system, I begged them to remove your surname. I couldn't risk Simon tracking you down. Oh, but I'm ever so glad you did find me," she said, stroking her cheek, "and I suspected you would."

"How?"

Arethusa leaned in, like she had a secret, and spun Nissa's bracelet around her wrist.

"It was you?"

Arethusa winked, tears streaming down her made-up cheeks.

It was like a sunbeam hit Nissa's chest. She fingered her bracelet, amazed at how far it had brought her. "And today, at the docks? How'd you know I'd come?"

Leaning in closer, Arethusa whispered, "Let me show you."

That afternoon, after a much-needed hearty lunch (smoked salmon and capers, fresh-baked bread, traditional Manx broth—a mix of beef celery, leek, and turnip—and more tea), Nissa was being led blindly, yet again, down a quiet country road.

"Almost there, pet."

"Where're we going?"

"Kewaigue Hill."

It didn't look like much. There was nothing but a farmstead and an old primary school in sight. "Is it, like, a famous hill? Where's the hill?"

"This way," Arethusa said brightly, steering Nissa towards a footpath beside the farmstead. Some untamed bushes came into view, and soon they'd entered a woodland crammed with tall, slim trees. They walked in silence for some time, listening to the sounds of the birds singing, leaves rustling underfoot, and the flow of water in the distance. When they reached a footbridge over a small, shallow river, Arethusa bypassed it, instead turning down an unseen trail alongside the water.

"Look ahead, ducky."

Through the trees was a site that quickly rendered Nissa in a state of calm. A very old-looking bridge stood between the surrounding trees and fallen branches, somewhat camouflaged by the vines that clung to its stone walls, as though nature was helping to keep its secret. Beneath it, a stream flowed through the rocks, bright autumn leaves drifting in its shallows.

"This is the ancient faery bridge. Not many know of it—only those who've already been here."

"More faery stuff?" Nissa blurted.

"Shhh, you don't want to offend them!"

Nissa wrinkled her brow. "Offend . . . the faeries?" She held back a chuckle, seeing that her grandmother didn't look to be kidding.

"Oh, faeries are very much real, pet. I can assure you of that."

"Have you seen them?"

"I don't have to. They show their presence in all sorts of ways. Through blessings, gifts, signs . . ."

"What kind of signs?"

Arethusa trod towards the arch of the bridge, where about a dozen stones lay on the ground, and smiled down at them. Nissa stepped closer: Each stone had a message written on it in thick, black ink:

> *Thank you for the great weather!*
>
> *Thank you for helping my family through this tough time.*
>
> *Please help Mom feel better.*
>
> *Please give my son strength.*

"Some of these are wishes," Nissa said.

"Go on . . ." Arethusa said, and pointed down at the rest. Nissa read every stone, her heart warming with each message.

Please help Nissa find her way home.

"I've been coming here every day since my return from Boston, leaving offerings to the fae folk. When I got here early this morning, I found this resting on my stone." She held up a long feather, a striking blend of yellow, orange, and indigo. "Feathers are messages from the divine, see? And this one, well, I'd never seen one so beautiful. Naturally, when I saw it . . ."

Nissa was lost for words. She reached out and squeezed her grandmother's hand and allowed the tears to fall, touched beyond measure that someone in this world had loved her all this time.

Port Soderick, Isle of Man
Present Day—October 30, 1991

The moment she stepped off the ferry and onto the Isle of Man, Mckenna felt a surge of energy enter the base of her feet and shoot upwards, as though magic lurked beneath the earth.

Perhaps it did. Esme's words rang in her ear: *Your intuition is stronger than you ken. You must always follow it.*

If the past two weeks under Esme's wing had taught her anything, it was that grounding was the only way to 'listen inward', as Esme would say. And so there, in the middle of the port, never minding the curious onlookers, she closed her eyes and inhaled, then let out a long, slow breath. Centring first, she released any tension trapped within her chakras, and grounded, picturing roots sprouting from the soles of her feet and into the pavement. The chatter around her dissolved, and she zeroed in on the noises of nature around her: the boats swaying in the harbour, the wind whistling high notes.

"Lead me to Nissa," she mouthed to the ether.

A buzzing sounded in her ear, followed by a hard tugging at her chest. Her toes tingled, then her feet, and her legs and onwards, as though every one of her limbs was falling asleep.

Was she . . . vibrating?

The tugging grew stronger. Instinctively, she resisted, putting as much weight on her feet as she could, but if she fought it any longer, she was afraid she'd rip in two. She loosened her muscles and let herself go.

POP.

She was lighter than a feather, floating upwards, her unconscious body lying beside the docks hundreds of feet below her.

Whoa.

Two dock workers ran to her aid. She squinted, trying to make out the scene, but it was drifting away as she soared higher . . . and higher . . . and higher still. She was a goddess, rising above land and water, omniscient; and there, the Isle of Man rested in the heart of the Irish Sea, an equal distance away from England, Ireland, Scotland, and Wales. It was literally one vast in-between . . .

This is like one huge faery doorway.

Another *POP.*

She was hovering above a woodsy area, not far from a farmhouse. Down the road below, a sign read: *Kewaigue Hill.*

Nissa felt at peace on the Isle of Man, and she was quite taken with the faery bridge. She and Arethusa walked over to the site every day to pay the fae a visit, leave out honey, chocolate, and silver coins ("They *adore* shiny objects!"), and pick up any trash left behind, something Nissa learned they most appreciated.

She also learned that faeries were sort of like angels, but for the earth. They tended to nature, and therefore were known in some cultures as nature spirits. Arethusa went on to explain the inner workings of devas, who smoothed weather conditions, and of nymphs, who oversaw the water and the woods.

"Leprechauns are faeries, too."

"No way! Aren't they known for being tricksters?"

"As are all faeries. They find it amusing to play wee pranks—you know, hide objects, spoil the milk, that sort of harmless thing. But if you *really* anger a faery, it won't be such a *wee* punishment."

Nissa's mind jumped to the tale of the old man who ended up

paralyzed after kicking a faery hill. "It sounds like they just want to be treated with respect. I see nothing wrong with that!"

"I quite agree, ducky."

There was a rustling sound behind them. "Same here," uttered a familiar voice, one Nissa had wished for weeks to hear again. Mckenna stood at the foot of the stream, her eyes hopeful, apologetic. Nissa ran over and threw her arms around her.

Mckenna returned her embrace. "I'm so sorry, Nissa. I didn't mean a thing—"

"No, don't! *I'm* sorry, Kenna. I just left you there. It was a crappy thing to do."

"Yeah, it was pretty crappy."

"*So* crappy."

"Lying to you was worse, though," Mckenna said solemnly. "But I'm ready to tell you everything."

"Like how you managed to find me here . . .?"

Mckenna laughed. "That, too."

Nissa's grin spread from ear to ear. "I'd like to think I had something to do with it, though."

"What d'you mean?"

Nissa glanced over at the wishing stones under the bridge, then at Arethusa. "I'll explain later."

Arethusa winked. Feeling giddy, Nissa linked her arms with Mckenna's, then with her grandmother's. "I'd like you to meet my best friend, Mckenna. Kenna, this is Arethusa—my grandmother."

Mckenna looked both stunned and elated. "It's an honour to meet you, Arethusa."

"How do you do, Mckenna. What an interesting name. Scottish, is it?"

"I'm actually not sure."

"And the honour's mine, my dear. Nissa's talked my ear off about you. She thinks highly of you, this one does. A very wise person, indeed."

Nissa noticed Mckenna flinch. "Should we head back for some tea?"

Arethusa clapped her hands together. "Excellent idea!"

As Mckenna led the way out, Arethusa placed a hand on Nissa's shoulder and leaned into her ear. "I daresay she needs you as much as you need her, ducky."

XVI

The Power of Samhain

Abredonia Woods, Massachusetts

Andre slammed the phone down on Seán and kicked the kitchen chair. Seán had been with Abby all this time—the woman who deserted her family through a vague explanation on a piece of paper.

Seán said he and Abby had a strong feeling Mckenna was in Ballycastle and that they would find her together "when the time was right." What did that even mean? *Immediately,* that was when the time was right. And this woman had no business *feeling* anything about *their* daughter.

"Abby says it's the safest place she could be," Seán had said, trying to reassure Andre.

"Right, if that's what Abby says," Andre scoffed. "Why are you letting her influence you?"

"Come off it, Andre, I'm not *letting* her do anything. She knows what she's talking about. You can't understand."

"Whose fault is that?" And that was when he had hung up.

Something wasn't right. She just happened to show up when Seán happened to be visiting the very spot they'd met seventeen years ago?

Andre was tired of waiting around. Seán was either being tricked or being drawn back into Abby's world; Andre had seen the way Seán spoke about her before he left. He'd never gotten over his grief, his heartbreak. He was still in love with her.

It was time Andre fought for him.

Cillian sat cross-legged on a sandy beach, staring out at the water drifting across the bay and playing last night's dream over in his mind. Mckenna had appeared to him so vividly, her hair wilder than ever and eyes piercing his own the way they so often did. But he couldn't make out what she way saying.

In a desperate attempt to locate her, Cillian had been practicing astral projection every day since she left Ms. Beattie's. He hadn't been successful the first several tries, but it must have been due to Abby's protection enchantment cast over Ballycastle. That, and the fact that he still couldn't astral project. His attempts failed each time, and he was about ready to give up all hope. The Priestess was right—he was a disappointment. As a high-level practitioner, he should have been able to master astral projection by now. He would never be able to warn Mckenna, to keep her from the High Priestess's grasp.

To be with her again.

Fear and self-loathing permeated his bones. The very thought of Mckenna being tortured into carrying out the High Priestess's plan made his chest rip to pieces. And to think just a month ago, Cillian's one desire had been to gain the Priestess's trust, to be the one to help the Wise One meet her fate.

Now, he cared little about the Priestess. In the end, they might have the same goal, but he could achieve the same outcome another way—one that allowed him and Mckenna to be together. He remembered how appalled he was, at first, when the Priestess disclosed the old witch's prophecy, that peace came at a cost: *billions of souls shall expire upon this Earth.* He was not a murderer, he'd said. "It's not a killing spree," the High Priestess had replied. "We are merely halting the reincarnation of souls—souls that should remain in the spiritual realm, that no longer have a physical place here on Earth." And in time, he understood: The Scrolls incited a righteous path, not an evil one.

Mckenna would understand that, too. She would come to believe in the new Earth, just as he had.

A thought occurred to him. What if she wasn't in Ballycastle anymore? There was a small possibility her mother wasn't there at all. What if he didn't focus on getting to Ballycastle and instead focused solely on *her?* In all his years as a mystic practitioner, he had only ever tried astral projecting to a location, but never to a person. It was a long shot, but he had to try. He knew the High Priestess would stop at nothing until she got her way. He'd been suspecting all this time that that thing she was working on had to do with lifting Abby's protection spell. And to be able to break a bond that strong, she would have to do it on the most magical night of the year—Samhain.

It was now or never.

It was this fervent desire that triggered what happened next: A loud buzzing noise sounded in his ear, and his body began to vibrate like it was mildly in shock. Then something popped, and he began to soar, leaving behind his dormant body.

In this new state of consciousness, limitations were a mere myth, and time was but a concept; with the power of intention, he could bend it. He suddenly found himself in a wooded area, floating above a stone bridge. He could feel Mckenna was here, wherever this place was, and that Nissa was with her. The magic here was strong and ancient, like faery magic. This was an in-between place.

The largest one there was.

DOUGLAS, ISLE OF MAN

She didn't know whether it was because she and Nissa had reconciled or if it was due to the three-course meal Arethusa whipped up the night before, but Mckenna awoke on Halloween morning bursting with energy.

"I slept like a log," Mckenna said, scooping up a mouthful of treacle tart, leftover dessert from last night's feast.

"A snoring log," Nissa said with a yawn.

Arethusa came around to fill their coffee mugs. "Happy to hear you got some rest—heard you girls chit-chatting 'til late last night."

Mckenna looked across at Nissa with mock guilt. She'd told her everything ("Took you long enough!"), from the incidents on her birthday, to Petronella's vendetta against Alice Kyteler, to being a Wise One tied to a terrifying prophecy. Nissa had been attentive to every word: "Where do you think Abby is, then?" Nissa asked.

"I don't know, maybe Scotland. I thought I'd try that thing I did to find you. But first, I was thinking we should go back to Belfast; last night, I dreamt of Cillian . . ."

Nissa sat up, propping her pillow behind her back. "Was it hot?"

Mckenna slapped her on the arm. "He was telling me to come back. He said it was important that he see me again."

"Do you know if it's a real message?"

"I don't know. I was thinking of the book you borrowed in Kilkenny. Remember the Wise One's ability to dreamwalk?"

"Oh, *right!* Freaky . . . of all books. I mean, it's fiction, but maybe some things are based on truth."

"I tried it."

"You tried to project yourself into someone else's dream?"

"Yeah, Cillian's—to talk to him somehow. I hate how things ended, you know? And there's something about him, it's like he can really see me."

"Mhm." Nissa winked.

Mckenna rolled her eyes. "*Anyway,* it didn't work. I don't even know if dreamwalking is possible."

"Kenna, did you think maybe you only dreamt that because you *want* him to want you to come back?"

Mckenna's face flushed.

That night, the girls stood out on Arethusa's porch, packed and ready to catch the ferry back to Belfast.

"Be good—both of you. And pick up a phone and call once in a while," Arethusa warned, squeezing them in a tight hug. "Look out for each other, whatever you do. I mean it, duckies."

"We promise, Gran," Nissa said. "And don't worry, we'll come visit!"

Arethusa beamed. "Mckenna, a word?" She placed her hands on Mckenna's shoulders and steered her out of earshot. Mckenna waited for the "keep my granddaughter safe" speech, but instead, Arethusa placed a smooth black stone inside her palm. "Black onyx. It absorbs negativity and helps the bearer resist negative influences. Think of it as a shield of sorts."

Mckenna found it strange but thanked her nonetheless. She couldn't shake the feeling that Arethusa knew more than she let on.

They waved at Nissa's grandmother from the road, and just as they began making their way to the town centre, Mckenna stopped in her tracks.

"You okay, Kenna?"

"Yeah, I just feel . . ." she started to say, but she couldn't put it into words. From the moment the wind stirred that morning, she had felt a mysticism drift through the air. "Is it okay if we make one last stop at the faery bridge? I'd like to say good-bye."

What Mckenna thought would be a peaceful walk down to Kewaigue Hill turned out to be the exact opposite. Dark shadows appeared out of the corner of her eyes, some at their heels, some gliding alongside them, and others appearing close enough to brush her cheekbones.

No doubt spirits that roamed the Isle, she thought. She could feel they were drawn to her, vying for her attention.

Shit. Not now.

"Do you think Halloween has something to do with it?"

Mckenna shrugged, then flinched at the sight of the shadow of a brawny man. "Can we just, like, quicken the pace?"

They half-walked, half-ran up the footpath and into the woods. At the sound of the water trickling from the stream, Mckenna's footsteps slowed, and she allowed herself to listen to its calming sounds. The spirits, whoever they were, seemed farther away now, like she had pushed them back somehow.

There was a rustling up ahead. They turned the corner and the bridge came into view, along with a visitor.

At the sight of Cillian sitting by the water's edge, Mckenna's stomach became the stage for a trapeze show again. "How did you . . .?"

Eyes growing wide at the sight of her, he jumped to his feet, took three long strides towards her, and grasped her hands in his. "You have to come with me, lass."

Mckenna swallowed, the touch of his skin shooting fire up her arms and down her body. "Where? What's going on, Cillian?"

"There's someone after you. And if you don't come with me now—"

"Whoa, whoa, Casanova, relax," Nissa said, stepping beside Mckenna. "Where she goes, I go. And whatever you mean to say, spill it."

Cillian turned to Nissa. "It's too dangerous for you."

"Nissa's not leaving," Mckenna said, pulling her hands back.

Cillian ran a hand through his hair. "Fine. Then you both have to leave with me right now."

"Where?"

Cillian sighed. "Ballycastle." *Did he know . . .?* "I'll tell you everything on the way, promise." When Mckenna hesitated, he said, "You see I'm telling the truth, don't you?" He took her hands again and lifted them to his heart, which was beating like a base drum.

She could. But Mckenna could also feel all sorts of other things—anxiety, fear, affection, guilt. "You've been lying to me."

Cillian bit his lip. "I have. I'm not now." His eyes were filled with pain as he gazed at her, unblinking.

Nissa looked from him to Mckenna. "Hang on. Kenna, maybe we should . . . deliberate?"

Mckenna turned to her friend, muttered, "It's okay," and then looked back at Cillian. "You'll tell me everything?"

He nodded, his hands still covering hers.

Wiltshire, England

"Come on, for old time's sake," Abby urged Seán over dinner. It was the evening of Samhain, the harvest's end and beginning of a new year. A time to honour their ancestors and leave offerings for the dead.

There was a magic around this time that had always pulled him in. Back in the day, he even participated in one of Abby's ritual ceremonies. But he felt it best not to get entangled with all of that again.

They'd been spending quite a bit of time together, meeting up every other day—Abby supposedly had 'business to attend to', but as always, she kept her explanations short. In the meantime, Seán hung back at the café and worked on his illustrations. The publisher would expect them soon, and he had fallen far behind.

"Would you watch, then?" she pleaded.

He looked into her persuasive eyes, which for an instant, he could've sworn flickered to a deep blue, like sapphire.

"Well . . . will you?"

He gazed down at his mushy peas, admiring the volcano he had shaped, then out the window. The town was growing still; children had already finished trick-or-treating, and the moon was at its brightest, a signal of the night's end.

"Fine. For old time's sake."

Looking as pleased as she did the day they met, Abby excused herself to freshen up.

Mckenna and Nissa followed Cillian back up the path.

"Wait, Cillian," Mckenna called after him. "Stop!"

Cillian turned, looking impatient.

"Why Ballycastle?"

"There's no time—"

"Tell us, Cillian, or we're not coming," Nissa said firmly.

Heaving a heavy sigh, he closed his eyes for a moment. He looked like he hadn't slept in days. "I think you need to go back there."

"Why?"

"It's the only place where you're protected. And I think it's the key to sensing where your mum is."

"How did you—?"

"I know who you are, Mckenna," Cillian said. "I've always known."

It was like she was falling from a hundred-storey building. Of course he did. Mckenna felt like a massive imbecile. What were the chances a perfect stranger would be there to chauffeur them around Ireland, offer them places to stay? "Who are you?" was all she could muster.

"I'm a mystic practitioner." Instantly, Mckenna felt faint. How could she not have sensed it? Could she have been so blinded by her attraction to him? "I've gotten good at hiding it," he added, looking both proud and ashamed. "I was sent to protect you on your quest to find your mother. It's important that you do, and you're the only one who can. There's someone after you; it's because of an old prediction . . ."

Elizabeth Dunlop's prophecy. He knew about that, too. Her mind froze and vision doubled, and her body went still, fighting hard to process the words that left Cillian's lips: *Prediction.*

Mystic. Scrolls. Finding her breath, she uttered, "Do you know what the Scrolls say?"

"Afraid not," Cillian said quickly. "Listen, there's a High Priestess who wants to use you to lead her to Abby. She needs both your powers to succeed. But when she's done with you . . ."

Maeve. "She'll kill us," Mckenna finished.

Nissa's hand flew to her mouth. Mckenna had known she was in some kind of danger, but not that her life was at stake. Nissa cleared her throat. "So . . . the, um, High Priestess can't find Abby without Kenna?"

"That's right. When Abby left you as a baby, she cast an enchantment on both of you—that you'd be the only one to find her when you came of age; that's seventeen for a Wise One. But the Priestess is performing a ritual *right now* to lift that enchantment *and* the one protecting Ballycastle."

"So that she can find us both no matter what." It was all starting to make sense.

"Exactly. She uses this ancient stone to dowse—dowsing is like searching for an answer or location using a pendulum," he added. "That's how she's known where you've been all this time."

"Why didn't she just find me and kill me then?"

"She needs both your powers, Kenna," Nissa said gently.

"Right, and if her ritual works tonight, there will be nothing stopping the stone from tracing Abby anymore. But if you find Abby first, you can warn her."

Mckenna let out a bitter laugh. "Impossible. How the hell am I supposed to warn her—?"

"Through astral travel," he said, his eyes desperate, pleading. That was how she'd found Nissa. She stared into them, sensing their sheer urgency.

"And the ritual—why tonight?"

"A complex ritual like this one needs all the power it can get. Tonight is Samhain, where the veil between the living and the dead is thinnest. The spirits, the ancestors she'll be able to invoke . . ." He trailed off, his expression grim.

Nissa gave her a light slap on the arm. "That must be why

you're seeing ghosts! Because of Halloween—uh, Samhain."

Mckenna felt like she was having another one of her nightmares. "How do you know all this? Who sent you to 'protect me'?" she said, using elaborate air quotes.

Cillian hesitated. "I'm sorry. I can't give them away."

Surely, it couldn't be her mother. "Esme?"

He cast her a remorseful glance, implying he couldn't say. Mckenna tried to read him, but all she could feel were her own emotions—of pain, betrayal, confusion. This was too much for her to bear. The feelings she had for him, the feelings she thought he had for her, had it all been merely based on his duty to protect her?

It was Nissa who broke the silence. "Um, so, how would going back to Ballycastle help Kenna sense Abby?"

"I believe she needs to be in a place she's connected to. One that's sacred to her." He stepped closer. "That's where your mum had you, and that's where she knew you'd one day come back to. We have to hurry, though . . ."

Mckenna seized his arm. "Wait. I know of a pretty magical place." Her eyes darted around the trees that loomed over them. "Right here. And I think I know how to find her." Spinning on the spot, she made for the faery bridge, Nissa and Cillian at her heels. Wind whipped her hair as she tore through the trees, imagining her mother's proud face when they set eyes on each other, and praying the High Priestess hadn't yet begun her ritual—

The shadow of the brawny man appeared again out of thin air, making Mckenna stumble backwards onto the path. His energy was heavy, dark. Frozen, she peered into its spectral eyes, black as the earth beneath her feet. *I'm not afraid of you,* she thought, keeping her head level with his. *I'm not afraid of you . . . I'm not afraid of you . . .*

A gravelly inner voice spat back, one that was not her own: *You should be.*

Gulping hard, adrenaline surged through her, her insides flooding with what felt like boiling water, and her eyes wide with fright; her heart was the spout of a kettle, about to burst and sizzle over. She was sweating, too. Was this what a panic attack felt like? Her knees buckling, she reached out to grab what was nearest, but her hand only snatched up air. *Uh-oh,* she thought stupidly, feeling nausea flowing up from her sacral chakra and straight for her head, and the trees blurring through her watery eyes.

Please don't faint. It'll be too late . . . the . . . the Priestess. As the world around her faded, her entire body began pulsing, then vibrating.

POP.

She was standing in some sort of back alley, the clattering of plates and cutlery sounding through the metal doors. Casting down was the glow of the moon, ominous in the dark passage. If it weren't for the graffitied walls that flanked her, she could've sworn she was back in that creepy alleyway in Kilkenny, where Petronella had flogged her until she practically passed out. No, this place was different. Where was she?

One of the metal doors swung open, and stepping out was one of the most stunning women Mckenna had ever seen. She was slender and leggy, with white-blond hair that poured down her back; she had pointed features, smooth and alabaster, like she'd been carved from clay; and her eyes were a deep, penetrating blue.

"You've learned to astral travel, I see. Such a quick learner. Beautiful form . . ." She took several paces towards her, admiring Mckenna's spectral silhouette.

"You're Maeve." From the moment their eyes locked, she knew; she held herself like no other: frightening but bewitching, graceful but commanding, imposing but transcendental. The woman was a walking paradox.

"It's a pleasure to finally meet you, Wise One."

"Where am I? How did you know I was here?"

"I sensed your apparition. What does it matter where we are? Your soul's found me, and for a reason, I'm sure." She waited, her lips forming a slight smile that didn't quite reach her perfect cheekbones.

"I'm here to tell you to stop. Just stop whatever you're doing!

Even if you manage to counter Abby's spell, you'll never get us to do what you want. You can screw your Scrolls."

"Hmm," Maeve began, feigning an innocence that didn't suit her. "I don't have to get you to do anything—you'll do that all on your own."

Mckenna's gut twisted. "What are you talking about?"

Her plump lips lifted into a full smile. "You were Elizabeth Dunlop. Don't you remember, Bessie?"

The name Bessie crashed in her ears like a gong. "You're lying," she spat. And yet she recognized the nickname as she did a childhood friend.

Maeve was scrutinizing her. "And those humans, how cruelly they treated you. An unforgivable punishment . . ."

Like a tidal wave, the image of an angry crowd and roaring firepit flooded her mind. The ropes straining her wrists. The shouting. The troll-like man. *"A quick snap of the neck, aye, Bessie girl?"* The flames catching her leather boots . . .

"My dear, it was you who had the prophetic vision, who wrote the Scottish Scrolls."

No. It couldn't be. "There's no way. I'm . . . I'm not evil!" she shouted, though was not the least bit convinced.

Her brow lowered slightly in concern. "Evil? I should think not. You, as Bessie, envisioned a utopia. Peace and harmony on Earth. The natural world thriving."

"At the cost of billions of lives!"

"Not lives, dear—souls. Oh, you've still so much to learn. I've forgotten how young you are. But I've faith in you; you'll soon ken that this is the only path. Tell me, which is the real evil: preserving the natural world, or allowing those who will cause its destruction to continue to have their place here on Earth?"

Before she could protest, she felt a tugging at her chest, like a yarn being pulled from a sweater, unravelling, loosening, until—

POP.

She was back in the woods, lying on the paved path and staring up at the concerned faces of Nissa and Cillian, the latter's warm hand cradling her neck.

"Kenna! Are you okay?"

"Are you hurt? You've hit your head—"

"I'm fine, I'm fine," she insisted, her voice hoarse. "There's no time. Help me get to the bridge . . ."

"What happened, lass?" Cillian asked as he lifted her to her feet.

She gulped. "A ghost came up in my face. I panicked and fainted, that's all."

Her head aching slightly from the fall, Mckenna sat cross legged at the edge of the stream. The mere act of touching the earth sent an outpouring of power through her body, like a current taking the path of least resistance. Only the leaves rustling, stones turning, and flow of water filled her ears. She felt for the small feather inside her coat pocket, the very one that flew into her bedroom window the night she left home. Raising it to her lips, she whispered to it her one wish, then tossed it into the running stream. She waited, hoping for some kind of vision to flash into her mind, like the one she'd had of Seán tucking Abby's note into his wallet. But nothing happened. "Lead me to my mother," she said aloud.

Still, nothing.

"It's not working. I can't do it."

Cillian dropped to the ground to face her. "You can. You're a Wise One, lass."

"I feel like I still don't understand what that really means."

"It means you've got centuries of magical abilities right inside of you. You've got it all, right here." He placed a hand to her heart. She wasn't sure why, but her eyes welled with tears.

Nissa rushed to her side. "You've got this, Kenna." She sat down, too, so the three formed a triangle. She took Mckenna's hand and nudged Cillian to take hers. He nodded and grasped it.

"Lead us to the Wise One's mother," Nissa said.

Cillian joined in. "Lead us to the Wise One's mother."

At last, Mckenna: "Lead us to the Wise One's mother. Lead us to the Wise One's mother."

The wind picked up, and steadily their voices grew stronger.

"Lead us to the Wise One's mother. Lead us to the Wise One's mother. LEAD US TO THE WISE ONE'S MOTHER."

Like flickering tea lights, hundreds of faeries appeared out of the air—specks of blue, yellow, green and white danced around the bridge, stream and trees, flooding the woods with light and radiance.

"Are those . . .?" Nissa whispered in awe.

Mckenna nodded, giving her hand a tight squeeze.

AVEBURY HENGE—WILTSHIRE, ENGLAND

When Seán and Abby reached the stone circle, he stopped just outside of it. "I'll watch from outside the stones."

"If you wish," she said, and stepped inside.

"Did you ask permission?" Seán grinned, remembering their first encounter.

"I always have permission." That wasn't the answer he expected. He meant to ask what she meant by this, but what happened next made words escape him altogether. Her eyes fixed on his, Abby undid her frock's buttons one by one.

Seán couldn't look away. He caught his breath as she lifted the garment over her head and tossed it aside, leaving a stone necklace as the only thing touching her silky skin. Oh, how she lit a fire in him still—one he couldn't seem to put out. Before he knew it, he had stepped past the stones and joined her in the centre of the circle. Then, piece by piece, he removed his clothing, too. She took his hands in hers and, together, they thanked nature for its gracious gifts, promising to continue giving back, from one living entity to another.

On the altar Abby created, a gust of wind blew out two candles, leaving just one to burn. In the dim light casting over her body, Seán found her lips. His mind didn't wander past the moment. He let himself fall at her mercy, their bodies greeting each other for the first time in seventeen years.

"Seán . . ."

"Yes?"

"Will you say something with me?"

"Yes."

"Briseadh an ceangal . . ."

"Briseadh an ceangal," he repeated in a daze.

"Eadar nighean is màthair."

" . . . eadar nighean is màthair."

The High Priestess looked down at Seán—the Wise One's flesh and blood and Abigail's one love. It was he who connected them, and so it was only he that could break their magical bond.

She waited for his body to give in, until all senses vanished and only his soul remained, overcome with ecstasy. Bridged with the divine.

"Briseadh an ceangal eadar nighean is màthair." They repeated the Scottish mantra for the final time.

Break the bond between daughter and mother.

Mckenna's body vibrated, until she felt the familiar *POP*. She was soaring through a dark tunnel, fast. *This isn't how it happened last time . . .*

Perhaps because now she was travelling much farther.

She landed in a valley, through which a narrow river rushed, and found herself standing in the shadows of a range of stony mountains; wisps of mist touched the green mountainside, dotted with sparkling pools of water. Had she entered a magical realm?

"Mckenna."

Slowly, she turned, hardly daring to believe who was staring back at her, looking pale, wild-haired, and beautiful. "Mom?"

Abby smiled a smile so warm, it could heat an entire island. "You found me." Her voice was velvety soft, and her accent resembled Esme's. It was everything she'd imagined it would be.

Mckenna reached out, but she couldn't touch her.

"You're not really here, you're astral projecting," Abby said sadly, but there was pride in her eyes.

"Where am I?"

"Isle of Skye. You must leave now and come to me. I'm in the village of Uig."

"Mom, there's so much I don't understand—"

"You are the bridge, Mckenna. The bridge between all of existence. But your destiny is not written. You *must* remember that."

She could feel herself being pulled away—her body was calling her back. "Mom—"

"I love you, swan."

"Mom!"

POP.

"MOM!" The woods echoed with Mckenna's cry. She was back on the ground with Nissa and Cillian, who was grasping her face in his hands.

He heaved a sigh of relief. "Thought we'd lost you."

"What happened, Kenna?"

The woods were dark again, but a brand-new light shone within. "I found her."

Epilogue

Mathis was too late. He surveyed the Wise One as she embarked on the ferry leaving the Isle of Man, his once ethereal body now fully flesh, blood, and bones.

He had been watching over her since she'd left on her journey. The Wise One's third eye was opening, he could tell from the glances she'd cast his way, likely feeling his Arcturian presence. But hovering around in his energetic form wasn't nearly enough—he had made his choice now; without warning the Council, he had left Arcturus and entered the third dimension. Though, his incarnation on Earth was only temporary—just until he completed his mission. The fate of the universe depended on it.

The Council would understand. How much did the girl know? Did she know of the Scrolls? He felt for her, truly. She had little idea what would become of this world if she continued on with Cillian by her side. How had his brother come to choose such an unrighteous path?

He examined their course. They were headed for Scotland. That was where the Akashic Records said it would all begin.

And he had to stop it before it did.

The boldest fae flees from our neighbour land
Her charge, the Wise One, and she the key
Whence the ancient passage tomb stands
United their magic, and so shall it be

—Scottish Scroll II, 1576

Acknowledgements

A deep, heartfelt thank-you to . . .

Mr. O'Neil, who sparked my love of writing and sheer fascination with Ireland.

Carmie and Signe Pike, who made me believe in faeries again.

Maggie, my editor, whose patient mentorship carried me through the tough times.

Laura, who spotted a spark and talent in me that, at the time, I failed to see in myself—and without whom I would have likely never pursued my master's.

Alexa and her wonderful team, who held my hand throughout the publishing process and made it the most exciting, surreal experience of my writing life.

Carol, who gave the ARC the final proofread it so desperately needed.

Nicola, who "Irish-proofed" this, and whose warmth and kindness is contagious to any who are lucky enough to encounter her.

Gen, my ultimate cheerleader. And I still don't fully understand why.

Aly, who despite our distance, makes me believe in myself every single day.

Jess, who's never allowed me to settle, and who constantly reminds me that we're all here to "do good".

Sophie, whose confidence in my writing makes me feel as clever and witty as Amy Sherman-Palladino.

Jess C., who keeps me good and weird when I need it most.

The Nerd Herd, whose friendship and ambition shaped me over all these years.

All my zias, who encouraged my writing pursuits no matter what.

Nonna and Nonno, who always tried their hardest to convince me that I didn't need a "real job."

Chantal, the best mother-in-law a person could ask for, who's supported my big dreams since the moment I divulged them to her as her son's high-school girlfriend.

My dad, Alex, and Nicky, who trusted in my creative aspirations even if they never quite understood them.

Vincent, whose enthusiasm over this book was overwhelming in the best way possible.

Jennifer, who helped make it the book that it is.

My mother, who read it first. She always does.

Andy, whose unwavering support is why this book exists.

Book Club Questions

1. What were the story's main themes?
2. What age group would you say this book is suited for?
3. What other books did this remind you of?
4. Which characters would you most like to meet?
5. How did you feel about the protagonist? Were you rooting for her?
6. If you were making this book into a film/TV series, who would you cast?
7. Did you feel there was chemistry between the main characters?
8. What feelings did this book evoke for you?
9. What ideas was the author trying to get across?
10. How would the story have changed if it were set in the present day?
11. Did the magic that was woven throughout the story feel real to you? Why or why not?

12. Which Celtic myth featured in the book was your favourite?
13. Which of the landscapes felt the most magical or meaningful to you?
14. Do you have any lingering questions about the book?
15. How did your opinion of the book change as you read it?
16. What surprised you the most about the story?
17. Did the story feel rushed, or was it more of a slow burn?

RECOMMENDED READING

Books that influenced, inspired, and informed me:

True Stories

Faery Tale: One Woman's Search for Enchantment in a Modern World, by Signe Pike

Scottish Witches, by Lily Seafield

Irish Myth & Folklore

In Chimney Corners: Merry Tales of Irish Folklore, by Seumas Macmanus and Pamela Coleman

Old Ways, Old Secrets: Pagan Ireland, by Jo Kerrigan

Myths and Folklore of Ireland, by Jeremiah Curtin

Irish Fairy Legends, by T. Crofton Croker

A Treasury of Irish Fairy and Folk Tales, by various authors

Irish History

Ireland—A Very Peculiar History, by Jim Pipe

The Princes of Ireland, by Edward Rutherfurd

For the Kids

Fairies: The Book of Secrets, by Russell Ince

Leprechauns and Irish Folklore, by Mary Pope Osborne and Natalie Pope Boyce

The Element Encyclopedia of Magical Creatures, by John and Caitlin Matthews

Magical Reads & Western Esotericism

The Western Esoteric Traditions: A Historical Introduction, by Nicholas Goodrick-Clarke

Enchantment of the Faerie Realm, by Ted Andrews

Earth, Air, Fire & Water, by Scott Cunningham

True Magick: A Beginner's Guide, by Amber K

About the Author

Katrina Tortorici Anglehart is a born and bred Italian-Canadian from Montreal. A devoted academic, she holds a Bachelor of Arts in Journalism; a graduate certificate in Scriptwriting; and a Master of Fine Arts in Creative Writing. After dabbling in TV writing and working as a digital marketing content manager, she left the nine to five to launch her freelance editing and coaching career. Today, she relishes helping aspiring authors to develop and refine their stories.

Besides English, Katrina speaks French, Italian, and Spanglish. When she's not writing, diving into magical reads, or Netflixing, she's travelling with her favourite human—her high-school-sweetheart-turned-husband, Andy—and obsessing over her pet bunny, Magic, and newly rescued pup, Nessie. Katrina currently lives in Toronto, Ontario.

www.ingramcontent.com/pod-product-compliance
Lightning Source LLC
Chambersburg PA
CBHW030425310726
48979CB00009B/1622/J
* 9 7 8 1 7 7 7 3 3 1 7 1 9 *